Forever Fake

TWISTED ARRANGEMENTS
BOOK THREE

CASSIA QUINN

Wednesday Ink

Forever Fake

For the girls who just want to be loved, cherished, and avenged.

Content Information

Dear reader, before you turn the page, please know that this romance has dark themes and potentially difficult situations. Please read the entire content list here: http://cassiaquinn.com/twisted-arrangements/

XX
Cassia

Forever Fake Playlist

Secrets and Lies by Ruelle
Babydoll by Ari Abdul
Too Sweet by Hozier
Cruel Summer by Taylor Swift
Heaven by Julia Michaels
Shameless by Camila Cabello
Dandelions by Ruth B.
I Wanna Be Yours by Arctic Monkeys
I'm Yours by Isabel LaRosa
Fake Smile by Ariana Grande
What Was I Made For? By Billie Eilish
Die For You by The Weeknd
Love Me Like You Do by Ellie Goulding

Listen on Spotify

One for Sorrow

One for sorrow,
Two for mirth,
Three for a wedding,
Four for death,
Five for silver,
Six for gold,
Seven for a secret never to be told.
Eight for a wish,
Nine for a kiss,
Ten for a surprise you should be careful not to miss.

Contents

CHAPTER 1

Blake

"I see you redecorated." Yve, my widowed step-mother, purses her collagen-stuffed lips while surveying the brownstone's renovated entryway. "Marble, stained wood, and antiques. How predictable. I don't know what I ever saw in this place, the penthouse is so much more modern. Its view of Central Park is stellar. Pity there's no decent view here. I still can't believe how much you paid for this old house."

Of course she'd rub that in. She held onto my ancestral home for years, refusing to sell it to me until I offered a price so astronomical that she simply couldn't pass it up. That back and forth was one of many games we've played since my father died three years ago and Yve gained control of everything, from the Baron family estate to our real estate investment empire.

As the eldest son, I should have inherited it all, but Father cut me out of his will a long time ago. Instead, handing over his massive fortune to this gold-digging bitch.

Gold-diggers are the worst kind of predators in my world. They seem to be everywhere.

I school my features in a bored expression and drawl, "If your urgent need to stop by was to comment on my home's features, you may leave now."

"Don't be ridiculous." She sneers, walking toward my office on the main floor like she still owns the place.

I stroll after her, refusing to let her get under my skin. Instead, I make her wait when she enters my office before I do, and takes one of two chairs in front of the desk. Unhurriedly, I round the sizable piece of wooden furniture and sink into the smooth leather chair.

Yve glares. Given the amount of Botox she's had in the last few years, her eyes are the only part of her face that naturally move.

I steeple my fingers, elbows on my desk, and return her stare. Another game. We've been playing one game after another for decades. We face each other like that for a solid thirty seconds before she finally breaks the strained silence.

"Lexa is now twenty-one, which means it's high time she found a husband. You are—"

"Not interested. For the *millionth* time, I'm not marrying my sister." The very idea makes my skin crawl, even though she's technically my step-sister. Not that there's anything wrong with the girl, except for the fact that I do see her as my baby *sister*. That we don't share blood is irrelevant.

Besides, whoever marries my *sister* will be under this monster's thumb, and that sorry fellow is not going to be me—anymore than I *already* am Yve's unwilling puppet.

Yve has been hounding me about this since the girl turned eighteen. For Christ's sake, give it a rest.

I find the very idea of being romantically involved with my step-sister repulsive on so many levels. She's a decade and half younger than me, and she shares blood with this viper who's seated in my office. The only reason Yve wants to pawn her daughter off on me is to make sure all the Baron family assets stay under her control. And to acquire the fortune I've made for myself over the years.

Just one big happy family. Forever.

Over my dead fucking body.

Though in all honesty, I'm surprised she hasn't moved on to arranging a marriage between Lexa and my younger brother Liam. They are closer in age. Also step-siblings. The fact that he's gay is not nearly enough of a reason for Yve to dismiss the idea of them together. In fact, it wouldn't deter her in the slightest. She's that sort of monster.

Either way, it's never going to happen. I'd welcome an arranged marriage to a stranger before I'd agree to marry Lexa.

Yve purses her puffy mauve lips. "You remember that you can't claim your little inheritance until you marry, right?"

Another of Yve's games. When I went away to boarding school as a teenager, she stole some things from my room—invaluable things. Over the years I've looked for them but keep coming up empty-handed. One day I'll get them all back.

"I'm well aware of your terms." Already bored of this conversation, I casually lean back in my chair.

"Well then, marry my daughter and you'll get what you want. One year of marriage is all I ask for you to claim what you want."

"Never." I let my boredom slip through in my tone. "I'd rather eat rusty nails."

A sinister smile touches her mouth. "If you're going to be so stubborn about it, I have no choice but to force the issue. If you want your inheritance, then you'll have to marry by your thirty-fifth birthday. The day after that, if you're not wed, I'll burn it all."

I'm about to protest, telling her she can't add this term on top of the other ridiculous stipulations regarding what she stole from me. Calling it *my inheritance*, doesn't alter the facts.

But she can change the terms, she can do whatever the hell she wants because my father gave her full control and the estate's lawyers always jump at whatever she wants to amend. Those bastards are entirely too accommodating.

Since my father's death, Yve has become unhinged. She's stepped into the CEO position at the company, she holds my little brother's inheritance over both his head and mine. How she convinced Father to give her carte blanche is still unknown to me. Though my father was a real bastard, his weakness was Yve, so I shouldn't really be surprised by his last will and testament leaving her in charge of the Baron family estate and business.

I simply have to deal with the consequences—for now.

My birthday's in six months. That's not a lot of time to find a wife.

"You must marry before then or risk losing what you

want most. And, if you choose someone other than Lexa, you must stay married for an entire year. Above all, I have to be convinced that your marriage will last. If either of you are caught cheating, then you'll never see your inheritance. If it's not a love-match, then our deal is off." She leans forward. "Wed Lexa and be done with it. You can cheat on her and I'll look the other way. Plus, I'll give you your inheritance immediately. Wed my daughter and you won't have to wait another year."

"I'd rather chew off my own fingers."

Her expression sours. She sighs, clearly exasperated. *Good.*

"She's the only option. Especially since I'll add that you may not pay a woman to be your wife. There will be a prenup in place for anyone you try to marry if it's not Lexa. Which means any other wife will be left with nothing if you divorce. We both know you're so intolerable that no woman would agree to be with you, if not for your money."

I cast her a bland look. "That is why you married my father. For the money."

Yve shrugs. Standing, she smooths down her Chanel suit and picks up her garish, monogram Louis Vuitton bag. The woman couldn't scream *new money* louder if she tried.

"I'll start planning the wedding." With a venomous smile she heads for my office door. "You won't find anyone else who'll marry you in six short months."

The viper leaves my door open, so I can hear the click of her heels all the way to the foyer. Good riddance.

When I'm alone, I pound my fist on the desk, once, and the few items atop it quiver. Then I pour myself a scotch from the bar cart. It's fucking five o'clock somewhere in the world. Though one brief conversation with my step-mother could drive a teetotaler to drink.

The scotch smoothly burns as it washes down my throat. Its peaty oak taste coats my tongue. I swallow the shot then pour myself a double, neat.

The truth of the situation is that I do need to find a wife before my birthday in November. One thing I know for certain about Yve is that she rarely bluffs. Her threats can be taken at face-value. November is my deadline if I want what she stole returned to me.

And I will have it. One way or another. No matter how many hoops Yve sets in place.

I need a wife.

A *fake* wife.

A knock sounds on my ajar door.

"What?" I snap.

Arianna Kozlov, formerly Arianna *Pontrelli*, before she married into the Russian Bratva, pokes her brunette head into my office. "I just wanted to give you an update, Mr. Baron. We're finished decorating in the garden and we've moved into the house. Catering should be arriving any moment."

I give her a curt nod and she disappears, going back to her work.

In celebration of finally owning my childhood home again and the recent renovation, I'm hosting a soiree tonight. One that my step-mother is not invited to attend.

When this idea came to mind, I knew the only event planner to hire was Arianna Kozlov—her connection to the Russian mafia of no concern. I've seen her work at Leonidas Gentleman's Club enough times to know she's the best. By tonight this place will be decked out in superb elegance and the party will go off without a hitch. I left the details in Mrs. Kozlov's capable hands so I'll be as surprised as everyone else tonight by its final presentation.

She sent invites out a while ago and the guest list is settled. It should be an interesting evening. I invited all the who's-who of Manhattan and beyond.

If only I could use this evening as an alibi while I off Yve... This isn't the first, nor even the thousandth, time I've considered putting my step-monster in an early grave.

I'd do it in a heartbeat if she didn't have dirt on me. One misstep when I was young and cocky, and now she has enough evidence to put me away for life.

I once asked her why she hasn't done it yet, and she confessed to enjoying our games too much. With me behind bars, she wouldn't have anyone to toy with and torment, knowing she can get away with everything. I can't touch her until I find and destroy that blackmail material.

The other problem is that I'd be the prime suspect. Naturally.

Not only would I jeopardize everything I've built in my life, but also my younger brother's inheritance, and our family company Titan Enterprises. Plus, I really don't relish the idea of life in prison just for offing one conniving gold-digger. The sacrifice is too much for the reward. I've come to terms with enduring her petty games. Even as she now forces me to come up with a willing bride in less than six months.

I don't think I'm as unpleasant in the eyes of most

women as Yve suggested. If anything, I could probably put out a call for potential candidates and be inundated with hopeful young women. More gold-diggers. Empty-headed arm candy.

The very idea has me cringing. I swallow the rest of my scotch and set the glass on my desk.

In truth, *I'm* the problem. I can't stomach most humans, and when it comes to blushing ladies who look at me and see my bank account balance and investment portfolio, I'd rather be buried alive than consider making one of them the next Mrs. Baron. Even temporarily.

In short, I'm fucked.

CHAPTER 2

Ginevra

"**G**inevra," Papa calls from his office on the main floor. "Where do you think you're going?"

I roll my eyes at his brusk, annoyed tone and walk through his open door to, yet again, remind him that I'm going out tonight. I told him and Mama over dinner that I had plans this evening.

"I'm going to a party, remember? Blake Baron has opened up the Baron mansion for the first time in at least a decade. Everyone will be there."

Papa sighs and pinches the bridge of his nose. "I wish you wouldn't get too close to people like Mr. Baron. He's a dangerous man."

Don't I know it. He completely destroyed our close friends, the Marino family, seven years ago. They disappeared without a trace, including my childhood best friend Viviana. Some people say they're in witness protection, others know they're most likely dead. When

Blake Baron sets out to ruin someone, he does a thorough job.

"I'm not going to see Mr. Baron," I explain. "Arianna did the planning for this event and she asked me to come." In fact, Mr. Baron never thought to invite me at all. The only reason I'll get through the front doors is because Arianna, after I begged and pleaded, put me on the guest list. But Papa doesn't need to know the details.

"Your sister should watch herself too. If I had any say in the matter, I'd have forbidden her from working for Mr. Baron."

Ducking my head, I hide my smirk. Luckily for all of us, Papa has very little say in any matter these days. We're grown women, and my two older sisters are married. We can all do whatever the hell we want. Well, sort of. I'm still living at home, so Papa thinks he can rule my life.

When I don't respond, Papa continues, "I forbid you from going."

"It's a little late for that." I sweep my fingers down my shimmery blue evening gown, as if he hadn't already noticed my attire. "I'm all dressed up and ready to go."

"Go upstairs and go to bed, Gin." He focuses on the papers in front of him.

My teeth clench. For my two older sisters, Papa will bend over backwards to accommodate them—which I know comes from a deep-seated sense of guilt. But he's never treated me the same as them. Even though he's wronged me worse than he ever did either of my sisters.

I cross my arms. "You can't tell me what to do. I'm almost twenty-one years old."

"You live under my roof, which means you'll do as I say." He doesn't even bother to look at me.

"Fat chance of that," I mutter.

Papa's sharp gaze snaps to mine. "What did you just say? I won't put up with your attitude tonight, girl."

He calls me *girl*, like I'm some street urchin instead of his own flesh and blood. The feeling's mutual—I'd rather not be related to him either.

I flip my perfectly styled, wavy blond hair over my shoulder. "Good night, Papa." I pin him with a winning smile and head out the door. When I'm in the hallway, instead of going upstairs to bed, I stroll to the front entrance and meet my waiting Lyft driver. Papa will throw a fit about my disobedience when he finds out, but I don't care. I also don't care about the consequences. Nothing he can do is worse than what he's already done to me—years ago.

As soon as I'm settled in the backseat, my phone chimes. Expecting it to be Papa, security already alerting him that I've left the estate, I ignore it.

I really need to find a way to move out of my parents' house. But I'm not super talented at anything like Arianna is at event planning. I'm also not college material like our oldest sister, Sophia, who's getting her degree in Art History. I'm the dud of the family. What does a dud do with her life?

Sighing, I reach for my phone. Negative thoughts won't get me anywhere good.

I am worthy.

I will figure out what I want.

I deserve a happy life.

All of these affirmations fall flat, but that doesn't stop

me from speaking them in my mind anytime I feel negativity threatening to swallow me whole. Someday I'll believe that I *am* worthy and happy. Until then, I'm all about faking it until I make it.

My phone chimes again, drawing my attention to the lit screen, and my breath seizes in my lungs. It's not my father texting me, it's worse... It's my ex-boyfriend. Oliver.

A shiver of disgust slithers across my skin.

I should ignore him and just delete his messages. My thumb hovers over the screen for several long seconds as I hesitate. I shouldn't keep reading his texts, but... If I block him I won't know what he's up to or what he's going to do next. I need to untangle myself from him without pissing him off.

I swipe and read the two messages he sent.

> OLIVER
>
> Hey babe, what are you doing tonight?
> We should talk. I don't understand why
> you aren't returning my calls and texts.

Really? After what he did, I think it would be obvious.

> OLIVER
>
> Why don't you come over to my place?
> Or we could meet for drinks?

I stare at the thread of unanswered texts going back two weeks. Since I resolutely broke up with him–again. By that I mean I've ghosted him. Total silence. I don't know how else to handle this situation. We've ended things in the past, but he has a way of manipulating me into giving him another chance. Not this time. It's final.

My pulse pounds in my temple as I consider replying. I should put it into words that we're over, through, totally done. Except every time I decide on that course of action, anxiety ripples through me. My heartbeat stutters and my skin flushes. I wipe a clammy palm against my thigh.

Before I can talk myself out of this again, I muster my courage and type out a text.

GINEVRA

We won't be seeing each other ever again. I hoped it was obvious, but we're done. Don't message me again.

OLIVER

I don't understand, babe. What happened?

I scoff. Is he serious right now?

GINEVRA

You know what happened. Leave me alone.

OLIVER

What? Are you angry about the movie we made together? That was hot, babe.

My stomach heaves. I feel like I'm going to be sick. He makes it all sound so innocent, but I...

Flashes of memory threaten to rise to the surface and I instantly shut them down. I can't deal with that shit right now. Or ever. I'm trying to shove that incident into a box in my mind and store it deep, deep down where it will never see the light of day again.

OLIVER

We're not over. There's no such thing as over between us. You're my forever girl and if you think you can break this off, you're wrong. I'd rather kill you myself than let you go. Do you hear me, you fucking whore? You're a worthless little slut, you know you are, and I'm the only one who cares about you. Who loves you.

Tears well in my eyes. I flip my phone over so I don't have to read whatever he sends next. Two more pings sound, telling me that he's not done ranting. I swallow past the lump in my throat, put my cell on silent and toss it into my clutch.

I can't fucking deal with this right now. I'm going to a party.

The driver pulls up in front of Blake Baron's enormous brownstone and lets me out. I'm late, so everyone is already inside and the party's well underway. Standing on the sidewalk, I give myself a short pep talk, inhale a couple of deep breaths, plaster a smile on my face, then climb the stairs to the mansion.

In the foyer, I give my name to the attendant and he checks it off the list. From here I'm free to roam. I should find Arianna and her husband, but I'm still too frazzled to immediately seek her out. Instead, I head for the second floor in hopes of finding a quiet bathroom where I can fully regroup in private. I'm going to have fun tonight, damn it, just as soon as I pull myself together.

I come across a candle-lit, unoccupied bathroom

about halfway down the hallway. Slipping inside, I turn the lock and press my back to the cool wooden door.

I'm okay. Or at least, I will be okay.

I repeat that mantra in my head for a solid minute.

I will be okay. I will be okay. I will be okay. Everything is fine.

The words—or perhaps it's the repetition—soothes my racing heart and fidgety fingers. Once I've regained some semblance of calm, I fix my already perfect makeup in the mirror and straighten my dress. Then I take in my surroundings.

The marble floor and walls gleam in the candle light. A crystal chandelier hangs above, suspended from the high ceiling. This humble space is no more than a powder room, yet it screams old money, wealth, and splendor. A promise of what the rest of the mansion has to offer.

I'm in Blake Baron's house, at his party, and I'm going to have fun tonight—*fun, fun, fun.* My sister might be a stuck up prude, or at least she was before she married, but Arianna sure knows how to organize a party. Only the best catering and booze will be here tonight. And damn, do I need a drink.

I smile at myself in the bathroom mirror. My expression almost appears genuine.

Ready to make the most of the evening, I stroll into the hallway. Further in the house are sounds of the party, but here it's quiet. There's not a soul around.

Which is why, when a sparkly figurine on a side table catches my eye, I pick it up. It's some kind of bird cast in clear crystal with black jewels decorating its head. Black and blue-green gems adorn the wings and tail feathers.

The piece is breath-taking. I've never seen anything like it.

Immediately, my palms itch. That familiar, exhilarating rush swoops through me as I reach out and stash the figurine in my clutch. It's now my little secret. A crime I got away with. The high is the best part.

A real smile strains my cheeks for the first time tonight. Warmth whirls in my chest.

Whenever I'm feeling down and depressed, taking something that isn't mine wipes away all of that negativity. A light airiness overtakes my body, my insides swell as if filled with helium. I very well might float away on this bubble of happiness.

The fact that I just stole from none other than *The Black Baron* himself, the most feared man in all of New York City, adds a layer of danger to my excitement. It's heady. Addictive.

More to the point, that fucker deserves it for murdering my childhood best friend. Viviana's gone because of him.

On bouncy toes, I spin around and collide with a wall of muscle.

Only an hour into this soiree and I find myself making excuses to drift further from the crowd that's taken over my house. The fact that I invited them all here, so therefore cannot escape them, leaves a bitter taste in my mouth.

I need some fucking distance from all these people. There are too many of them.

Which is how I end up on the second floor, in a quieter part of my home, hiding from my own guests. Well, not *hiding,* I don't hide, just seeking some fucking privacy.

The bathroom door down the hall opens and out steps a curvy woman with bouncing blond waves. Her back's to me, but I recognize her immediately. Ginevra Pontrelli. My party planner's youngest sister. Who I most certainly did *not* invite.

How the hell did she get in here? Oh wait, I did tell Arianna she could invite a friend, an obvious error on my part. What the fuck was I thinking?

I watch her from the shadows, remembering the first time I laid eyes on the youngest Pontrelli girl. Yes, girl, she can't be any older than twenty or twenty-one. Which means back then she was barely eighteen. I inwardly cringe.

She was at a club dancing with her sisters and cousin. My best friend, Roman, only had eyes for his fiancée Sophia, but my gaze latched onto the gorgeous blond who had tits and ass for days. She was the only blond among them, petite, and curvy in all the right places. Then Roman warned me off of her.

For one, she's much too young for me.

And she's trouble. Not the fun kind.

Which I mentally note while I watch her pick up a diamond encrusted figurine my grandfather brought back from his travels to India. The piece is utterly priceless.

Stealthily, I approach Ginevra, who seems too lost in the glittering gems to notice her surroundings. I'm right behind her when she drops the figurine into her tiny bag with a soft chuckle. What she finds so amusing, I haven't a clue. However, I can guarantee her mirth will be short-lived once she realizes she's been caught.

So she's not only a gold-digger but also a thief. How intriguing...

No one steals from me and lives to tell about it. Much less *chuckle*.

With a dazzling smile, she spins on her heel and plows right into my chest. Automatically, my muscles tense at the impact, and my fingers wrap around her upper arms to steady her.

She takes two quick steps back, hiding her clutch

behind her back, and slowly her gaze travels up my body to meet mine. Her wide brown eyes are the color of dark chocolate and caramel. Fear skitters through them and I can't help but smirk. She recognizes me. Good.

Because she's in trouble now.

"I believe you have something of mine," I drawl, leaning one shoulder against the wall. As casual as my stance is, my gaze never leaves hers.

"I..." She summons a blindingly bright smile that shows straight white teeth, but it doesn't reach her eyes. "I have no idea what you're talking about, Mr. Baron." Her voice is smooth and thick as honey. It oozes over me, filling in all of my crevices, and for a moment I believe her lie—even though I saw her steal the figurine with my own eyes. She's that convincing.

"I'm talking about the crystal magpie figurine you have in your purse. It's small, decorated with black and blue-green diamonds. Normally, I wouldn't give a shit, but that particular piece happens to be a family heirloom. So, I must insist that you return it."

She blinks, not giving any ground. Audacious.

Then she holds out her little purse. "I swear I don't have it. You can search my clutch if you'd like, sir." Again she shoots me that disarming grin. My chest tingles with the strangest sensation, and I shake it off.

I eye her purse. So, she wants to play games? Game on, sweetheart.

I certainly won't be outsmarted, or duped, by one barely adult girl. I have years of experience on her, which she'll learn soon enough.

Stepping closer to her, I take the clutch. It's soft and

shiny. A blue satin that perfectly matches the color of her evening gown.

I upend it, emptying the contents on a side table. She lets out a surprised gasp as her belongings scatter. A whole bunch of girly crap falls onto the polished wooden top, but notably missing is my figurine.

Just as I thought. Was it sleight of hand? There's no way she'd incriminate herself. I know she has the diamond magpie. *Where* is the only question.

I glance at her, my gaze skims the skin-tight sparkly dress that dips low in the front to reveal her ample cleavage. Any fool would say there's nowhere else she could have hidden the figurine except for in the bag.

Luckily, I'm no fool.

"See?" she says. "I don't have whatever you think I stole."

A wolfish grin spreads across my lips. "Oh, I'm not done searching for it yet."

"But you emptied my clutch. You can see there's nothing in there except for what's mine."

"I'm done searching your bag, but I'm not done searching *you*."

Her smooth brow pinches with confusion. I step closer, until I'm towering over her and then I finally see it, the flicker of comprehension in her eyes. Her lips part as if she's shocked or perhaps it's the beginning of a silent protest.

Either way, it doesn't matter. She brought this on herself.

"Turn around and put your hands on the wall. Now."

She visibly shivers under my commanding tone. Then lifts her chin and pins me with a glare.

"Go to hell. I'm not going to—"

"Right now," I warn.

"You can't make me—"

I grab her hips and spin us so her back's against the wall. Holding her there, I cage her in with my much larger frame. She's not going anywhere until I've thoroughly searched her. My cock stirs at that idea and the heat of her supple body beneath my palms.

"Don't move." I run my hands down her hips. The dress ends mid-thigh and below that she's wearing a pair of strappy gold heels. Certainly nothing's hiding in her shoes.

Wedging one hand between her legs, and the other on the outside, I slide my palms up her thigh. She stiffens. Her breath catches and she swallows hard. I let my hands do the searching, never dropping my gaze from hers. When I reach the apex of her thighs, I expect to encounter the barrier of her underwear. But there's no tiny scrap of fabric. She's bare and smooth beneath her dress.

Fuck me.

Her breath hitches, and my cock grows harder. A mix of desire and fear swims in her brown eyes. Now I have her full attention.

I drop my hands, only to slide them up her other leg, still under the guise of searching for what she stole. A completely unnecessary move at this point. Logically I know that, and I don't care. The feel of her soft skin beneath my rough palms is too alluring to resist.

This time, as I slide my hands up, she whimpers a

soft moan. I take in her flushed cheeks and the rapid rise and fall of her chest, liking the way my touch affects her.

When I release her, she reaches for my upper arms to steady herself. Our gazes remain locked as I take her hips, then explore the dip of her waist and the underside of her luscious breasts. I get a sudden, vivid mental image of her tits shaking with each of my powerful thrusts as I fuck her.

No. *Not happening.* Ever.

I'm well aware of her reputation as a party girl, an easy lay, she's probably slept with half the city's bachelors. I'm sure she's keeping her options open until she comes across the man with the right figure for his net worth.

The very thought makes me want to punish her for being such a little gold-digger. I learned to loathe women like that after my father's second and third marriages, before he settled down with Yve–the worst of them all.

I consciously shift my hips backward, putting some space between us, so she can't feel my raging erection. When all I really want to do is tie her up and fuck her until she confesses to her crime–all of her crimes. Too bad that's not an option. I won't fall for the temptation.

Her hold on me tightens as I search every inch of her breasts through the thin fabric, but she never protests. Her nipples pebble beneath my thumbs, making my mouth water with the need to suck on her delicious peaks. An urge that I, thankfully, resist.

I run my hand between her cleavage. The actual feel of her soft flesh lights a fire deep in my stomach. We're so close, our breaths mingle. I inhale the sweet scent of her perfume.

I've been with plenty of women, but not one of them has ever affected me the way Ginevra is right now. I'm mesmerized by her shining, glassy eyes. It's taking every shred of self-control I have to resist biting her parted, pouty lips, the curve of her smooth neck, and her heaving breasts. I want to lick every inch of this woman—then punish her for making me lose control.

The need is visceral. And rather unsettling.

Is it because I've told myself she's forbidden fruit? Too young. Too innocent. Too... tempting.

Or is it—?

My fingers touch the distinct hardness of clustered diamonds. From her breasts, I pluck the magpie figurine and hold it between us.

"Found it." My voice comes out strong and surprisingly steady. It belies the whirling of my thoughts, and the twisted, pulsing sensation in my gut. "What do you have to say for yourself? Are you ready to confess your sins?"

She licks her lips. "I—I wasn't expecting you to be so thorough."

"I'm always thorough. You can count on that." My mind fills with all kinds of dirty thoughts involving other ways I could be quite thorough with her tonight.

We continue to stand much too close together. The figurine sits on my open palm between us, my other hand resting on her waist. Her hold has moved to the crook at my elbows. She should be pushing me away, but she's not. She's holding on for dear life, like she's drowning in a fathomless sea and I'm her life line—her only hope.

The next words out of my mouth have me questioning my sanity, because I certainly haven't thought this through. And I *always* think things through.

"We both know that you tried to steal from me." Against my better judgment, I lean closer, noting the floral scent of her shampoo. "No one steals from me and gets away with it. So I'm going to give you a choice, Ginevra, you can either go to jail for your crime—that's at least two years locked up once I'm done with you in court—or you can agree to be my wife."

"**M**y *fake* wife," he clarifies, but the damage to my malfunctioning brain is already done. "Marry me and be my fake wife for one year. Then I'll say you've done your time and are free to go."

All I can do is gape at him. I've never been more speechless in my life. He can't be serious. But I'm having trouble getting a read on him because he's too close. His body heat, his spicy masculine scent, his mere presence is too much.

Overwhelming.

Overpowering.

I've never felt like this around a man before. He radiates raw, primal *predator* energy, but my anxiety has yet to rear its head. This proves that I'm beyond broken. The guys I'm drawn to and I think are nice end up being psychos, but when I'm in the clutches of an *obviously* dangerous man, my alarm bells fail to ring.

No red flags here.

No big flashing red lights.

Nothing at all—except this insane need to hold onto him, to draw him closer. Do I have a death wish? I *know* this man is bad news. He's the devil himself.

I inwardly sigh at myself.

Releasing his arms, I slide my back against the wall and side-step to escape him. I step away until there's plenty of distance between us. Until I can breathe again. Clearly think again.

I can't believe I just let him grope me. I mean, if I was drunk, sure, that kind of thing happens all the time and I let it. But I'm sober—too fucking sober for this situation. What was I thinking?

He's no different from any other man. They're all perverts.

"Well?" he lazily prompts. "What will it be?"

My laugh comes out high-pitched and slightly hysterical. "You aren't serious."

"Dead serious." The heat in his bright blue eyes from earlier has dimmed to indifference. Was the lust ever there, or did I imagine it? He looks every inch the foreboding, moody billionaire that he is. One who has no interest in me, at least not in any way that's good.

"I can't. I have a boyfriend." I make the first excuse that comes to mind. He'll get tired of this game soon enough, laugh at my expense, and call it a night.

"Break up with him," he drawls, as if that's the obvious solution.

"I can't."

"You will if you don't want to go to prison."

I wave him off. "Even if I was single, I can't marry you."

"Why?"

"Because you're old and boring." I do my best to act unaffected by him, smoothing down my sparkly dress.

"*Old?* Boring?" His jaw ticks.

Did I hit a nerve?

Why am I poking this beast? What is wrong with me?

I fake a yawn. "So boring. In fact, you're boring me with this game."

A ruthless gleam sparkles in his astonishingly blue eyes. Those beautiful blues should belong to someone who deserves them. Not this evil man.

"This is no game, Ginevra." His tone sends a chill up my spine.

"I'm calling your bluff." I fold my arms under my breasts. His gaze flicks to my tits then is gone so quickly that my head spins. Did he really check me out? Or did I imagine that too?

Do I *want* him to find me attractive? When I know he's wicked and I should avoid him?

"Fine. Have it your way." His bored expression almost convinces me that he doesn't care which option I choose. I don't buy it. He needs a fake wife for something, otherwise why try to blackmail me into filling that role? "Just know that I've destroyed people much more powerful than you—for the fun of it. Your daddy can't get you out of this. I'll eat you alive in court. See you there." He pulls out his phone.

"Wh-what are you doing?"

Without glancing up, he replies, "Reporting a theft. My security cameras caught it all." Turning away, he casually strolls along the hallway toward the stairs.

He's not bragging, or lying, about his capabilities. I know that he's dangerous, powerful, and can make me disappear with a snap of his fingers. He did it to Viviana, to her *and* her entire family.

Poof. Gone.

My hands tremble at the memory. Fourteen year old me was devastated.

"Wait!" I stumble after him.

Blake Baron, rightly called *The Black Baron* by everyone who knows he has a rotten soul, stops and angles toward me. He waits, phone in hand.

"Why? Why do you want me to pretend to be with you?" I ask.

His jaw muscles work, like he doesn't want to tell me the truth. "That's none of your business."

I force a coy smile. "Tell me, or the answer is a hard *no*."

How badly does he need me? I'm about to find out, I hope.

The idea of being temporarily married to this man makes my stomach twist, but spending two years in prison would be far, far worse. I'm not prison material. I'd never survive.

But Blake Baron? I might not be able to survive him for twelve months either.

He rakes his fingers through his blond waves. "There's something I want. To get it, I have to take a wife before I'm thirty-five."

Thirty-five? God, he's ancient.

"When do you turn thirty-five?" I ask more out of curiosity than anything, noting that his explanation was vague at best.

"November."

Fucking hell, we only have a few months. Like six months. I'd be married in less than six months.

Am I really considering doing this?

What choice do I have?

I clear my throat and smooth my sweaty palms down my dress. "Why me? Surely you could blackmail or bribe any woman into being your fake wife."

Pocketing his phone, he shakes his head. "One of the conditions is that I cannot, in fact, bribe or pay a woman to marry me. However, my step-mother overlooked the possibility of blackmail, so... here we are." He shrugs, as if he's not altering the course of my entire life to get what he wants, all seemingly on a whim, on a seized opportunity.

Whatever he's after must be important to him. But... he's a selfish bastard for putting me in this position.

An annoying little voice reminds me that I put *myself* in this position by stealing from the wrong man. Did I really think I wouldn't get caught?

Yes, yes I did.

Obviously, I've gotten far too brazen. Arrogant in my actions. Of course there are security cameras in his house —duh. Now I have to eat humble pie—in the form of whatever Mr. Baron decides to serve up.

I'm so fucked. But the alternative is worse.

With any other situation, I might be able to rely on my father's contacts to help me out of this, but even Papa knows not to go up against *The Black Baron*. I could turn to other powerful men, either one of my sisters' husbands. Roman De Luca has half this city in his pocket, but he's also Blake's best friend. Dimitri Kozlov is a Bratva leader, but Mr. Baron saved his life last year so... I'm shit out of luck.

"You said it's only for a year?" I want to make sure I heard that right.

"That's correct. A year from our wedding date. We'll marry this summer, well before my thirty-fifth birthday, give it exactly twelve months and then divorce. As long as our act is convincing, everything will work out."

"Convincing to who, exactly?" I need to know who we're deceiving.

My god, I can't believe I'm agreeing to this, but I don't see a way out of it. I've survived worse than Mr. Baron. I can do this. Can't I?

"Everybody," he says. "We will never know who's watching, so we must convince everyone. Your family and mine. Our friends, too."

I balk at that. "My sisters will see right through this."

"Not if you convince them otherwise." He cocks his head. "I know you're a good actress, I've seen it for myself, just tonight. I have faith in you to lie your way through this situation. If you let me down, our deal is off."

I scoff at him. "You really love tossing around threats, don't you? This sounds like I'm damned if I do and damned if I don't."

He bites down on his lower lip, considering, and it's sexy as hell. "I suppose you're right. The question is, are you going to give up now and go to prison, or fight like hell to come out of this on the other side?"

I lift my chin high. I might not know what I want to do with my life, and I might have terrible taste in men, but one thing I'm sure of is that I'm a fighter—through and through. Mr. Baron will rue the day he forced me into this. I'll make sure of it.

"You'll have the contract drawn up in detail," I tell him, straightening to my full petite height. "I'll strike anything I don't agree with before I sign. I'm available Thursday afternoon to seal this deal. Now, if you'll excuse me, I have a party to go to." And a fuck ton of booze to drink because I think I'm still in denial about what I just agreed to do. Over a year with this... *man.*

A predatory smile curves his full lips. "Good girl."

Those two words punch me right in the gut, then melt and slither down to pool between my legs. I involuntarily shiver.

This is a terrible idea. But there's no turning back now. I don't have any other choice. I'd never survive prison. I'm beginning to question whether I'll survive *him.*

Shit, shit, *shit.*

CHAPTER 5

Blake

"One more thing before you go." I stalk toward Ginevra, a delicious warmth washes over me to know that for the next fourteen months, more or less, she's *mine*. When I figured I had to find a fake wife, I dreaded the outcome. But this... *her*... I can handle this. I can make it work. I might even enjoy it.

She won't be some blushing virginal bride. I know her reputation. She's wild, and I'm sure we'll have plenty of fun together. Her body will be mine to do with as I please.

I'll make sure to insist on monogamy in the contract because there's no way in hell I'm letting another man touch her while she's mine. After our year is up, she can do whatever and whomever she wants. My jaw clenches at that thought.

Until then, she's mine. My little liar. My toy. My thieving magpie.

It's perfect.

I don't have to worry about some woman getting clingy. Ginevra's too independent for that. Judging from tonight, she's also not my biggest fan. As long as she does as she's told, and occasionally spreads her legs for me, then she can hate me all she wants. We both have physical needs, which neither of us should ignore while we're married.

And she certainly doesn't have to be concerned about *me* catching feelings. She's a means to an end. That's all.

If she's a very good girl, I might even give her a parting gift once this is over to reward her for her services. I know she won't turn down such a thing.

"What?" she asks, sounding exasperated as I slowly approach.

She can act as disinterested as she wants, but I saw the yearning in her eyes when I touched her. She wants me as much as I want her in my bed.

"Let's get this ball rolling." I pull her toward me and snap a picture of us. Our first couple's photo. She looks slightly stunned, but that's fine. I set the picture as my cell phone's lock screen background, then show it to her. "See? Now we're officially dating. Here's proof."

She rolls her eyes. "That's only proof of how bad you are at taking selfies."

I glare down at her. She needs to cut the sass, or she's going to get spanked.

Ginevra snatches up her phone, then grabs my tie and yanks me toward her.

"Gin," I warn.

She ignores me. With a pouty smile on her face, she

snaps a picture. She looks sexy as fuck in it and I'm scowling.

Figures.

"That's much better." She grins at the photo and sets it as her phone's background. Collecting her belongings, she shoves them back in her clutch, then turns on her heel and struts down the stairs to enjoy *my* party.

When she's finally out of sight, I drag my fingers through my hair. *Fuck...*

I'm going to enjoy having Ginevra Pontrelli on my arm and in my bed. She might be too young for me, but fuck it, I've already crossed that line in my thoughts, may as well take it all the way to reality and damnation. She's exactly what I need to deceive my step-mother and get my inheritance. Gin is an actress, a seasoned bullshitter, if anyone can convince Yve that we're in love, it will be the woman I just blackmailed into becoming my fake girlfriend and future fake wife.

I'll admit, even for me, this is a new low. Yet, I have no regrets, not an ounce of remorse.

Ginevra's not nearly as innocent as her years would suggest. I can't wait to show her what a *real* man can do to her—not those boys that she entertains herself with all the time.

And this *boyfriend* will have to be dealt with too, whoever the fuck he is–if he's even real.

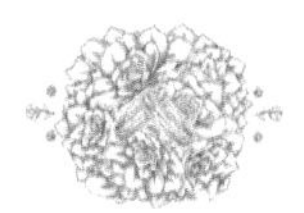

When my mind is set on a certain course of action, I don't believe in wasting time. Which is why I'm sitting in Mr. Pontrelli's office the morning after my party. The poor fool has no idea of the reason for my visit, but he's already beginning to sweat through his silk shirt.

It's good to know my reputation still precedes me. I've worked hard to earn it.

"What can I do for you, Mr. Baron?" he asks, now that the basic niceties are out of the way—such a waste of time in my opinion.

I make him sweat for a few more moments before I speak. "I'm here to ask for your daughter's hand in marriage."

His bushy brow pinches. "I... I don't understand. My eldest two daughters are already married and you can't possibly mean—"

"Ginevra." I lean slightly forward. "I have every intention of marrying your youngest daughter."

Mr. Pontrelli's mouth opens, then closes, only to open again. I find his imitation of a fish annoying.

"W-why?" he asks. "What did she do? Did she cross you in some way? I deeply apologize for my daughter's actions, she's out of control these days."

It seems he knows his youngest daughter pretty well. Though that's not the angle I'm playing at today. If this is to work, then *everyone* needs to believe that Ginevra and I are actually dating—and worse, in love.

"Of course not," I clip. "It's nothing sinister. Have your daughter come down here. She'll explain."

He rings for her and we sit in strained silence until she decides to grace us with her presence. When she comes into her father's office, her face is clean of makeup, her curls are a mess, and she's wrapped in a satin robe. She's delicious. It's nearly seven in the morning and she looks like she just got out of bed.

What a lazy little magpie.

Groggily, she takes in the two of us sitting at her father's desk. She blinks once, twice, then pops open that pouty mouth. "What are you doing here?" The question is, obviously, directed at me.

I show my teeth—a grin. "Good morning, darling. I've come to ask your father for your hand in marriage. It's time we told him the truth about us." I turn my attention on Mr. Pontrelli. "Ginevra and I have been secretly dating for several months."

He eyes me. "That can't be true. What about Oliver? You're dating Oliver, aren't you?" His gaze seeks out his daughter.

Who the fuck is Oliver? The boyfriend? He's a dead man walking.

She visibly swallows. "That was last year, Papa. Oliver and I broke up. I've been seeing Mr. Bar—Blake— in secret, like he said. I lied last night when I told you Arianna invited me to Blake's party. It was actually he who invited me so we could see each other."

The lies roll off her tongue so smoothly that I almost believe them. She's lying right to her father's face without batting an eye. No tells, nothing to give her away. She's a wonder to behold.

I store that information away for later reflection.

Mr. Pontrelli looks to me. "You want me to believe that out of all the women in the world, you want to shackle yourself with *her*?" He points at Ginevra. "A girl who's likely to either end up in prison or dead before she's thirty? She's a disgrace to this family, a slut, and she'll only ruin your reputation."

Ginevra flinches.

Heat rises up my neck. My fingers briefly curl into fists before I deliberately flex them.

"If you think that's true, then you've forgotten my reputation." My icy tone drains the color from his face. "Don't you ever call her a *slut* again, or you'll experience my wrath first hand. I'll fucking destroy you, Pontrelli."

I'm the only person who will be calling her a *slut*. My sweet little slut, as she takes my cock like a good girl.

"I-I didn't mean to offend—"

"Good." I cut him off. "Then you'll apologize to your daughter."

His eyes bulge. I know he was trying to apologize to me, but I'm not the one who needs to hear it. No one, not even her own father, will speak of her in that way. I won't allow it.

Sitting back, I wait, expectantly. The seconds tick by, tossing fuel on the fire of my irritation.

"Now," I prompt him.

"I'm sorry." His words come out in a rush, but at least they're aimed at Ginevra.

I finally glance her way. She's pale, her mouth hanging open in shock.

"It's okay, Papa—"

"Don't forgive him," I snap. "Mr. Pontrelli, what are you sorry for?"

He looks pained as he elaborates. "I'm sorry for calling you a slut and a disgrace to this family."

"Now simply accept his apology," I instruct Gin.

She licks her lips, her gaze flicking to me then back to him. "Thank you, Papa."

She's being much more obedient this morning and I wonder if it's because she's not fully awake yet or simply my unexpected visit.

"Now, where were we..." I drawl, my usual calm having returned.

"You have my blessing, sir." Mr. Pontrelli extends his hand.

In our world, many of the most important deals are done on a handshake. So I firmly grip his palm in mine and look him in the eyes.

"Welcome to the family." The pleasantry falls flat. He doesn't want me anywhere near his family. Which is interesting because most fathers would love to have ties to the Barons. In this case, I can only assume Mr. Pontrelli's fear outweighs his enthusiasm. Or perhaps he knows that he won't be making any demands of his soon to be son-in-law—not if he values his life and current position as a mafia don, one of the four remaining Italian families. It's no secret that I took out the fifth.

I give him a curt nod. This deal is done. First one of the day.

On my way out, I stop at Gin's side. She turns those chocolate eyes on me, there are so many questions racing through them. I almost want to stay and soothe her— almost.

Stooping low, I murmur in her ear. "I'll pick you up at eight tonight. We're going to dinner."

My fingers brush her satin-clad hip, and the heat of her body sears my palm.

Without thinking too much about it, I place a chaste

kiss on her cheek. That's what normal, loving couples do, right? I wouldn't know, I've never officially had a girlfriend. Never saw the point, honestly.

"See you tonight, darling," I call as I head out the door. "Eight sharp."

Papa waits until Blake has left the house before he turns his wrath on me. "What are you playing at, girl? Either that man is a fool, you got yourself into trouble, or you've somehow snared him into this situation. So which is it?"

I guffaw. *Me* snare *him* into marrying? Fuck, I need a drink and it's not even noon.

"This isn't funny!" My father rounds his desk, coming toward me and I instinctively back away until my legs hit a sofa. He grabs a fistful of my hair, wrenching. "Tell me what the fuck is going on. The truth, for once in your life." Spittle sprays across my face.

Papa hasn't hit me in years, but he seems close to violence right now. Even so, I keep up the charade. Mr. Baron is far scarier than Papa.

"I met Blake through Roman and Sophia." Which is technically true. "We've gotten to know each other over the last couple of years and this just kind of happened.

We thought keeping it a secret was the best thing to do until we were sure—"

He shakes me by my hair. Pain erupts through my scalp, but I swallow my whimper.

"I don't believe you," he says right in my face.

"It's the truth! I swear." Tears prick my eyes.

Papa studies me for a long moment, then with one last ruthless tug on my hair, he releases me and paces his office. "You never should have kept this from me. Baron is a dangerous man, scheming. What is he after?"

I rub at my sore head, wrapping my other arm protectively around myself. Papa's rarely violent, but he has his moments—only with me, of course. I'm the only one in this family who brings out his fury.

He's not actually angry about my supposed secret relationship with Blake, he's furious because of what Blake made him do—apologize to me.

No one has ever stood up for me the way Blake did, especially against my father. I'm still rattled by it. Most of all because I don't understand why he cares about the horrible things my father says to me, and the names he calls me? I'm sure it's just a power play. That's the only rational explanation.

But... for a moment it felt like he really cared. Like he saw me as a person who deserves a sliver of respect.

I let go of that thought before it anchors deeper inside my mind, my heart.... my soul. It doesn't belong there.

Papa continues, "You should have told me about your ties to Mr. Baron."

"Why?" I snap. "So you can use my relationship with him to your advantage?"

Papa's fingers curl into fists, and I recoil. "Don't make me hurt you, girl. Why are you always so difficult? Why can't you be more like your sisters, or your mother?"

I fall silent as he berates me, pointing out how I'm lacking compared to my siblings. He's been telling me for years how I'm not as good as them, how I never will be either. How I'm lucky to be living under his roof.

"You are a disgrace," he says, pacing again. "The only reason I haven't thrown you out of my house is because your mother and sisters would object. But now, just maybe, you're good for something." He stops and stares down at me. "Don't fuck this up. Make Blake Baron my son-in-law. With him as family, I'll become the most powerful and feared don in the city. But if you two break up or divorce then that's it. I'll cut you off and toss you out of here. Don't ever bother coming back—this won't be your home anymore."

I nod again.

He's not bluffing. He'll make sure I never set foot in this house again if I disappoint him. Too bad my fake marriage to Blake Baron will inevitably end in divorce. He's sure to have an airtight prenup in place, which means I'll be on the street, penniless.

I'll deal with those consequences later. For now, it seems my father has completely bought this fake relationship. That's one family member down. Now all I have to do is convince Mama and my sisters.

CHAPTER 7

Only Yve would call a board meeting on a Sunday afternoon. In her perfect world, everyone would work seven days a week, there's no such things as weekends or holidays. Which is why we're all gathered around this table today instead of waiting until Monday morning.

Partly, I think she does this to fuck with me, since she knows I have my own business to run. The only reason I'm sitting on the board of directors for Titan Enterprises is to keep my brother Liam's seat warm while he's in college. He'll inherit this position as soon as he graduates, and I'll be damned if I let Yve run the company without keeping an eye on what she's doing.

So for the past three years, this is where I've spent the majority of my weekly working hours. In this hell.

Peter, Titan Enterprises CFO, drones on and on about last quarter's financial reports. This board meeting should have ended at least an hour ago. Everyone around the table's getting antsy, toying with their pencils, or zoning out on the whiteboard behind Peter's head.

Everyone except for my step-monster. Yve keeps glancing at her watch. I look at mine and discover it's three minutes past four in the afternoon. She must have hired a new assistant. One that isn't punctual.

I can't wait for this shit-show to go down.

Sure enough, the boardroom door bursts open, drawing everyone's attention to the frazzled mess of a young woman standing there. Her dress suit's wrinkled, hair frizzy, and cheeks flushed. In one hand she holds a venti Starbucks beverage. Ducking her head, she makes a beeline for Yve, whose heated scowl could light the devil on fire.

"I said four PM *sharp*, Erica." She grabs the drink from her assistant. "It's almost five minutes after the hour. *Five* minutes. If I wanted my latte at four-o-five, I would have told you so."

The young woman withers under Yve's vicious gaze. Everyone else in the room shifts uncomfortably in their seats. Even Peter stops talking for a minute.

Yve sips her drink and her face scrunches in disgust. "Is this made with *milk*?"

"It-it's a latte, ma'am." Erica nervously twists her fingers together.

If I weren't used to Yve's tirades, I'd cringe at the girl's poor choice of explanation.

"I didn't ask you if this was a latte, you brainless idiot. I asked if this is made with milk!"

"Y-yes, ma'am."

"From a cow?" Yve's shrill voice causes temporary hearing loss.

Her assistant hesitantly nods.

Yve hurls the cardboard cup against the far wall. Several board members duck in order to dodge the steaming missile that paints the white wall in brown liquid.

"I don't drink cow's milk!" Yve shrieks. "I said almond milk, you moron! You're fired!" She makes a shooing motion. "Get out of my sight."

Erica bolts out the door. No arguing. No begging to keep her job.

Another one bites the dust.

Yve glares around the silent room.

Unflinchingly, I gaze at the creature who rules over the Baron family business that my father left behind. He left everything in her tainted hands. The woman has never worked a day in her life until three years ago. Until she became acting CEO until Liam's old enough to take charge.

As much as I hated my father, my other reason for being here is to keep Yve within my sight. I'm ninety percent sure she had a hand in his death, whether she did the deed, orchestrated it, or paid someone else to do it, hardly matters. She influenced him to change his will to suit her own needs and then did away with him.

If only I could prove my suspicion that Yve murdered my father. But I can't prove it. For three fucking years I've been trying to find something to pin on her, only to keep coming up empty-handed. Frustration burns through my chest.

The fishing boat explosion left no evidence behind. Not a shred.

For the past three years I've been waiting and

watching for Yve to slip up. Everyone does eventually. And when she does, I'll be there to help her fall to ruin.

It's what I do best, after all.

My phone rings and I fish it out of my suit pocket, ignoring Yve's sharp glare. To further annoy her, I take the call in the boardroom, not bothering to budge from my seat.

"Baron," I say into my cell phone.

"It's Dimitri Kozlov."

I sigh. "Yes, I know. What do you want?"

Thankfully he gets right to the point. "I'm having some trouble at one of my clubs. Roman said you could help."

Did he now..?

"Go on."

"Someone's raped and murdered two of my waitresses right behind *Riot*. The security camera I put out there turned up disconnected and my security team can't catch this guy. I think he works at the club. I need someone from the outside to deal with him."

Interesting.

Without a single glance at the board members, I step out of the room. This meeting is fucking over anyway.

"Why not have your Bratva men take care of it?" I ask, strolling in the hallway.

"Some of my men work at the club. I don't know if he's Bratva or not."

I step into the elevator and push the button for the lobby level. "So you want me to set up a little sting operation?"

"I want you to do whatever will catch this fucker before he kills someone else." Dimitri pauses, and I can practically hear him raking his fingers through his short hair. "Money's no object, so name your price."

I *tsk*. "You know I don't do favors for money, Kozlov." *Silly boy*.

"Fuck," he mutters. "Fine. I'll owe you a favor in return. Just make sure it's not something that'll piss off my wife."

"I can't promise you that, as I don't allow conditions placed on favors owed. Do we have a deal or not?"

He hesitates. "We have a deal."

"It probably won't be tonight, I'm busy. Send me what info you have."

"If not tonight, then when—?"

I hang up on him, not in the mood for stupid questions. I'll deal with his problem later, after dinner with Ginevra.

And Roman's going to help me because he sent Kozlov my way. I swear my best friend's going soft since he married the eldest Pontrelli girl. He and Kozlov are brothers-in-law by marriage, and he treats the young Bratva *pakhan* like family.

Shit, I just realized that *I'll* be joining that family when I wed the youngest Pontrelli—even temporarily. Roman's going to give me hell for marrying her, then dig my grave when I divorce her, supposedly breaking her heart. For a fleeting second, I consider letting him in on this game Gin and I are playing, then dismiss the idea. No one can know the truth. Not even Roman.

Ginevra

Once upon a time I thought it would be romantic to be kidnapped and fall in love—*nope.* I was wrong. Not that I'm being kidnapped exactly, and I'm certainly not falling in love with Mr. Baron. How could I? The guy's not only blackmailing me, but he sits across the table and literally scowls at everyone in the restaurant. He might look pretty on the outside, aside from the deep crease between his eyebrows, but his insides are rancid. He's murdered women and children.

I was fourteen when he took away my best friend and her entire family. Viviana had two older sisters, the same ages as mine, and the six of us were close. Our world was turned upside down when the Marino family disappeared one night, never to be heard from again. The fifth pillar of the mafia families just... gone.

Now I'm sitting at dinner with the man responsible.

I smile at our server, letting her know that she's done

nothing wrong despite Blake's expression. "I'll have the chicken, please. Thank you."

She offers me a quick grin and a nod before taking our order to the kitchen.

I turn my full attention on Blake, who continues to glower at the dining room. Reaching out, I touch his fingers and he twitches, his bright, steely gaze locking on mine.

"What are you doing?" he demands.

"Acting." I take his hand in mine. "That's why you brought me here, right? So we can look like a couple in public?" My casual tone belies the twisting of my stomach. I can't help that he makes me nervous. I mean, I *should* be nervous, right?

Besides becoming his fake wife, I don't know what he has in store for me.

He sits back in his chair, but doesn't remove his hand from mine. "Actually, I brought you here to discuss terms, specifics of our agreement. I figure we should date for one month before announcing our engagement, then we can have a quick late summer wedding. It'll be a whirlwind romantic affair. Do you think you can handle that?"

I lift a haughty brow. "Can *you*?"

He interlaces his fingers with mine and gives them a squeeze. Our body language is in complete contrast to the topic we're discussing—business, strategy, how to fool everyone in our lives into thinking this relationship is real. While on the outside we look like every other couple enjoying dinner at *Spades* this evening.

I'm pretty sure this is the same restaurant where

Roman proposed to my sister Sophia after they talked terms. What is it about this place?

"I can handle anything thrown at me," Blake says. The arrogance in his tone has me rolling my eyes. "Let's talk rules."

Before I can respond, he's listing off the rules we're playing by—or at least the ones *he's* playing by.

"One, no falling in love or catching feelings for one another." His gaze roams my face.

"No worries there." I flash him a dazzling smile, but the bite of my words still hit their mark.

He gives me a slight glare, but continues. "When the time is appropriate, you will move in with me. My stepmother has a sharp eye and in order to pull this off we must live together. She'll—"

"As roommates, right? You don't expect... anything more. Do you?" I really should have asked about this before agreeing to fake marry him, especially with the way his hands roamed my body at his house last night. We both know he didn't need to do that to find his figurine.

Unexpectedly, a flush warms my body. The slow, sensual way he searched my body still makes my skin tingle. No man has ever touched me like that before. It was so sensuous.

Blake lifts my hand to his lips. His warm breath caresses my fingers. "I expect fidelity. You won't be sleeping around on me."

"And how about you? Are you going to be faithful to me as well?"

"Absolutely. I can't risk getting caught with another woman by my step-mother, and she will be the most difficult to convince. I won't do anything to put my goal in jeopardy. However... I don't expect someone with your reputation to be celibate for an entire year. I'm sure we can come to an arrangement that fits both of our needs." Blake's heated gaze never leaves my eyes.

My *reputation?*

I shouldn't be angry considering that I purposely crafted and fed this reputation he's talking about. But I'm fucking livid that he sees me as an easy lay. A slut. Does he think I'm going to be his own personal whore? Heat creeps from my chest up to my ears. With my free hand, I toss my hair over my shoulder.

Blake leans in and lowers his voice, so only I can hear him say, "I want you to be my good little slut."

I flinch at that last word, then quickly cover it up with a smile that makes my cheeks ache. My heart gallops across my ribcage as I grit my teeth.

Sucking in a steadying breath, I will myself to calm the fuck down. "I'm all yours."

A devilish grin touches his lips. "You'll be well rewarded."

Is he talking about money? Compensation? Or something else?

My gut wrenches with disgust, and my racing heart won't slow down. Slipping my hand from his, I excuse myself and manage to make my way to the restroom on shaky legs, without faltering. Once safely inside a stall, I inhale a long, shuddering breath and blink away the moisture that threatens to fall. I'm not usually this emotional. Normally I can just roll with whatever people toss at me and laugh it off.

Why do I loathe that Blake sees me as a toy? Did I

really expect him to be different from other men? He's not, and I'll deal with him the same way I've dealt with all the others. Preferably intoxicated enough to not care.

Angrily, I swipe at my wet cheeks. Life's too short to cry about every little thing. Plus I hate wallowing in the darkness, when I prefer the light.

Everything will be fine. I'm fine.

What I need is more fun in my life. Blake's party last night was okay, but not the escape I desperately desired. Both of my sisters were there and, as much as I know they love me, I can't let loose under their watchful gazes. Arianna's always telling me not to slouch, to drink less, to behave.

I'm so tired of being told what to do. When will they get it, I don't want to behave, I'll never follow their rules or anybody else's.

Now Blake wants to tell me what to do? He wants me to be his *good little slut*? I shiver. I don't belong to any man. Except... now I do, and it's all my fault. For the next fourteen months, Blake Baron all but owns me.

My pulse spikes. My hands shake.

To take off the edge, I pull the small flask from my clutch and gulp down its entire contents. The vanilla flavored vodka burns my throat on its way to warming my stomach. My head spins a little since I haven't eaten much today—not with having to answer a million and one questions that my father bombarded me with after Blake left this morning. Blake never should have made my father apologize to me. After the inquisition that followed, I fell back to sleep until the late afternoon, then spent some time getting ready for this dinner.

The alcohol settles in my belly and I immediately feel stronger, floaty, and ready to face the world—and Mr. Baron.

I exit the stall, only to come face-to-face with the devil himself. He pushes off from the wall and strolls toward me, his gaze evaluating, running along every inch of my body.

"I upset you," he states, but there's no remorse in his tone.

Stepping around him to wash my hands, I shake my head. "It's nothing. Don't worry about it."

Just then, a woman comes into the restroom and gives us a disapproving glance before shutting herself into one of the private stalls. Blake doesn't seem to notice her. Does he even realize he's in the women's bathroom? He probably does, and he obviously doesn't care. He's the kind of man who thinks the rules don't apply to him —and for the most part, he's right, they don't.

He folds his arms and leans against the wall closest to me. "I didn't mean to offend you. One of the reasons I think this can work between us is that you're no blushing virgin. We're both experienced adults who know how to give and receive physical pleasure without catching feelings. That's all I meant."

"I said don't worry about it. It's fine." I dry my hands, avoiding his stare. "I know my reputation. I'm the one who built it, after all."

It's my shield against the truth. I never want anyone to see the darkness that lurks beneath what I choose to show them of myself.

He's quiet for a moment while he scrutinizes me,

seemingly unable to believe that I'm fine. I am fine—thanks to the triple shot of booze flowing through my veins.

Blake nods once, as if he's made an important decision about something. "I'll take your word for it."

Ignoring him, I leave the restroom, returning to our table, and Blake follows me.

"No sex until our wedding night," he states, sitting down. "We'll both be celibate for the duration of our engagement. However, we must keep up appearances, so we should kiss and touch in public, the same as any happy couple."

Finally, I give him my attention. No sex until marriage gives me the time I need to process all of this. It's generous of him.

The thought of kissing him makes my stomach flip-flop. I can still feel his touch from last night, the sensation of his hands all over my body lingers like a phantom. My lips part and his gaze drops to my mouth.

"Are we in agreement so far?" he asks, his eyes lingering.

My gaze slides over the man seated in front of me. His broad shoulders fill out his suit perfectly. Wavy blond hair, that looks like it'd be soft to touch, falls loosely over his brilliant blue eyes, a square jaw, and full lips. He's incredibly handsome. A gorgeous devil.

I nod, and sip my wine, wishing it was something stronger.

"Good. No catching feelings, no sex before we're married, and last, but not least, no more stealing."

I huff out an objection. "You're not the boss of me."

"Until we sign divorce papers, I am your boss and more. This is a business arrangement and you are working for me—therefore you'll do as you're told. No more stealing. I mean it."

I groan. "This is hell. You're just trying to punish me on top of blackmailing me into this, aren't you?"

"Wouldn't be the first time I killed two birds with one stone." He leans forward and lowers his voice. "Believe me when I tell you this could be a lot worse for you, Ginevra. How the next year goes is up to you. Behave, be a good girl, and you'll get rewarded. Misbehave and I'll have no choice but to punish you."

I swear my brain momentarily glitches. A very vivid picture of Blake *punishing* me as I writhe beneath him pops to mind. Liquid heat sears my core—so unexpectedly, like *what the actual fuck?* My upper body sways towards his and I catch myself, for once sitting up straight with my shoulders back like Arianna nags me about.

What is wrong with me tonight? Have I really had enough booze that my body wants whatever this man has to offer? If that's true, then I've become a real cheap date. Normally, I need a lot more to drink before I'm ready to jump into bed with someone.

"What will it be, Gin?" There's a warning edge to his voice. "Good girl or naughty girl?"

Our dinner arrives, and I immediately dive in, effectively avoiding answering him. Throughout the meal, we shoot glances at each other. From the outside it probably looks like we're nervously flirting, but in reality it's a test of wills. His gaze demands an answer, while I refuse to give him what he wants. His stare hardens, but I refuse to crack.

I'm not sure if I could resist the urge to steal even if I wanted. It's an impulse, maybe an addiction, and the high I get from it is worth the risk. What is Blake going to do, kill me?

We both know he needs me alive for his little ruse. So it's not like he can off me and bury my body in a shallow grave—or wherever he normally puts people that he's done with.

He needs me, and that gives me some leverage.

As we're finishing up our entrees, our server returns. "Would you like dessert—"

"No," Blake barks at her.

"Actually, yes." I take my time perusing the dessert menu, hemming and hawing over which one to get, just to annoy Blake. I can tell my behavior is irritating him from the deepening of his scowl, and that slight glare aimed in my direction. I inwardly chuckle at his growing annoyance, I'm not sure why I find it so amusing, but I do.

"Okay, I'll have—"

He cuts me off. "We'll take one of everything."

"Very good, sir." The server darts off to do his bidding.

"I was going to make a decision," I tell him. Eventually.

"Not any time soon, so I made it for you. There. Done."

"Do you always have to be in control?"

He takes a swallow of wine. "Yes."

"Tyrant." My tone's light, almost giddy as I

tease him.

"Brat."

"What, are you name calling now?" I narrow my eyes at him. A playful Mr. Baron is totally unexpected.

He shrugs. "You started it. Besides, I'm only stating a fact."

A dozen desserts arrive at our table and I don't bother to suppress the grin that curves my lips. Each little dessert is a work of culinary art, a slice of the divine. I can't wait to taste them. My spoon hovers in the air as I debate about which to sample first.

"Start with the one in front of you," Blake impatiently suggests, so I grab the plate that's in front of *him* and place it before me, scooping up a bite of exquisite chocolate mousse. "Brat," he murmurs, but there's a tiny spark in his eyes as he watches me eat.

"Oh *my god*." I moan around a lemon tart. "The zest in this is perfection."

Happily, humming low to myself, I make my way from one dessert to the next, getting a taste of them all. I'll never tell Blake this, but I'm glad he ordered one of everything—having to decide on only one would have been a travesty and broken my heart.

He intently watches me, but doesn't comment. One corner of his mouth twitches, and I can only figure that he finds my moans and gasps amusing. He really doesn't know what he's missing by not having dessert.

Once I've sampled each one, I set my spoon down and sigh. "That was delicious."

"Aren't you going to finish them?" He surveys the dozen desserts with a single bite missing from each.

"Are you joking? Do you have any idea how many

calories that would be in one sitting?" I shake my head in disbelief.

"Very well." He snaps his fingers and our server appears. "We'll take these to go."

"You could have some," I urge him.

"I don't do sweets."

"Why? Would they ruin your bitter disposition?"

His lips twitch again. "Probably."

My dessert's packaged up and Blake pays the bill, then we're on our way out of the restaurant. As we weave our way through the occupied tables, my fingers tingle with the need to defy his orders. I mean, seriously, what's he going to do about it? Without overthinking it, I swipe a silk Hermes scarf from a woman's handbag and tie it around my wrist.

We wait at the cloakroom to get our coats, and Blake turns to me. His gaze immediately latches onto the scarf. How is that even possible? Is he really that observant?

Under his scrutiny, a shiver runs down my spine.

"Where did you get that, magpie?" His tone's low and dangerous. It sends a slight thrill through me and I lift my chin.

"None of your business." My voice comes out breathy.

His fingers curl around my upper arm and he pulls me close. "I said no more stealing. I meant it."

He removes the scarf and gives it to the attendant. "Put that in Lost and Found." Then he hauls me out of the restaurant like I'm some disobedient child. He shoves me, and the leftovers, into the waiting car the valet brought around, then settles into the driver's seat. "You like to test people, don't you?"

I eye him from the passenger seat, but don't answer.

"Test me all you want, my little magpie, but I promise that every action you take will have a consequence. So be prepared."

With those ominous words, he drives me home to my parents' house.

Blake

Turns out I am helping Kozlov tonight. After I drop Ginevra off at her parents' house, I go home and read through the information Kozlov sent me about his club problem. It doesn't take me long to find the killer's pattern. He always strikes at the end of the late night shift change. While *Riot's* legitimate business closes down in the early morning hours, the underground gambling doesn't finish until well after dawn. Those are the waitresses he's targeting.

I hack into *Riot's* security cameras, as well as those from surrounding businesses. Then I wait. When a heavy-set man enters the dead end alley and never reappears, my gut tells me it's the rapist we're seeking. He's lying in wait for his next victim.

I make the drive to *Riot* in record time, while texting Roman De Luca to meet me there.

Slamming my door shut, I sprint along the alley, toward the sound of a woman's screams, with Roman at my side. I hope we're not too fucking late. His victim must have clocked out early tonight. To her own peril.

Our soles pound against the grimy asphalt as we round the corner to the alley behind the club. The only light comes from a flickering bulb in a fixture on the building, leaving most of the corridor in deep shadow. Grunts and muffled cries draw us to the far corner.

Roman and I pull the bulky man off the woman with enough force to send him stumbling backward. He lands on his ass. Before he can get to his feet, I'm on him, shoving him to his knees.

"Get out of here," Roman barks at the terrified wait-ress, who darts away, seeking refuge in *Riot* through a side door. As soon as she's gone, he turns toward me. "What have we got here?"

I grip the guy by the hair and pull his head back, then punch him in the face. His nose makes a satisfying crunch as inky blood streams down his chin and drips to his chest.

"You broke my nose!" His garbled wail is swallowed by the night.

"That's the least of your worries," I tell him, sliding my knife from its sheath.

"Blake, don't you think we should—"

Tugging on his hair, I angle his head back and draw the blade slowly across his exposed throat. In the dim light, his eyes widen with shock and horror—a look I'm quite familiar with by now. Bubbles form in his blood where the oxygen escapes his lungs. In seconds, a wash of crimson soaks his front and his gaze dims.

I watch, feeling only satisfaction that there's one less fucker like him in this world.

Once his heart stops pumping, I let him go. He falls forward, sprawled on the gritty pavement in a pool of his own blood.

Roman clears his throat. "Don't you think Kozlov might have wanted to question him?"

I shrug. "Kozlov called me in to deal with the situation." I glance down at the dead man. "I've dealt with it."

Roman sighs, shaking his head.

I send a quick text on my phone to my clean up contact. He should be here soon.

Glancing up, I mutter, "Speak of the devil."

Dimitri Kozlov rounds the corner of the building. His steps falter when he spots the mess I've made. "*Christ!* Baron, I wanted the guy alive."

"You omitted that detail. If you're not happy with this outcome, that's on you."

"I thought it'd be obvious," he grumbles, slowly approaching us.

"Only idiots think things should be obvious. If you don't specify, then you get what you get." Bending down, I search the man until I find his wallet, then toss it to a glowering Kozlov. "Do you know him?"

He checks out the guy's ID. "Yeah. He's one of my poker dealers. But he's not Bratva, so he's not one of my men, just a club employee." His shoulders visibly sag with relief. Kozlov's dealt with enough upheaval in his Bratva over the past year, he doesn't need any more drama within the brotherhood. The city's finally settled after all of that—which is the way I like it. Quiet and somewhat predictable. Manageable.

An old Cadillac kills its lights and backs down the alley as we watch.

I shoot a smirk at Kozlov. "Don't worry, I always clean up after myself."

Dante, my cleaner, steps out of the car and eyes the company I'm with, taking us in with a sweeping glance. He's dressed in a dark suit, the greying hair at his temples —the only indication he's older than me—gives him a distinguished quality. A scar slashes across his cheek to his chin.

"Baron," he dips his head in my direction, "you called."

"I have a cleanup job for you. As you can see," I drawl, motioning toward the spreading puddle of blood.

Dante grunts. "For the hundredth time, I'm a hitman, not a cleaner."

"Meaning?" I lift a brow.

Roman snorts. Kozlov crosses his arms and watches our exchange with interest.

"Meaning, I eliminate people, I don't clean up other people's dead bodies."

I consider his explanation for a moment. "Yet, you always come when I text and you have no issue taking my money."

"Then I guess it's my own damn fault you keep calling me." With another grunt, he pops the trunk and grabs a sheet of plastic.

"And you say you're not a cleaner." I scoff, taking note of the cleaning supplies in his car.

"Well, I do clean up my own messes. Don't trust anyone else to do a decent job."

I bark a laugh. "Therein lies my confusion. See? You are a cleaner."

"Whatever you say," he grumbles, getting to work.

"But you need to stop calling me for these jobs, I don't work for you, Baron."

"I know. But as long as you keep taking my money, I'll keep calling on you." I motion to Roman that it's time for us to leave. "I've always been satisfied with your level of service, Dante."

As Roman and I head toward the mouth of the alley, Kozlov catches up to us. "Thanks for dealing with this, I appreciate it," he says. "You know how to contact me when you need that favor."

"Two favors," I remind him. "One for tonight, and one for what I did for you in Russia."

"You're taking credit for that rescue? Arianna led that—"

"I am. It was my jet that saved your ass."

He scowls. "Fine. Two favors." He glances at Roman. "Next time I have an issue, remind me to call someone who'll just take my money. None of this favors bullshit. Who knows what he's going to ask me to do."

"Might I remind you that you called in a favor of your own just last year." I lift a brow at him. "You weren't complaining then."

"That was different," he grumbles.

"Hardly. You're lucky everything turned out happily between you and your wife. Otherwise there would have been hell to pay. You know how Roman's gone soft for his sisters-in-law since he married into the Pontrelli family. He'll shred anyone who messes with them."

"I know. Now that *I've* married into that family, I feel the same way." Kozlov shoves his hands into his pockets. "Too bad Ginevra's a walking disaster. It makes protecting her a nightmare."

"Neither of you need to worry about her." My tone's harsher than I intended. A strange, ugly sensation twists in my gut. "Just worry about protecting your own wives."

Roman halts and eyes me. "Why, exactly, shouldn't we be bothered with Gin's safety? Has something... occurred?"

When I blackmailed Ginevra into being my fake wife, I hadn't taken my soon to be brothers-in-law into consideration. I mean, I thought about the potential consequences, but I didn't *really* think about them. When I divorce her, they're both going to come after me with flaming torches and sharp objects. Which means... she needs to be the one to leave me—except these two will still think *I* did something wrong, and it's somehow my fault.

Damn it, this is a lose-lose situation. There goes one of my favors owed. I'm going to have to use it to make sure Kozlov doesn't kill me for presumably breaking Ginevra's heart. Roman's my best friend, surely he'll dish out a good beating, but stop short of putting a bullet in my head. Right?

Now's as good a time as any to take this ruse to the next level, so I fully face Roman and Kozlov. "We're dating."

They exchange a confused glance.

"Who's dating who?" Roman asks. "You lost me."

I grit my teeth. "*I'm* dating Ginevra Pontrelli."

Kozlov sputters a laugh. "Nice joke! We're not falling for it, so you can stop right there."

"It's not a fucking joke. Look." I pull out my phone and show them the photo of Gin and me together at my party. I ended up swapping it out with the picture she took of us because it was much more flattering. She's right, I suck at taking selfies. *Selfies*—what a stupid sounding word.

"Holy shit," Kozlov murmurs. "When? How?"

Roman's gaze latches onto mine. "I recall warning you to stay away from her," he growls.

I roll my eyes. "That's when she was eighteen. She's twenty now, almost twenty-one. All grown up."

"She's still in over her head with a man like you, and you know it." He glances at the photo again, his lips twist with disgust. "You damn well know she's too young for you."

I bristle. Sliding my phone back into my pocket, I point out, "Your wife is ten years younger than you."

"That's different. Sophia's mature beyond her years. Ginevra is not, and you're almost *fifteen* years older than her."

I start walking again, done being lectured by my best friend. I know our fucking age gap, he doesn't need to remind me about it. It's not like I was *planning* on fake marrying a woman who's barely an adult. That's just how this situation has turned out. I probably shouldn't be thinking about fucking her, and if she were a virgin then I wouldn't even consider it, but she's not.

Kozlov slips through a door, going back into his club, leaving me and Roman alone in the alley. We probably scared him off with our strained conversation. Either that, or he's running straight to his wife to tell her the news. I'm not sure if Ginevra's told her sisters about us yet. Everything's happening so quickly.

"Are you listening to me?" Roman barks out.

I wave him off. "My love life is none of your concern."

"It is when I promised Sophia I'd always protect her sisters. So you can confess right now, what's your angle? What are you doing with Ginevra?"

My lips briefly quirk up at the corners. Roman knows me too well. Deceiving him is next to impossible, and will only make matters worse when my time with Gin comes to an end.

We stop at the mouth of the alley. It's late, after one in the morning, and the club's music spills from the entry around the corner where a line extends in the opposite direction in front of *Riot*. The place is busy for a Sunday night.

Leaning against the side of the building, I consider how best to tell Roman the truth. Every which way I spin the situation, it doesn't sound good. So I just let it out.

"I'm blackmailing her into being my fake girlfriend and future fake wife." I inwardly cringe at those words. Normally, I don't feel an ounce of remorse, but confessing to Roman leaves a burning sensation in my chest. Heartburn, perhaps?

His fist comes out of nowhere. It solidly connects with my jaw and if I weren't already leaning against a solid structure, I'd have stumbled. Pain sparks across my face and has me seeing stars. I blink them away, rubbing my chin.

Fuck that hurt.

Roman steps away, shaking out his hand. "I'm sure you have a splendid explanation, but right now I don't want to hear it."

Fucking hot-headed Italian. He might look calm, his

voice even and steady, but I can tell he's seething. He's just waiting for a reason to punch me again.

Straightening up, I shoot him a pointed look. "It's not like I kidnapped her from her fucking fiancé. From her own engagement party." I motion toward the club, indicating Kozlov with the gesture. "Or drugged and dragged her to a church in the middle of the night."

"No, you're just blackmailing her into walking down the aisle," Roman snarls. "If you were anyone else I'd cut off your fucking balls! As it is, I don't want to speak with you again until you've pulled your head out of your ass and let the girl go free."

"I can't. I won't. I need Ginevra to play her part." I stand tall, but don't make a move. I have no intention of fighting Roman.

"Let me guess... this has something to do with your step-mother." Perceptive as always.

I nod.

"Even more of a reason not to get Gin involved. She's too young and naive for the vipers nest that is your family."

"This is happening, there's nothing you can do about it." I take one step toward him. "Yve has to believe that Gin and I are in love, that our marriage is legitimate." I mutter a curse. "I never should have told you the damn truth. Especially if this is how you're going to react." Brushing my thumb over my bruised jaw, I scowl. "You can't tell Sophia the truth."

"Well, I'm not fucking lying to her." He glances away and shakes his head. "I'm staying out of this. Don't you dare come crawling to me when the shit hits the fan. And you know it fucking will."

With those ominous words, he strides from the alley, leaving me alone with my aching jaw, and a deep sense of foreboding.

Fuck him. I'm in control of this situation. I've thought of every angle, and have backup plans if anything goes awry. Everything will turn out exactly as planned. It has to. I won't rest until I have my inheritance.

"What do you think you're doing here?" Father's voice booms in the hallway outside my door, jolting me awake.

"Just following orders, sir. We'll be in and out as quickly as possible." An unfamiliar female voice answers him and I roll out of bed to see what is going on.

As soon as I open my door, no less than seven people swarm my room and immediately start packing up my belongings. I stare at them in shock, unable to utter a single coherent word.

"Did you know the movers were coming today?" Papa demands, annoyance written across his features.

Movers?

"I..."

"Answer me, girl."

"Honey," Mama enters my room, stepping around Papa. "Are you really moving in with Mr. Baron? Already? Isn't this too soon?"

My brain finally wakes up the rest of the way and I

puzzle the pieces together. He warned me that my actions would have consequences last night. What I didn't know then was that by stealing that Hermes scarf, he'd up my move in date—to today, apparently.

My fists curl in outrage, but I release them, taking in a deep, steadying breath. I have to uphold my part of our deal—even if I don't like it. There's no way I'm going to jail over a trinket.

"I'm so sorry, Mama. I forgot to mention it. Yeah, I'm moving to Blake's brownstone today. I must have gotten the date wrong, I thought it was next week." I caress my mama's arm to reassure her and flash her a smile.

"Empty-headed, girl, you'll never learn," Father mutters and sees himself out.

Ignoring him, Mama holds me at arms distance, searching my face. "Are you sure you're ready for this? Moving in with someone is a huge leap forward. I wish you were at least engaged before doing this."

Don't worry, I will be in a matter of weeks. My stomach sinks.

"I'm ready. Besides, I need to get out of here. Now that Sophia and Arianna are both gone, you know how Papa and I grate on each other's nerves."

Mama huffs. "That's no reason to move out."

"It's not my only reason. I promise."

Mama doesn't know the half of what goes on with me and Papa. She doesn't realize how much he hates me, and how living here, under his roof, is suffocating.

"Do you love him?" She abruptly asks.

I blink at her. "Who? Papa?"

"Blake Baron." Her lips thin as she states his name. "You know what he did to our friends, the Marinos. You know his reputation. They don't call him *The Black Baron* for nothing, sweetie. I just want to make sure you want to be with him, and that you haven't gotten mixed up in something you shouldn't be."

I swallow hard. "It's nothing like that." I plaster a smile on my face. "I love him. He's the one for me. This has been slowly building between us for years, it's only recently that we both realized our feelings for each other."

Mama scrutinizes me for a moment, and I desperately try not to squirm. I'm outright lying to my own mother, right to her face. All because I don't want to go to prison. Does that make me a terrible person?

I'm not usually one to ask for forgiveness, but God above, please forgive this sin. The same sin I'll have to repeat to convince my sisters that my relationship with Blake is real.

Shit. I didn't expect this to be so hard.

"If you say so, sweetie." Mama pulls me in for a hug. I briefly close my eyes and soak in her warm embrace, drawing on her strength. She's never gone easy on me, but I know without a doubt that she loves me.

Pulling back, we watch the movers make quick work of my bedroom. They're like an army of ants who've descended on a dead beetle.

"You'd better get dressed before they pack up all of your clothes and you have to wear this nightgown all day." Mama lets me go, and I grab an outfit from a still open box, then hurry to my bathroom to change.

As soon as the door closes behind me, my wrath returns. So Blake thinks he can just order his people to come in here and upend my life? Well, he has another think coming. Yes, *think*, because despite my best efforts, some of that proper English those tutors rammed down my throat growing up actually stuck with me.

And I'm going to make sure Blake knows, beyond a shadow of a doubt, that he cannot do whatever he wants with my life. I have boundaries—and he just crossed them. Actually, he bulldozed right through them. Which is not okay.

After I'm dressed, have run a brush through my hair and a toothbrush over my teeth, I grab my phone and head out. I need to get to Blake's place before the movers do so I can direct them. I give my family's driver the address and settle into the back seat.

My cell chimes and I glance at the screen. Two messages from my ex, Oliver, sit unread. I have no intention of interacting with him, so I darken the screen.

Then... my curiosity gets the better of me—or maybe it's my anxiety that spurs me to do it, just to make sure things haven't gotten worse, but I read his texts.

> OLIVER
>
> Hey baby, I'm sorry for what I texted the other night, I was drunk. You know I love you. We can't end like this.

> OLIVER
>
> I'm begging you. Please.

I sigh, dragging my fingers through my barely tamed curls. Oliver runs hot and cold, mean and nice, like this enough that it leaves me second guessing myself. Which version is really him?

He was great the first few months we were together. We had a ton of fun. I even introduced him to my family.

My first long-term boyfriend—first actual boyfriend, instead of a one night stand. I thought I was finally on the right track with my love life, but then... He started acting differently. Just little things at first, a cutting comment, pushing me to do something I didn't like, always wanting to know where I was when we weren't together.

Then he started to get violent during sex. He'd call me a slut and a whore, and slap me around. I'd break up with him. He'd come crawling back, apologize, and stupidly, I believed him. The final straw for me was when he made that video of us. That video...

Bile rises up and I quickly swallow it back down. I can't think about that right now. I have more immediate problems.

The crazy thing is, I half expected Oliver to use that video to blackmail me. Instead, I'm getting blackmailed over a trinket. Yeah, I never saw Mr. Baron coming, that's for sure.

When I arrive at his brownstone, he's not home, but the housekeeper lets me in.

"Do you know when he'll be back?" I ask her.

"I'm sorry, I don't. He doesn't keep a regular schedule, so I can't say for sure. However, he did leave us all instructions for moving you in. If you'll come with me, I'll show you to your room and give you a tour of the house."

"I'd like to see my room, please."

"Yes, miss. This way."

We climb the staircase to the second floor. All the way at the end of the hall, she opens a door and steps aside. "You're in here, Miss Pontrelli."

One glance at the bedroom and my heart stutters. Maybe it's the scent of his cologne drifting through the air and the sight of his clothes hanging in a small walk-in closet that has me on pins and needles.

"This is Blake's room," I blurt.

"Yes, I know." She gives me a confused look. "Were you expecting something else?"

"I, uh…" Shit. How am I going to explain this? "We're not even engaged yet, so I thought I'd be staying in a guest room."

"Oh." Her brows draw together. "I don't think Mr. Baron's concerned about that sort of propriety. He specifically left instructions to put your things in his bedroom. I'm afraid you'll have to take it up with him, but until then…" She shrugs.

Until then, there's nothing I can do about it.

Just as I turn to follow her on a tour of the house, the movers arrive and start bringing all of my worldly belongings into Blake's room. This is really happening.

Shit, shit, shit.

My whole life is moving under his roof, into his domain, and I know for a fact that he's going to try to control every bit of it—of me. For the next fourteen months, I'm his puppet. His to do with as he wants.

Why the fuck did I agree to this? I must have been insane.

My new reality sinks beneath my skin, grows claws, and scrapes at my pounding heart. All I've ever wanted was freedom, and now I'm more trapped than ever. This is a nightmare.

"I'm sorry, I can't." I turn on my heel and literally run out of the house.

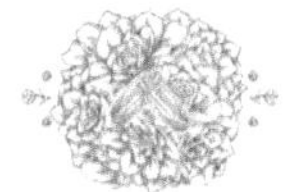

As I sway my body, the beat hammers deep into my bones, pulsating and pounding. It's around ten in the evening on a weeknight, but *Riot* is packed with writhing, sweaty bodies on the dance floor. My head spins as I undulate up against the solid walls of muscle around me. I've been dancing for hours, I can tell by the burning and shakiness of my limbs.

But I'm going to keep dancing, and drinking, until all thoughts of Blake are out of my head.

I stumble toward the bar and wave the bartender over. "Tequila. Two shots, please."

She briefly studies my face, but doesn't cut me off. Not yet anyway. When she sets the shots in front of me, I down them one right after the other. I've lost count of how many I've had today, but it's enough that the burn's barely noticeable in my throat.

I put the drinks on my tab, then step back onto the crowded dance floor. Immediately, I'm swallowed whole by hot bodies and jostled deeper into the club. Wordlessly, we all move together as one writhing mass.

Hands grope my hips, slide over my shoulders. A stranger presses himself against my back and I grind my ass into his crotch. I lose myself in his touch, in the beat of the music, I let it all go. All of my anger, worries, and fears. They spill all around me and disappear into the crowd. It's bliss. Relief. Just for one night.

Another man comes close and sandwiches me

between their two hard bodies. He says something, but I can't make it out over the music.

The room begins to spin, tipping to one side, and I blink sweat out of my eyes. If this were any other night, I might go home with one of these guys. Only to wake up in the morning without a single memory of what happened, just vague impressions. But even as drunk as I am, I know that tonight's different. I don't belong to myself anymore. Not really. Because I belong to *him*.

The Black Baron. Wicked. Cruel. Devious.

The devil in a tailored suit.

His face swims before my eyes, as if I've summoned him with my thoughts. His deep rumble vibrates in my core. Then I'm floating through the crowd.

CHAPTER 11

Blake

"**G**et your fucking hands off of her." My tone's menacing enough that even over the deafening music the two younger men step away from Ginevra. She sways in place, her eyes glassy, and I catch her before she falls. Lifting her into my arms, I carry her through the club to the exit, where my car's waiting.

Rage rips through my veins. Dimitri owns *Riot*, it's his club. While, yes, he called me to let me know Gin was here getting sloshed on the dance floor, he should have put a stop to this, to her, before she got wasted. Places like this are full of predators who like to prey on drunk women—or worse, spike their drinks, drugging and abducting them.

What was Dimitri thinking to let Gin be this vulnerable? If I demand an answer, he'll probably give me some shit about keeping an eye on her via his security cameras. But that's not good enough for me.

Ginevra murmurs a protest when I slide her into the

backseat of the town car and duck in after her. I buckle her in, then tell my driver to take us home.

She tilts in her seat, her head landing in my lap, and I tense. Nuzzling my dick with her face, I begin to harden.

"*Fuck*," I mutter under my breath. "Gin, stop it. Sit up."

She groans. "Fuck me. You know you want to."

Her palms slide up my thigh and over my chest. The heat of her touch goes straight to my swelling cock and burns low in my stomach. I'm tempted to unfasten my slacks and feel Gin's sweet, hot mouth around my dick. I want to thread my fingers through her blond curls and pump my release into the back of her throat, to remind her who she fucking belongs to now.

Witnessing her body moving against those two men still has me seeing red. She's mine. She belongs to me, and I don't like other people touching my things.

I twine my fingers through her hair and pull her up, off of me. My gaze finds hers, those gorgeous brown eyes unfocused, and I realize she might not even know it's me. I could be any man right now. Just a cock to get her off. Fuck that.

Roughly, I shove her away. Disgusted.

She slouches in her seat, her head falls to one side, and she's unconscious. Passed out drunk.

If I was a more depraved man, I'd take her right now in this back seat, fast and hard, then spank her ass in punishment for what she did tonight. For her disobedience, and for putting herself in danger. But I swore not to touch her until our wedding night, and my word is binding.

Why the fuck did I make that one of our terms? Oh

right, because she seemed nervous and vulnerable during dinner. A kind of unexpected innocence shone in her eyes and I wanted to do the honorable thing.

But looking at her now? She's the gold-digging, cum-slut that I know her to be. The first time I fuck her, she's going to be sober, lucid, and screaming *my* name—no one else's. She's going to remember every single wicked thing I do to her body, then beg me for more.

In the meantime, she needs to understand that if she ever touches another man again, I'll kill him.

I put a passed out Gin to bed last night, then left for work before she woke up this morning. That isn't exactly the way I pictured our first night together going, but *c'est la fucking vie.* We have many more evenings ahead of us.

After a rough day of dealing with Yve's bullshit at the office, the last thing I want to come home to is an angry blond in my living room, but... here she is, that fake smile she greets me with, barely concealing her rage.

With a weary sigh, I settle into one of the leather chairs because we sure as fuck need to talk. Gin's perched on the sofa across from me, her hands folded in her lap.

"Speak your mind," I prompt her, and it's like setting off a bomb.

"How dare you send people to invade my private space and upend my life! We agreed I'd move into your home, but I am not sleeping in your bed–not again." She throws a decorative pillow at me, which I catch and set on the Persian area rug. She huffs, clearly frustrated. "I'll pretend every which way you want, but I draw the line at you dictating every second of my life."

"Hm... Actually, that's exactly how we're going to do this." I lean forward, my elbows on my knees, and catch her eye. "You are going to be a good girl and do as you're told—or else our deal is off. After last night's drunken debauchery, you should be grateful that I'm feeling forgiving right now. You crossed the line and you won't do it again. Am I clear?"

"That's not fair. All I was doing was dancing."

"Bullshit. We both know you were acting out. That may have worked with your daddy, but you will not do that shit with me. Do you understand?"

She stares me down for five seconds before she nods. "Fine."

"Fine, what?"

"Fine. I understand that you're horrible and unfair."

I sigh. "I loathe to explain myself, but the reason you're staying in my bedroom is because when my stepmother comes around—and she will—we need to convincingly appear as a couple. Couples don't sleep in separate rooms. And mark my words, she will sense anything if it's off. So you will sleep in my bed, is that understood?"

Ginevra looks away, hopefully she's taking a minute to consider what I just told her, and see the logic behind it. When she doesn't respond, my patience wears thin.

"You will also answer me when I ask a question. Do you understand?"

"Yes," her reply is barely audible.

"Good. Now come here."

Hesitantly, she stands and approaches my chair, eyeing me. When she's within reach, my fingers curl around her wrist and I pull her into my lap. She lands on my thighs with a sharp gasp. Immediately, my senses fill with the honey scent of her hair, my hands indulge in the soft dip of her waist, and her warmth presses against my skin.

All these years I have been fucking leggy, small breasted, athletic types—I'm not entirely sure why. Habit, I suppose. Or expectation. But I realize now that I was never fully attracted to those women. I didn't salivate at the very thought of tasting their breasts or burying my face between their thighs.

But Ginevra and her delicious curves? I want to smother myself in her breasts, fuck her tits, mark them with my teeth. I've never been this feral in my attraction to a woman before.

She pissed me the fuck off last night, but nothing that's happened has dimmed her allure. I can't wait to fully claim her as my own little fuck toy. To use her the way I want.

Lifting her, I adjust her on my lap to make room for my growing erection. Her cheeks color and she licks her lips. There's that vulnerable, naive expression again.

Lies, it's all lies. It has to be because she's no innocent girl.

"What are we doing?" Her pulse visibly flutters.

"Getting used to each other, and having a conversation that won't be overheard by anyone else." I wrap one arm around her waist and settle my free hand on her thigh. She stiffens, but only for a second. "You were out most of the day. Where did you go?"

She shoots me a glare. "That's none of your business."

"Don't test me, Gin." I lean down to speak into her ear. "I require monogamy. If you were with another man—"

"I wasn't. I was on my own."

I squeeze her thigh. "Then you've dealt with the boyfriend?"

She swallows, her throat flexing. "There was never a boyfriend, only my ex. We've been broken up for a couple of weeks."

So she has an ex-boyfriend. The thought of another man touching her makes my blood boil all over again. My hold on her tightens and I force myself to relax before I squeeze her to death. This ex better not come around or I'll fucking kill him.

"He knows it's over between you two?" I ask, needing assurance.

She nods. "I've made it clear."

"Good girl." Knowing she's all mine has my cock growing painfully hard. It throbs beneath her shapely ass. "It's time for bed."

She sharply inhales. "I, um... Are you sure we have to share the same bed?"

"I'm not going to fuck you tonight, Gin, remember we aren't doing that until we're married. Even so, yes, we have to sleep in the same bed. Though I doubt we'll see each other that often. I have several hours of work ahead of me tonight and I will wake up early."

"But it's already late." Her confused frown sets off a

tingling sensation in my chest. Is she concerned about my long hours? How sweet.

I shrug. "I'm a night owl. Don't worry, I won't disturb you when I come to bed." Standing up, I set her on her feet. She's so petite, the top of her head barely reaches my shoulders. "Off to bed with you."

"Okay."

She's being obedient again, and I'm not sure if I should be suspicious or if the fight's left her because of exhaustion. She's obviously been fuming all day long, and probably nursing a hangover after drinking her body weight in tequila.

"Good night." Cupping her face, I plant a delicate kiss against her lips. The urge to taste her, to plunder her mouth with my tongue, nearly overwhelms me, but I resist.

All in good time.

When I release her, she's blushing. I have the strangest sense that she's never been kissed like that before. But I must be wrong, this girl's been kissed a thousand times, a hundred different ways.

I scowl. Possessiveness coils in the pit of my stomach. The urge to claim her mouth resurfaces.

"Good night," she whispers and scurries from the living room before I can drag her into my arms and devour every inch of her. At least if I have to have a fake girlfriend, she's actually someone I find attractive. Sexual chemistry won't be a problem in our short marriage.

Willing my body to chill the fuck out, I head to my office, where I login to the dark web chat room that serves as my inquiry form. People post jobs they'd like me to consider, and I either accept or decline depending on my mood. I certainly don't need the money like I used to, but this is the work I enjoy. This is how I gained freedom from my father and wicked step-mother.

Once upon a time, in high school and then college, I did need the money. Even then, I clearly saw what Yve was doing to my father, how she manipulated him at every turn. He was too weak, too infatuated to see what was happening. She slowly sank her claws into everything from our home life, to my father's social circle, to Titan Enterprises.

Watching her ruin him solidified my determination to never fall in love, to never let a woman in that close. Vipers, all of them.

I realized then that I needed independence. Financial freedom.

Spending so much time locked in my room to avoid the step-monster, I discovered my talent for hacking into computer systems. What started as a game quickly became a way to earn an outrageous amount of money. My own money, untouchable, as I kept it hidden in off-shore accounts. Watching the balance in those accounts climb to astronomical heights also felt like a game.

By the time I graduated college, I was a multi-millionaire and had a sizable investment portfolio. In the years since then, I've turned my millions into billions, all under the guise of a tech services company that runs a multitude of shell companies around the world. I pay enough in taxes that the IRS shakes my hand and doesn't look too closely into my business. Not that they'd find anything if they did.

To this day, Yve doesn't know how I became independently wealthy. The fact that I am, frustrates her to no end. When she realized she couldn't control me with money, she turned to blackmail–and my only weakness: my love of my siblings.

I scroll through the encrypted messages. There's everything from requests to hack into a banking system to steal money, to pyramid schemes, to political sabotage. A couple of personal vendettas where they want me to destroy their rival's career.

Boring. All of it's boring.

Until I run across one that wants to sabotage a certain import-export company... De Luca Global Trades. Seems like someone wants to fuck with Roman.

Not on my watch, even if he did punch me in the face the last time I saw him.

I accept the job and start a chat with the client. He's happy to pay a cool million for the job. All I have to do is hack into the company's systems and install a virus that will incapacitate their communication and scheduling operations. Easy.

Except, while I have this guy in the chatroom, I run a program to pinpoint his location and get into his system. It takes a while, jumping around the globe until I finally have him. But I do find him. I always find what I seek. Then I upload my own virus onto his devices. It's stealthy, quiet, its job is to watch and listen and record every email and text he sends, every webpage he browses. I want to thoroughly know this fucker before I destroy him.

Now *this* is a fun game.

He pays me half up front, the rest to be collected when I complete my task. Though that's an ending we'll never arrive at. I think when I'm done playing with him,

I'll empty that bank account he just logged into to wire me the down payment, his username and password safely tucked away for future use.

He signs off and I go onto my next order of business. It seems my little birdies were busy today. I have six thousand snippets of gossip and information that's come in over the last twenty-four hours. My program has already sorted it all into relevant categories, flagged priority messages, and added everything to my searchable database.

I have eyes and ears everywhere that matters, and many places that don't. My little birdies upload everything from photos, to sightings, to general gossip of celebrities, criminals, the wealthy, and the underdogs. Because of them, I have my fingers on the pulse of sports, politics, and the underworld—and honestly, everything in between. They give me information and I pay them in bitcoin for each little piece.

This is my empire. How I work from the shadows.

I finally glance at the clock. It's two in the morning. I pour myself a scotch and head up to bed. Quietly opening the door, I'm greeted by Ginevra's steady breathing and a sliver of silver light peeking through the curtains.

I stop short, amusement curling my lips as I take in the barrier of pillows she's constructed down the middle of the king size bed. Her message reads loud and clear. Stay away.

It's going to take more than a few pillows to keep me away from her, but for tonight I'll leave her be. Quickly undressing in my closet, I neatly hang my clothes for dry cleaning, then slip under the covers on what's clearly been designated as my side of the bed.

Sleep pulls me under like a riptide.

My alarm buzzes, waking me at six in the morning, and I instantly freeze. There's a warm body pressed against mine, a honey scent permeating the air. I glance down to find Ginevra wrapped around me like an angelic boa constrictor, her arm embracing my chest, her leg resting over mine. She's tucked into my shoulder, peacefully asleep. So much for the pillow barrier.

I stay there, holding her as she sleeps for a couple of minutes, as a series of slightly uncomfortable sensations wash over me. I've never actually *slept* next to a woman before—certainly never *cuddled*. I'm pretty sure this qualifies as cuddling. It feels... strange, intimate. More intimate than sex.

I'm undecided on whether I like it or hate it.

Gently, I untangle myself from her limbs. Gin softly murmurs and rolls over, fast asleep. She sleeps like the dead. Obviously she cuddled with me by accident. That was never her intention.

With a heaviness in my gut I don't dare to try to explain, I get ready for my day. Falling back into my established habits.

As the days go by, we keep to a certain routine. Ginevra wakes many hours after I do, and is asleep by the time I turn in around two or three in the morning. While we hardly see each other, I do notice the growing amount of discarded clothing draped on my bedroom furniture. My bathroom counter has become a cosmetics display, swallowed up by an alarming number of scented products, makeup, and nail polishes. The living room looks like a girls slumber party descended, leaving destruction in its wake. It's chaos.

If this keeps up, I'm going to have to move out. Which I suspect is Ginevra's endgame. The little vixen is trying to drive me crazy with clutter and messes everywhere.

My housekeeper cleans twice a week, but I might have to up that schedule to once a day at the rate this is going. How can one adult woman cause so much chaos? I have this ominous feeling that she's slowly taking over the entire house. Soon I'll be buried in high heeled shoes, takeout containers, and heaps of laundry.

I'll drown in it all. Ginevra's clutter will be my demise.

It's time to set some more rules.

CHAPTER 12

I wish I could honestly say that I hate living in Mr. Baron's house. That I'm miserable. But I'm not. In fact, I don't miss my childhood home at all, and moving here may actually be the best thing that's ever happened to me.

Blake's never home, so I have the entire place to myself, instead of being stuck in my bedroom like I was at my parents' house. I no longer have to worry about catching my father's attention when I venture into the hallway, or to the kitchen, or heading out for the day. There's no one here to scold me either.

Honestly, it's heaven. I spend my days doing whatever I want, which is mostly watching TV, eating takeout from a different restaurant for dinner every night, and hanging out with Kyla. She's Blake's cook.

She's offered to make me food on numerous occasions, but I don't want to take advantage. I'm sure she's stressed enough having to cook for Mr. Nothing-is-ever-good-enough. But every day I find myself drawn to the kitchen, mostly for the company.

Kyla and I lean against the kitchen's massive island and watch a cooking competition show on her iPad. I've probably said it a hundred times today, and I'm sure she's getting tired of hearing it, but I state again, "It's so cool that you won that competition!"

She laughs. "It seems like ages ago now. And I never expected to end up as someone's private chef. I thought I'd be cooking at one of those high-end restaurants or something. Still, working for Mr. Baron, living in Manhattan, and doing what I love is a dream come true for a poor, Midwest girl like me."

"I love your story so much." When the episode comes to an end, the next one auto starts. "It's so inspiring. And it's wild that I actually watched this show when it was streaming five years ago. This show was the highlight of my week. Never thought I'd actually meet you in person."

Yeah, I'm totally fan-girling.

She waves me off. "I just got lucky."

"No. You're amazingly talented." I glance around the pristine, high-end kitchen. "What are we making today?"

"What do you want to make? Anything you want is fine by me."

Kyla is seriously the coolest person I've ever met.

"Really? Okay. Hm... Cookies. I'm craving something sweet and chocolaty. If it's not too much trouble."

"Not at all." Her grin widens. "Chocolate chip cookies it is. I'll show you my super-secret recipe if you promise not to tell anyone else."

"My lips are sealed." A smile stretches across my face.

We spend the next hour baking the most gigantic, delicious, chocolate chip cookies I've ever tasted. They're heaven in my mouth. I moan and do a little dance while I devour the second one in a row.

"It's nice to have someone appreciate my baking skills," Kyla says around a mouthful of cookie. "Mr. Baron doesn't do sweets, so I hardly ever get to bake desserts."

I'm about to make a snarky comment about Blake's lack of a sweet tooth, but then I remember that we're supposed to be a happy couple. So instead, I say, "Hey, it's his loss, and that just means there's more for me. We should do dessert every night, because I love sweets."

She exhales an exaggerated sigh of relief. "Thank God. Finally, someone who will eat all the fabulous dessert recipes I've created over the years."

"But," I hold up a hand, "you have to teach me how to make them."

Kyla eyes me. "Do you have an actual interest in the culinary arts?"

"I think so. I'm pretty sure I've watched every cooking show that's ever been made." My exuberance dies down a little when I think of my old home life. "But my parents' kitchen was always off-limits to us unless we wanted to cook with Mom. She only showed us how to make traditional Italian dishes, nothing fun or experimental. So I haven't really had the chance to try."

"Well, now you live here and this kitchen is always available to you." She spreads her arms, gesturing to the wide, open space. "And I'll help you create anything you want. I know you've been eating a lot of takeout for dinner, but... I could cook you any of those dishes."

My face heats as I realize that I've probably been offending her by eating food from restaurants every night instead of whatever she cooks for Blake. But until today, I've thought of her as *his* cook, not mine. I didn't want to be a burden.

"I didn't mean to be rude—" I start.

"It's no problem." She leans her forearms on the counter. "I'm sure you know this but, Mr. Baron eats the same boneless, skinless chicken and vegetables every night for dinner. I'm sorry, but I'm so bored," she whispers.

A grin splits my face. "Then, let's fix that. How do you feel about a turducken, or beef Wellington? Oh, I know! Sausage stuffed croissants."

Kyla laughs and pushes off from the counter. "I'm game for all of those. Which one do you want to make for dinner tomorrow?"

"Beef Wellington? But only if you eat with me. Otherwise I'll feel guilty and just weird."

"Deal. I'll pull together the ingredients and let that beef chill overnight."

I grab another cookie, stoked about diving into a complicated and time-consuming recipe tomorrow. From what I've seen on cooking shows, it'll take a good chunk of the day.

"Why are we making beef Wellington?" drawls a familiar, deep voice from the doorway.

Kyla offers him a professional smile. "Ms. Pontrelli requested it, sir."

"Did she?" he says, leaning against the door frame. "Why?"

I square my shoulders and face him. "Because it will be fun."

"Fun?" He scowls. "Food's not supposed to be fun."

"Says who?"

"Says me."

I roll my eyes. "You know what you need?" Taking one of our creations from the cooling rack, I saunter up to him and slap it to his chest. "A cookie."

He catches it, probably afraid it's going to stain his perfectly starched white shirt. Seriously, how does this man look so pristine this late in the afternoon? It's like he's stepped out of a fashion magazine page, not just arrived home from the office.

I plant a kiss on his cheek—because we're keeping up appearances—then stroll out of the kitchen.

With an irritated growl, Blake follows me to the living room. "You can cook whatever you want, just clean up after yourself," he demands. "This place is a mess."

"Hardly," I mutter. This morning, I cleaned up the takeout containers and loaded the silverware and cups into the dishwasher. The living room looks tidy enough to me.

Blake picks up a lap blanket from the couch. "These need to be folded, and the pillows all have places. They're not to be thrown about wherever."

Seriously? This guy has issues.

"They are called *throw* pillows for a reason."

He blankly stares at me.

"Fine, okay..." I sigh.

"We need to address the situation in the bedroom

and bathroom as well." He continues folding blankets and arranging pillows. It's so... domestic. It's an interesting, unexpected look on him.

"What *situation?*" I prompt.

He glowers. "You know exactly what I'm talking about. The explosion of your stuff all over the place."

"My stuff doesn't have anywhere else to go." I fold my arms. "Your closet's too small to hold my clothes and there's nowhere to put anything in your bathroom either. If you'd let me move into a guest room—"

"That's never happening, so drop it." Finally satisfied with the state of his living room, he turns to me. "You need to keep my house tidy. It should look like this at the end of the day."

"*Your* house? Don't you mean *our* house? You're the one who moved me in here."

All of my joy over the past few days dissipates. Why's he being such a grouch?

Blake steps closer to me and lowers his voice. "Just remember, in the grand scheme of things, this is temporary. You'll be out of here in a year."

Ouch. Heat blazes behind my eyes. So in other words, I'm not welcome here. This *isn't* my home, just a temporary lodging.

"I'll remember that." Turning on my heel, I head for the front door.

"Where are you going?" he demands.

"Out."

"Gin," he uses that warning tone, which I ignore.

"It's none of your business."

He catches up to me at the door and grabs my arm, spinning me toward him. My body collides with his chest. "It is my business." His blue gaze searches my features. "I swear, if you're fucking someone—"

"I'm not fucking anyone! Give it a rest. I know the terms of our agreement and I'm not going to risk going to prison for a bit of dick on the side. How stupid do you think I am?"

He leans toward me, then his lips are crushing mine. My startled inhale gives him full access to my mouth and his tongue sweeps in, tangling with mine. He licks and sucks and devours me with ruthless passion. The sensory overload renders me motionless.

I've never been kissed like this. Men have tongue-fucked my mouth and drooled all over me, but they've never *kissed* me like Blake. This kiss is possessive, claiming, passionate—almost desperate, but for what I don't know.

His arm loops around my waist, holding me to him, and my hands find the warm skin of his neck. Then, surprising myself, I kiss him back.

The heat between us turns into a raging inferno. We've caught fire and we're blissfully burning alive in each other's arms. The intensity nearly bowls me over.

Blake's hold on my arm loosens as he skims down my waist, my hip, my thigh, until his thumb finds my clit. I jolt at the new sensation. Moaning, I press into him and he circles my bundle of nerves with more vigor. His touch becomes rougher, more demanding of my body.

Then I smell it—the stench of stale cigar smoke and body odor. *His* hands on my skin, trapping me beneath his heavy body. *His* voice in my ear, *"That's right, come for Uncle Lorenzo before I fuck your tight little-girl cunt."*

I squeeze my eyes shut and push away from Blake.

"No! Get away from me!" The foyer spins around me, and I stumble, catching myself on the entry table. My heart pounds in my ears. My vision blurs and I realize it's because of the tears in my eyes. I blink them away and focus on calming my nerves.

Why is that horrible memory springing up now?

Blake keeps his distance, a deep frown etched on his face as he watches me hyperventilate. Without a word, he turns and walks away, leaving me here to deal with my own shit.

Fair enough, I know I'm a mess, no matter how hard I try to hide it. But for some reason his abandonment still... hurts.

A few seconds later, he returns with a cold glass of water. "Drink this. Slow your breathing. In through your nose and out through your mouth." He demonstrates, filling his lungs, then exhales slowly through his parted lips. "Do it with me."

He came back. For me.

I hold the water glass in my shaking hands, and follow his lead. Gradually, my breathing and heart rate calm down enough that I can sip the icy liquid. I swallow down the glass's contents, and place it on the table.

"Come with me." He extends his hand. After a moment's hesitation, I take it, his palm warm and dry—strong, and he leads me upstairs to our bedroom. There, he sits me on the edge of the bed, disappears into the bathroom and comes back with a cool, damp washcloth. He dabs the cloth against my flushed cheeks and neck.

Closing my heavy eyelids, I relax into his touch. My emotions are in such turmoil that I don't question or resist the way he's caring for me right now. No one's ever treated me like this before.

"Do you want to tell me what happened?" his tone's calm, soothing even.

I shake my head, the gesture small, but he understands and doesn't push me for an explanation.

"Whoever hurt you, I'll *kill him*."

I lean forward, resting my forehead against Blake's solid chest. Exhaustion threatens to pull me under. His arms wrap around me like a cocoon and for the first time in my life I feel safe in a man's embrace. It's the most odd, unfamiliar sensation, but with him it feels right. I don't know why. There's no logic behind it.

But that sense of safety lowers my defenses. For the first time in many years, I allow myself to vaguely acknowledge the past instead of denying its existence.

Softly, I murmur, "You can't kill a ghost."

CHAPTER 13

Blake

Yve waltzes right past my secretary at Titan Enterprises and straight into my private office. "I've waited long enough, Blake, the wedding date has been set."

"Oh?" I arch a brow. "Whose wedding is that?"

"Yours. You're marrying Lexa." She folds her spray-tanned arms. "You'll never find a woman to marry you before your birthday. That's a fact. Rumor has it you're not even trying to find a wife, you're just keeping to yourself like always. So here's the deal: You marry Lexa and then you get your inheritance. We'll both be happy."

I doubt this woman's been *happy* a day in her life.

"No." My tone's flat. I'm done humoring her on this subject.

A cold smile curves her lips. "The date and location are set. On June 11th you'll be wed."

I lean back in my chair and meet her gaze. I don't want to miss a moment of her reaction to what I'm about to say. "I'm not marrying Lexa. I have a girlfriend and we'll be engaged soon."

Her jaw drops, before she catches herself, snapping it shut like a Venus flytrap. Fury sparks in her eyes. "Who?" she demands in a low, frigid voice.

"You'll find out with everyone else when we publicly announce our engagement." I tap my keyboard to wake the computer screen. "Now if there's nothing else, you may go."

Her jaw's clenched so hard she's likely to crack a tooth. "There is something else." Much to my chagrin she takes a seat in front of my desk. "We have a new project. It's prime real estate right on the Hudson river. We want it, but we're not the only ones. The seller's from an old money family who's finally willing to part with the property after having it in the estate for several generations."

"Send me his information and I'll make sure the deal goes through." Why does she think it's necessary to tell me this face-to-face when an email would suffice?

That cold, calculating expression returns to her face. "Good. Because if this deal doesn't go through, then I'm giving Titan Enterprises to my daughter. Poor Liam won't have an inheritance any more. He won't see a dime of this company's money, nor will he ever get a position on the board."

This fucking bitch sets my teeth on edge. I should be used to all the game playing by now, but she still manages to throw me off at times. She's always changing not only the rules, but the stakes. There's no way in hell I'm letting Liam's inheritance go to anyone but him.

Titan Enterprises is his, end of story. I'll do whatever it takes to make that happen.

"Fine," I easily agree. She likes to get a rise out of me, but this time I'm not going to give her the satisfaction. "Who's our competition?"

Her grin's pure evil. "Eion Bane."

Finally, I glower.

Fuck the fucking Banes. They've been a thorn in my side since college. If they weren't the most powerful billionaire family in New York City—practically royalty—I'd have figured out a way to wipe them out. But the Bane family is just as dangerous as I am, and there's a fuck ton of them too. Six Bane brothers and a sister.

Eion Bane's going to be tough competition for this property. He owns his own development company and we're often pitted against each other. But losing to him before never had stakes this high. My brother's inheritance wasn't on the line then.

"I'll get it done. Now get out," I bark.

"You'd better." Yve prances out of my office with a victorious smile. She knows I'm riled up, she succeeded in her mission.

The next few months I need to be on top of my game—across the board. To beat Eion Bane and convince the seller my company's the better option, I'm going to have to go above and beyond.

I'm also going to have to be careful with Ginevra and our upcoming fake engagement. It needs to be perfect. As does the wedding.

I can't let anything slip. Yve must be convinced that Gin and I are a real couple, committed for life.

Thinking of marrying Gin turns my thoughts to last

night and her panic attack. One moment we were kissing —she kissed me back—and the next she's having a full blown meltdown in my foyer. I know someone hurt her, even if I don't know the details. She seemed fine with the kissing, but when I touched her...

Rage simmers in my gut. Someone touched her, hurt her, and ghost or not, I'm going to get to the bottom of it. The one who hurt her may be dead, but there could be others. I'll find out. It's my new personal mission.

I've been so focused on her, that I quickly tired of toying with the man who hired me to fuck with Roman's shipping empire. Last night I ended that game by draining his account. Then I sent a quick text to Roman so he can deal with the man himself. Which he will do, thoroughly. No one messes with Roman De Luca's business and lives.

Now I'm free to focus on Gin. That beautiful young woman has far too many secrets. I can't wait to unearth them one by one. She's a puzzle that I'm determined to solve.

Friday night, I decide to forego my dark web surfing, any messages can wait a day, in favor of going to bed with Gin for a change. I've been thinking a lot about her, and us, this week. If the man who hurt her is dead, there's nothing I can do to hurt him. But I can still help her. At least I think I can. I'm willing to try.

I've seen trauma, and PTSD, in others many times

before. If I can help her... *heal* ... that might be beneficial for both of us. She's going to be my wife—fake wife—and I want to touch her in the most intimate ways while she's sober, not a drop of alcohol to cloud her mind. More importantly, I want her to want to be touched *by me.* Only me. In fact, I want her begging for it.

So tonight, we're going to try some things. Ease her into what I can only assume will be new experiences for her. Which begs the question about her reputation. If she panics when a man touches her through her clothing, how in the hell has she slept with half of Manhattan's bachelors? I'm confused.

Either she made it all up–probably to piss off her parents–or as a shield against society, to keep herself safe. That's some twisted logic, but I won't judge her for it. I'm sure she has her reasons.

Or she only fucks when she's drunk, too trashed to let her past haunt her, to let her demons claim her mind. But that's...

My gut wrenches at that thought. I scowl, imagining all those boys taking advantage of her when she's inebriated and clearly not in her right state of mind. She'd never let them touch her otherwise.

Either way, I'm going to help her, and ruin her for any other man. I'll break down her defenses until her ghosts vanish and she's begging for my touch.

Armed with these new insights, I find her curled up in bed watching a cooking show on her phone. I guess her blossoming friendship with Kyla, my cook, isn't a bunch of bullshit. Gin's genuinely interested in the culinary arts. How unexpected.

However, the pillow blockade is alive and well.

Doesn't she realize how she busts through that thing every night in her sleep and ends up snuggled at my side, her limbs tangled with mine?

When I stop at the foot of the bed, she eyes me, then sets her phone on the nightstand. "Are you coming to bed early tonight?"

"You could say that." I shrug out of my suit jacket then loosen my tie, my gaze roaming over her appreciatively. "Come here, I want to kiss you."

She visibly swallows. "I don't think that's a good idea. After last time—"

"I don't want to kiss your lips."

"What do you mean?" She frowns in confusion. "W-where do you want to kiss me?"

My gaze drops to the apex of her thighs. "I want to taste you there."

Gin's face flames a bright tomato red, and she sits up, her back to the headboard. But she doesn't appear frightened, merely alarmed at my blatant desire.

I continue, "Has anyone ever tasted your pussy before? Don't lie to me, I'll know if you're lying."

She hesitates, then shakes her head. Raw possessiveness courses through my veins and I can't wait to get my hands and mouth on her, but I have to take this slow. I don't want to scare her away.

"Do you think you'd like that?" I ask. "Or would it cause you to panic?"

Her lips twist as she thinks about her answer before giving it. "I-I think that might be okay."

I try to suppress my wolfish grin and fail miserably. I'm going to eat my little magpie tonight until she's screaming my name.

"Come here. Slide to the end of the bed and remove your panties." My tone's a soft command, and like a good girl, she does as she's told. Her satin nightgown drapes over her curves, riding up as she slides to the edge of the bed, showing me how she's not wearing any panties. I swear I start to fucking salivate.

"Are you sure this is a good idea?" Her tone's so soft it's barely above a whisper. My heart pinches at seeing the more vulnerable side of this sassy woman.

"It's just pleasure, baby girl." I drop to my knees. "Now lie back and enjoy yourself. If it's too much, just say so. Use your words."

She bobs her head and settles back on the bed. Her lips parted, pupils blown wide, she watches me as I grip her hips and drag her butt to the edge. The kiss I plant on her inner thigh sends a shiver through her body. Her skin erupts with tiny goosebumps.

I kiss and lick my way toward her bare, pink pussy. She tastes like sugar, so damn sweet, and I grunt my approval. At my urging, she drops her knees, spreading her legs wide to give me better access. I lick from the bottom of her slit to the top, and she jumps.

Holding her hips in place, I circle her clit with my tongue, reveling in her sweet, earthy taste. I knew she'd taste fucking divine. She's a little demon in the body of an angel.

The sudden urge to mercilessly devour her spurs me forward, but I hold back, I don't want to frighten or overwhelm her. This is supposed to help, not reveal the kind of monster I am in bed. I need to ease her into this or she'll never willingly come to me.

Gin's moan catches my attention. She's enjoying herself. That's good.

Leaving her clit, I drag my tongue to her opening and thrust inside. Her startled gasp goes straight to my throbbing cock. Lazily, I tongue-fuck her until she's writhing beneath me, her hips rising up to meet my face. Her moans, gasps, and shudders spur me on, harder and faster. When her thighs begin to shake, I ease off. Her whimpered protest is music to my ears.

I kiss her swollen lips, then suck down hard on her clit, locking her hips in place with my arms as she comes apart.

Gin screams out my name. *Fuck yes.*

"Blake!" Her body tenses, flushing a bright pink, then quakes as her orgasm rockets through her. I don't let up until her trembling subsides.

I hum against her sensitive flesh. Satisfied. Then stand up, admiring my work. Ginevra's hair is a wild mess of curls, her breasts heave as she catches her breath, and her unfocused gaze rests on me. I can't help but round the bed and capture her lips with mine. She opens for me, and I sweep my tongue into her hot mouth, letting her taste herself. She makes a small noise of surprise before she sucks on my tongue.

Fuck me. I'd love to have her suck on something else right now, but that'll have to wait for another time. Tonight's about her, not my raging hard-on.

Peeling myself away from her, I drop one last kiss on her forehead. "Sleep well. I'll be in later."

"Oh. Okay." Her gaze falls to the significant bulge in my trousers. "Don't you want me to—"

"No." My tone's clipped, and at the way her expression crumbles, I mentally kick myself. "I mean not tonight. I have work to do." *Like jerking myself off in the shower.* "Oh, and we're going out of town this weekend. The car will be out front tomorrow at ten. Be ready."

"Where are we going?"

"It's a surprise. Just be ready by ten."

Murmuring an affirmative, she curls up under the blankets, her heavy eyelids drooping closed. She's asleep before I've even stepped into the bathroom.

I make quick work of stripping, turn the shower on cold, and step inside. Even the frigid temperature isn't enough to calm my painfully hard cock. So I take myself in hand and jerk off like a teenage boy bursting with hormones, while picturing Gin spread wide on my bed and savoring the taste of her on my lips.

CHAPTER 14

Ginevra

Another text pops up on my screen and I do my best to ignore it, but my sisters and cousin are relentless. Someone told Arianna about my relationship with Blake and the news has spread. Now they're past the point of asking, and demanding I give them answers. Of course they are. I expected this.

When Sophia and Arianna were taken against their will and forced into twisted marriage arrangements, they were free to tell their family what was actually going on. I'm not. I have to lie to everybody I love, or risk going to prison. It's been over two weeks since Blake's party and I still don't know what to tell my sisters and cousin.

"You're popular this morning," Blake says. He's seated beside me in the back of the town car. "Are you going to answer those texts or just let them pile up?"

I sigh. "My sisters are after me."

"Oh? Have you told them about us yet?"

"Nope." I pop the *P*. "I don't know how to lie to them without actually lying to them. How did they find out that we're dating anyway? Actually, never mind, Mama probably told them."

"Or Dimitri Kozlov. I ran into him a while ago and told him we're seeing each other. He probably went straight to his wife with that information." Blake sounds disgusted by the idea of Dimitri sharing our news with Arianna.

"Hm. Well, either way, they all know." I fidget with my phone. "What am I supposed to tell them?"

"How about the truth, except you can leave out the blackmail part." He turns his full attention on me and continues. "We're dating—which we are. You've moved in with me–which you have. We like each other–which we do."

I snort. "Do we?"

"I can tolerate your company, so I think that qualifies as liking someone." He actually sounds serious.

"Wow, what a great compliment. Well, I'm not sure if I *like* the man who's blackmailing me."

"You can like me without liking the blackmail part."

I squint at him, assessing. Yeah, I suppose that's true. "I don't know. I still think *like* might be too strong of a word."

He gazes past me to the passing city scenery. "I'd say you more than liked the orgasm I gave you last night."

Instantly my skin heats and I glance away from him. I don't know what on earth I was thinking last night, but when he suggested the idea... I couldn't bring myself to say *no*. In fact, I wanted to know what his mouth would feel like on me, what it would be like to orgasm in his strong arms, and maybe, just maybe my decision had something to do with how sweet he was when I had that meltdown. He was so caring.

In the past, I'd never put the words *Blake Baron* and *sweet* in the same sentence, but that was before. This man is much more complex than I gave him credit for and I can't wait to see more sides of him. I know he's a killer, blackmailer, and clean freak. But he's also caring, gives pleasure without expecting anything in return, and I swear he sees me in a way no one else does.

I'm not sure if that last part is good or bad.

God, he's still the man who murdered my childhood friend and her family. I can't believe I let him touch me the way he did. Never in a million years did I think I'd be sitting in a car bantering with him, pretending to date him.

A prickle of guilt slithers across my skin. Am I betraying her memory by, maybe just a little, starting to like Blake? Definitely.

I clear my throat, changing the subject. "Where are we going this weekend?"

"To a mountain lake resort. Mohonk Mountain House. It's quaint, I think you'll enjoy it."

"And we're going there... why?"

"I thought it would be an ideal location for a marriage proposal."

My heart lurches—what a strange physical response. Of course, I knew a formal, and very public, proposal was going to happen. But it's too soon. Isn't it? I guess not, if that's the plan.

Not when the wedding ceremony has to happen before the end of summer. It's mid-May and before the end of August we'll be husband and wife. Holy shit.

Blake eyes me up and down. "You are ready to be engaged, aren't you?"

"Sure." I squirm in my seat. "Can we just keep it quiet for a little bit longer? I still need to tell my sisters we're dating, then I can surprise them with the news of our engagement."

"Fine. But I won't keep quiet about it for too long," he grumbles.

"Fair enough." Picking up my phone, I start to type out a response to my sisters' group chat, then delete it and start again—and again. Frustrated, I finally send a text saying I'm fine and we'll talk later, then drop my cell into my purse. I'll tell them everything after this weekend.

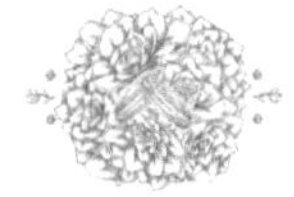

"Hello, beautiful, are you here by yourself?" The guy sitting at the bar slides one seat closer to me and smiles. He's about my age, with tousled brown hair and a suit that's a bit too large in the shoulders.

I grin back at him. "For the moment."

"Then let me buy you a drink."

"Sure. I'll have a lemon drop, please." I toss my hair over my shoulder. Blake's not here yet, he sent me off to the salon shortly after we arrived and now I'm waiting for him to finish up work and come down for dinner. In the meantime, I can entertain myself with this very nice looking guy—a little flirting never hurt anybody. Or maybe it's simply that old habits die hard.

"Coming right up, beautiful." He flags the bartender and orders our drinks, then gives me his full attention. "Are you here with family, or is it a girl's weekend?"

"I'm here with a friend. How about you?"

"Bachelor party. We've got one of the big suites. You should come up, bring your friend if you want." He appreciatively takes me in, his gaze pauses at my cleavage before sliding down to my hips.

I clear my throat, bringing his eyes back up to mine. Why are men so predictable? "If you're at a bachelor party, then why are you hanging out at the resort bar?"

"Just looking for some classy ladies to join us upstairs, if you know what I mean."

That gives me pause. It probably shouldn't, they're just some guys looking to have a good time. But a slithering sensation coasts across my skin and I shiver.

"Well, I'm sorry but I'm busy tonight." My lemon drop arrives, and I sip it.

He shoots me a charming smile and takes a swig of his beer. "Are you sure? It's going to be loads of fun. The groom's super rich so there'll be endless booze, even champagne, food and dancing and some games. You'll have an unforgettable night. I promise." He winks at me. The expression gives me the ick.

"I really can't. Sorry."

"Oh, come on." He gives me puppy dog eyes, sliding closer.

"She said *no.*" The deep, smooth voice behind me sends a delicious shudder down my spine. Immediately, I feel safer with Blake near. "Now get the fuck out of here before I *make* you leave."

The guy's cheeks tinge pink, his brows pull together

right before his eyes widen and the blood drains from his face. The series of expressions that cross his features is fascinating to watch.

"Sorry, sir." He grabs his beer and practically runs out of the bar.

I turn around and face Blake. He looks good enough to eat in his navy blue suit, his blond waves artfully styled. His eyes though, they burn with the promise of danger. He's a killer, I remind myself, anyone with a brain would run far away.

That fire dims as soon as he looks at me. "Have you been down here *flirting*, naughty magpie?"

I give him a shrug, realizing all I want to do is run toward him instead of away. See? Broken.

His bright blues flash with warning.

"I was just having some fun." I down the rest of my cocktail and beam up at him, the disturbing encounter with that guy almost forgotten. "I even got a free drink out of it."

Blake glowers, obviously annoyed by me. "Come. It's time for dinner."

"Okay." I slide off the stool and wrap my arm around his as he leads us to the restaurant.

Quaint is not the word I'd use to describe this resort. The outside has the appearance of a sprawling European castle and the interior's decorated with Victorian antiques. Our suite's two stories tall, overlooking the mountains, with a wet bar, two balconies, a fireplace, and luxury ensuite.

The host leads us through the crowded room to our table by the window, where a silver moon peeks over the horizon and casts its reflection on the lake's dark waters.

The restaurant's atmosphere is both luxurious and old world.

Blake strikes me as the type of man who prefers modern luxury—I'm not sure why, considering his home's filled with antiques. He just gives off that vibe. But in his heart, he has a soft spot for artifacts of the past. I can see why he likes the Mohonk Mountain House. It's so *him*.

And this is where we're going to get engaged. I'll never be able to stay here again without thinking of this night, I'm sure of it.

How many other places in New York, or around the world, will be imprinted with memories of my time with the infamous Blake Baron? As it is, his kisses are seared into my skin, his touch branded on my flesh, and his scent is anchored in my soul. My pulse stutters. He's affected me so much in such a short amount of time. A year might be my ruin.

Blake orders us the seven course dinner and the dishes begin arriving shortly thereafter. Each dish is accompanied by a wine pairing, and by the fifth course I'm buzzed. That lemon drop on a practically empty stomach may have helped too.

"I scheduled you for a spa day tomorrow," he announces, swirling his wine.

My stomach drops. "So we're here for the weekend, but we're not actually going to spend any time together?"

He glances at me, his gaze briefly flashes with surprise. "Did you..." He clears his throat. "Did you *want* to spend time together?"

I lift my shoulders and let them drop, doing my best to appear nonchalant. "Maybe. I mean not a lot of time, but maybe we could go out on the lake or something. Unless you're too busy with work—"

"No. I'm not too busy." He frowns into his glass. "We can go out on the lake tomorrow around sunset."

The lake at sunset? How romantic. Heat sweeps over my skin and my heart soars.

"Okay. Sure." I bounce in my seat, giving away my enthusiasm. All things considered, I shouldn't *want* to hang out with Blake, except that since moving in with him, I've felt more free and alive than ever in my life. Like I'm finally able to discover who I am without judgment or restrictions. And this new me that's forming wants to spend time with this alluring man. After all, I won't have him in my life forever. Each minute with him should be savored like a delicious dessert.

He's a killer. He murdered your friend and her family. That insistent little voice won't let me forget those details, even if it happened seven years ago. Almost everyone I know is a killer, so really, Blake's not that different.

Am I making excuses for him now? We're not even engaged yet.

By the time the dessert course rolls around, I'm practically vibrating in my seat with jittery nerves. He's going to propose. It's fake, I know it is, but I'm still nervous. We have a captive audience in this dining room who are going to witness this next step in our ruse.

For some reason, this feels like a point of no return. If I accept his proposal, then I'm in this fake relationship to the end. There's no going back after tonight. Calling it off would create a scandal.

With each step forward, I become more and more... *his.*

We're in the middle of dessert—which Blake hasn't touched—when he clears his throat and stands up from the table. For a moment, he looks as nervous as I feel. But that can't be true. The mighty Blake Baron's never anxious about anything. Unless he really is human after all.

He goes down on one knee and my heart leaps into my throat. From his trousers pocket, he pulls out a small, black velvet box and pops the top open. Inside is the largest diamond I've ever seen.

Oh my god, this is happening. Breathe.

"Ginevra, I first saw you on the dance floor a couple of years ago, and I immediately noticed your beauty. I realize that we've only been officially dating for a relatively short time, but in that time I've decided that I don't want to live my life without you." His brilliant blue eyes capture mine, boring into me, all the way to my soul. He's lying, every single word is a sweet lie. "I absolutely adore you, and I would be honored if you'd be my wife. Ginevra Pontrelli, will you marry me?"

The diners around us all silently stare, seeming to collectively hold their breath. You could hear a pin drop in this restaurant right now.

"I-I—" Inhaling deeply, I will my nerves to settle. "Yes. I will."

Applause erupts all around.

He slides the ring on my finger, and astoundingly, the grin that splits my face doesn't feel forced. Blake takes me by the arms and stands up, then he dips me, his lips crashing down on mine. The crowd goes wild, applauding louder, and several whistles split the air.

But at this moment, all I know is Blake. His strong arms around me, his tongue roughly invading my mouth, and the heat that rushes through my body. We're in our own little bubble.

Blake straightens, setting me firmly on my feet again, and I think he's going to pull away when his fingers slide around the side of my neck and he dips his head, his lips taking mine in a slow, sensuous and tender kiss.

CHAPTER 15

Blake

That first, dramatic show of a kiss was planned—this one is not. After letting her up, I simply had to come back for one more taste of her sweet lips. Except this isn't a taste, it's an indulgence. One I reluctantly put to an end after several long, exquisite seconds.

We reclaim our seats, everyone else in the restaurant goes back to their own business now that the show's over.

"What do you think of it?" I ask, motioning to her engagement ring.

She lifts her hand, gently rocking it and watching the diamond glimmer in the light. "It's... breathtaking." Her smile sags, and I lean forward.

"What's the matter?" I demand to know.

"Oh, nothing." The corners of her lips turn up, but the mirth doesn't reach her beautiful eyes anymore.

"It's something. Tell me."

"It's silly."

"I don't care how silly it is. Tell me."

She bites her full bottom lip, snagging my attention. With a sigh, she quietly says, "I was just thinking about how gorgeous it is, and how it's too bad I'll have to give it back to you when this is all over."

"Give it back?" I frown. "Why would you give it back to me? I have no use for it. Its only use is to adorn your finger."

Her gaze darts to mine. "Why wouldn't I give it back? Isn't this some family heirloom or something? You'll want to keep it in the Baron estate and pass it on to someone else."

A slow grin spreads my lips as realization dawns. "No, it's not a family piece. I had it custom made. Don't get me wrong, I looked through the family jewels but couldn't find anything suitable. So I went to Maçon Jewelers and had them create a piece suitable for my little magpie. That's yours. Created specifically for you. You're keeping it."

She's literally gaping at me, mouth open. "Wait. *What?*"

"Did I slur? It's yours. Custom made by Maçon. You get to keep it."

"You got Maçon to make you a ring in less than a month? It takes months to even get on their schedule, and that's if they agree to take you on as a customer."

Of everything, *that's* what she's fixated on? My jeweler's turnaround time?

I shrug one shoulder. "They owed me a favor."

She huffs a laugh. Her attention returns to the forty-four carat, round cut solitaire engagement ring.

"I get to keep it." Awe colors her tone. She glances at me and beams. "I get to keep it! Thank you. Thank you so much. It's... I don't even have the right words to describe it."

"Magpie-worthy?"

Gin laughs. "What's with the magpies? Is it because of your grandpa's figurine that I... tried to liberate?"

"Only partially." I lean back in my chair, amusement flowing through my chest. "It's because you love shiny objects. The myth is that magpies steal shiny things, just like you."

"Myth?"

"Yes. The bird is actually afraid of pretty much anything flashy, including shiny things, but the myth lives on regardless."

"Huh. I didn't know that."

"It's pointless information really." I wave our server over. "Would you like a nightcap?"

"Sure. I'll have a lemon drop."

I grunt at her choice of the sugar-rimmed drink, and order myself a whiskey, neat. Neither of us really needs another drink, but we're celebrating tonight, so we can indulge a little. After all, we're recently engaged.

"Tell me about your family," Gin says when our drinks arrive.

Her inquiry catches me off guard. I'm hesitant to divulge too much information about my relatives, but she'll be subjected to them all soon enough. "What do you want to know?"

"I don't know. I'll be joining your family soon, so I feel like I should know at least something about them."

"You've met my younger brother, Liam, at numerous events."

"Yeah. I know of him, but we're just acquaintances. He's always been polite but aloof."

"I see. He graduates from college next month, then he's set to inherit my family's real estate development company, Titan Enterprises."

"So nepotism is alive and well."

I snort a laugh. "It is indeed."

"If that's his inheritance, then what's yours?" She sips her lemon drop.

"That's not important. Besides Liam, I have a step-sister who's about your age. Her name's Lexa. She's quiet and sweet." I take a swig of whiskey. "That's pretty much all you need to know about her. Then there's Yve, my wicked step-mother. It's best if you avoid her at all costs."

"Oh?" She quirks a brow. "Why's that?"

"She is evil incarnate. A manipulative, terrible woman. If you come within her sphere of influence she will relentlessly use you for her own gains. That's a warning, Gin. You'd do well to heed it. Avoid her throughout our marriage and you'll be fine."

"Okay." Gin finishes her drink. "I heard your father passed a few years ago."

I give her a curt nod. Everyone seems too aware of the late Mr. Baron's demise. His abrupt end startled much of Manhattan society and started the rumor mill going. Some people assume a rival took out his fishing boat—with him on it. Others think it was an unfortunate accident. But, oddly enough, no one voices their suspicions of, or accuses, his sweet young wife, Yve.

Only I seem to see the blood on her hands.

Abruptly, I stand and down the rest of my whisky. "We should go."

Gin rises from her seat and sways. I catch her against my chest, steadying her on her feet. I note her flushed skin and glassy eyes. She's obviously had a bit too much to drink, so I hold her against my side as we make our way out of the dining room.

By the time we get upstairs, she's hugging my middle and giggling—over nothing, as far as I can tell.

"What's so funny?"

She lifts her hand, showing me her glittering engagement ring. "We're getting married." More giggles. "That's just crazy!"

"If you say so," I mutter, letting us into our suite. Gin's feet drag and she's grown more unsteady, so I pick her up bridal style and carry her into our bedroom.

"You're so strong," she slurs against my chest. "Do you work out?"

"Yes, obviously."

She hums with approval. "Mm, and you smell so good."

I glance down to find her sniffing my neck. My blood heats when her tongue darts out and leaves a hot, wet trail from my collar bone to my chin. She just fucking licked me. *And I liked it.*

She's drunk, I remind myself. All of her inhibitions are obliterated.

I drop her onto the bed and she lands with a soft huff. We both need to sober up.

Going into the bathroom, I get her a glass of water, and when I return she's stripped down to a pair of lace panties and a bra. My gaze travels over her stunning body, taking in the smoothness of her skin and delicious curves. The sight goes straight to my dick.

"Drink this." I sit on the edge of the bed and thrust the water glass toward her. Thankfully, she takes it and downs the liquid in one go. She sets the glass on the nightstand, and before I know it she's in my lap, straddling my thighs.

"Gin. Don't." I wrap my hands around her waist to lift her off, but she clings to me like a feral cat.

"Why?" Her breath warms my neck. She peppers my skin with open-mouthed kisses.

"Because you're drunk. Because I don't want you to have another panic attack."

She giggles, grinning up at me. "I'm fine. Really. We should have some fun. Touch me, Blake."

The temptation is strong. She's throwing herself at me, grinding herself against my achingly hard cock, and all I want to do is bury myself in her sweet cunt.

Which sets off alarm bells in my mind.

"You're not fine, you're drunk," I finally tell her.

"Same difference."

The alarm bells are now accompanied by flashing red lights. Something's not right, but I can't put my finger on what exactly. I've fucked drunk women before. Sober, drunk, doesn't really matter to me so long as I know they're willing and they sign an NDA before things get too interesting.

But with Gin... her entire demeanor changes when she's intoxicated. I barely know this person.

When I touched her clit through her clothes she spiraled fast. Then when I ate her pussy she was shy and uncertain. But in the car after the club, and now, she's living up to her reputation as a horny, eager, confident woman who wants to get fucked.

And I'm not buying it. Something's off. Which version is the real Gin?

I come back around to the thought that she only wants sex when she's trashed, when she has temporarily silenced her demons.

Her small hands are inside my shirt as she sucks on my neck. I swallow hard, warring with the side of myself that wants to throw caution to the wind—not to mention our agreement to only have sex after we're married—and fuck her now. She's so damn eager. And I'm so fucking hard that it hurts.

But somehow, my moral and heroic side wins out. *Fucking pathetic.* I didn't realize that part of me still existed. It hasn't shown itself in years.

"Gin, that's enough." My harsh tone gets through the haze clouding her brain. She freezes on my lap. "I'm not fucking you when you're drunk. Now go to bed."

Pushing her away, I make a beeline for the door and don't glance back. I can't. She's too tempting.

CHAPTER 16

Ginevra

Blake turned me down last night. Humiliation washes through me again as I spend the day at the spa getting pampered and treated like a queen. But I can't relax, not totally, because I keep replaying the snippets of last night that I *do* remember, which aren't many. I know I acted like a fool and that he left the bedroom and slept on the sofa.

My stomach twists and my chest tightens. If I could crawl under a log and hide forever, I would. I'm so embarrassed.

I shouldn't have had so much to drink last night, because when I do, my inhibitions disappear and I'll do pretty much anything. Luckily for me, I usually don't remember much of what happens, just vague impressions and sensations. Or maybe that's not a good thing? I don't know. All I know is that the wild and carefree version of myself doesn't have panic attacks, she's happy and freed from her trauma, and she does whatever the hell she wants.

I'd love to be her all the time. There was an era in my life not so long ago when I downed a shot of vodka first thing in the morning. It helped with the hangover from the night before. Since moving in with Blake, I haven't been drinking as much, if at all. When did that change? I don't actually recall.

Never mind, it's not important.

Mostly, I'm embarrassed about last night because Blake's the only man who's ever turned me down—as far as memory serves. But do I really want to have sex with him when I won't remember it the next morning?

That thought gives me pause. I've always been fine with not remembering. Most of the snippets I do recall leave me feeling dirty and used. Why would I want to have all those details seared into my mind forever? I don't.

My thoughts wander to Blake... Would having sex with him leave me feeling gross and used? Hmm... Somehow, I doubt it. He made me come on his face and that felt downright heavenly.

Even so, I've never fucked anyone while sober, and since he won't do it when I'm drunk, we're at an impasse. The truth is, I'm afraid to do it sober, I don't know what thoughts or feelings will come up, and that terrifies me. I don't know how to be vulnerable like that without freaking out.

As my day at the spa comes to an end, I make my way back to the suite, in a much better head-space and ready to go out on the lake with my fake fiancé, only to find him on his phone, pacing the living area.

"What do you mean by *he dropped the ball?*" Blake's cold tone could make hell freeze over. "I see. Find his crew, and make them get it done tonight. No, I'll deal with him later. Personally."

Blake glances at me, then out the window at the sun's position low on the horizon, and shakes his head. He mouths the words: *Not tonight.* I nod, understanding that he's too busy with work for us to go out on the lake. Which is fine. Our relationship's fake anyway, we probably shouldn't do romantic stuff like watching the sunset from a rowboat. I'm not even sure why I originally suggested spending time together while we're here.

Blake turns his back to me. "I don't care what it takes, Marcus, I want it done tonight. If you have to hold them there at gunpoint to get the job done, then do it." A pause. "Yes, I'm fucking serious," he growls. "Good. I'll send you the plans I sent that fucker. Hold on."

He goes upstairs to the bedroom and doesn't come back down for the rest of the night. From what I can hear, he's either on his laptop or the phone dealing with this work crisis. So I curl up on the sofa in front of the cold fireplace and watch my cooking shows. Room service arrives with our dinner, and Blake takes his meal up to the bedroom.

I'm not disappointed in our last night here. Not at all. We really should try to keep this kind of distance from each other and not get too attached. Not that Blake's the type to get *attached* to anybody. Tonight proves that I'm low on his priority list.

Brushing off my sadness, I focus on what makes me happy—my television shows.

Morning brings pretty much the same dynamic as last night. Blake continues to ignore me in favor of his laptop and cell phone for the three-hour ride home, so I take in the beautiful scenery and try not to let his behavior get me down.

I shouldn't want his attention. He's blackmailing me, using me to get something he wants from his step-mother—I'm assuming. I should distance myself from him. The fact that I do want to spend time with him and get to know him shows that I'm seriously messed up. It seems the more toxic the relationship, the deeper I fall into it.

My ex, who runs hot and cold—who's apparently on a cold streak because I haven't heard from him in a while —had me pining for him. Hell, I thought he was my first true love in the beginning. So stupid. So *naive*.

Now Blake's blackmailing me into this fake relation-ship, and I suggest a romantic boat ride on a lake. Worse, I'm irritated when I'm not the center of his attention. I crave to know who he really is beneath that frigid exterior. He intrigues me to no end.

What. Is. *Wrong*. With. Me?

This is all *fake*. We're not friends. He's a dangerous man I should stay far away from. I know all of this, but it doesn't stop me from sliding fast toward getting my heart broken—again. And this isn't all my fault either, is it? I mean he was so nice to me when I had that panic attack, then he was amazing when he licked my pussy, and that proposal was pure perfection. I almost believed his lies. But that's what comes out of his mouth whenever he opens it—lies.

I need to rally my defenses against him. He's far better than I am at any game of manipulation. He's a pro, and I just realized I'm in over my head.

When we arrive home—his home, my temporary living situation—Blake's in a much better mood. I can tell because his scowl lines are more relaxed than they were earlier. His shoulders look less tense too.

As we step out of the car, a tall, beefy guy appears and takes our luggage in hand. He gives a single nod to Blake, some kind of silent communication passes between them, then he disappears inside the brownstone. What was that all about?

Blake opens the front door for me. "Go straight to the bedroom."

I choke on air, and blink up at him. "*Excuse* me?"

After he turned me down last night, now he demands that I go to his bedroom? I don't think so.

"There's something I want you to see. Come on." He takes my arm, and I give in as we head upstairs.

We enter and I immediately notice the change. The bedroom's clean and tidy...

I turn toward him. "Where are all of my things?"

"Open that door." Blake releases me at the same time that I notice a door in the wall, one that didn't used to be there. My chest tightens with apprehension, but curiosity wins out and I turn the knob and step over the threshold.

My gasp catches in my throat.

Lights automatically turn on all around me, illuminating the largest walk-in closet I've ever seen. It's an entire room with an island in the middle, a crystal chandelier hanging over it. My clothes, shoes, and bags are beautifully displayed in a custom closet system. Part of the island is a glass jewelry case. There's even a makeup vanity and mirror in front of one of the two huge windows.

"This is..." I trail off, I have no words.

Blake leans casually against the doorjamb, arms folded. "Magpie-worthy?" he asks.

My heart skips a beat, and a foreign kind of warmth spreads through my limbs. He did this... *for me*. I can't believe it.

Spinning toward him, I ask, "Is this why you were on the phone last night and this morning?"

"Yes. The contractor did half the job then vanished, so I had my assistant Marcus and his team finish it up before our return. Do you like it? I can have them change anything—"

With a squeal, I rush to him and throw my arms around his neck. "I love it! Thank you so much."

He grunts. "Now you have a place for all of your stuff."

I kiss his cheek, then pull away. "I know you want me to think you did this to get all of my clutter out of your way, but I know that's not entirely true. You did this for me. Admit it."

"Never. I did this for my own selfish reasons, and that is all." He states those words as fact, yet my heart flutters at the warmth in his eyes. *Liar.* He did this for me.

"Whatever you say." I bounce on my toes, unable to contain my excitement. "I'm cooking you dinner tonight." That statement's out before I lose my nerve. "Your boneless chicken and vegetables can wait one more night. I know you eat delicious dishes, you did at the resort."

He sighs. "I only eat delicious dishes made by world-renowned chefs."

"Snob."

"Quite."

"Well, I promise you that you'll love whatever I make for you."

"Gin, don't." He frowns. "I'm not a polite person. I'm not going to tell you how good your home-cooked meal is just to make you happy. I don't believe in false praise."

I dryly chuckle. "Oh, I know."

But I don't care. Nothing he can say will dissuade me from thanking him by cooking dinner tonight. With that goal in mind, I go in search of Kyla. We have work to do.

"Gin," Blake growls as I make him sit down at the dining table with me. He's like a fussy toddler who doesn't want to eat his food.

"Stop protesting. It's too late now. Sit down so we can have a nice meal together." I take my seat across from him. Nerves skitter beneath my skin as Kyla serves the dinner we worked so hard on. I wanted to do this one mostly by myself, so she provided the ingredients, then sat back and watched, only speaking up when I was about to do something wrong. Under her masterful guidance, I think I did okay.

Blake sniffs at his forkful of braised pork in a sweet and savory sauce before tentatively putting it in his mouth. I roll my eyes. He's acting like I might serve him poison—or worse, prison food. I know he eats pork because he ordered it at *Spades,* when we had dinner together.

He chews, makes a small noise in the back of his throat, swallows, then goes for another bite. I tasted everything in the kitchen along the way, so I know it's good—excellent even. Blake tastes the braised pork with the accompanying rice, then the sautéed bok choy and mushrooms topped with basil, all in silence.

I can't stand the suspense any longer. "Well?"

Leaning forward, I wait for him to speak.

"It's good." He scowls at his plate, like he's blaming it for being so tasty. "Actually, it might be the best braised pork dish I've ever had."

I grin so wide my cheeks ache. He'd never say that if he didn't mean it. The anxiety twisting my stomach morphs into tiny bubbles, so light and airy I could float away. Finally, I dive into my own meal. It is good. I'm very proud of myself right now.

Blake arches a brow. "You made this under Kyla's supervision?"

"Yep. She corrected me twice. Once when I almost skipped a step, and again when I grabbed the wrong spice. Other than that, it's all my creation."

He nods, chewing. "You have a true talent here, magpie. Why haven't you pursued it?"

"Oh, um." I swallow. "I've been watching cooking shows for years, but I didn't realize I could actually cook until I moved in here."

"How's that possible? Didn't you grow up with a working kitchen in your home?"

"I did. But we weren't allowed in there very often. I didn't have anywhere to cook until Kyla let me use the kitchen here." Explaining it all aloud sounds kind of sad, but it's the truth. Moving in with Blake has changed my life in more ways than one.

That's something I can never repay him for, I wouldn't even know where to start.

CHAPTER 17

Blake

My phone's incessant buzzing wakes me. It's five thirty in the morning, who the fuck—? I swipe to see multiple text messages from my housekeeper, Fleur, saying Yve's at the front door. If she's on my front step, she won't stay out there for long. Sure enough, the clicking of stilettos rings through the hallway.

Now what the fuck am I going to do..? My gaze slides to Ginevra's peaceful face nestled against my bare chest.

Toppling the pillow-wall to destroy it, I murmur, "Gin, wake up. It's show time."

"What?" She blinks awake, pausing to take in our close proximity. "What time—?"

"Shh. That's irrelevant. Yve's here and it's time to put on a show. Are you up for it, magpie?" I run my palm over her satin-clad waist. She feels divine in my arms and lust pulses through me, making my morning wood grow rigid.

"Mm-hm." She rubs sleep from her eyes and blinks

up at me. How is she so fucking gorgeous in the morning? This is a side of her I haven't seen before because I'm always up and out of here before she rises. I've been missing out on this sight every morning. My cold heart twists.

"Good." My voice comes out huskier than intended. I clear my throat. "I have an idea."

"Yeah? What are we going to do?" Her gorgeous chocolate eyes draw me in and I'm tempted to kiss her, just once.

Bang, bang, bang! "Blake, I know you're in there." Yve's irritating voice comes through my door. "Open up. We need to talk."

I groan. Keeping my voice low, I say, "Let's do what couples do in the morning." That innocent expression on her face unravels me from the inside out. "They fuck," I clarify, then hurry to add, "We're going to *pretend* to fuck. Okay?"

Gin bobs her head in agreement, and I roll us over so I'm on top, while trying not to crush her beneath my weight. Her nightgown and my boxers create a barrier between us, but I know she can feel my erection—it's challenging to miss. At first she's tense, her breath coming in shallow pants, and a light sheen of sweat breaks out on her forehead. She's nervous.

"We're just pretending," I whisper in her ear. "I know you're an amazing actress, Gin. Act for me. Give me the best performance you've ever done."

"Mm," she moans, loud enough that Yve takes a break from pounding on my bedroom door. "Oh, yes!"

"Good girl. Just like that." I settle between Gin's legs, but keep my weight off of her and grip the headboard, rocking it against the wall. From the sounds we're making there should be no doubt in anyone's mind what we're doing in here—or what they *think* we're doing.

My door bursts open just as Gin really gets into our role-playing and screams, "Yes! Yes!"

Gin's covered from the waist down by her nightgown, and our bottom halves are under the blanket, but my bare chest is on full display.

The stricken look on Yve's face is amusing enough to make my lips twitch before I scowl and shout at her, "Get the fuck out! Can't you see I'm busy?"

Yve's over-plumped lips twist with disgust, but she retreats, closing my door behind her. But she's not that easy to scare off. I know she's in the hallway, waiting, listening. So I pick up my pace on that headboard, slamming it against the wall with enough force to crack the plaster.

Gin giggles, then shouts, "That's it! Oh my God, that's right big boy, give it to me harder. Faster! Harder!" She releases a loud moan. "Fuck me, Blake. That's right, split me in half with your huge cock. Oh! Oh! Oh!"

A laugh rumbles in my chest at her over the top acting. She's like listening to a badly directed porno. But she's doing exactly what I want—perfectly. Hopefully, Yve will be scarred for life.

"Give it to me, big boy. Stuff your sausage in my hole. Oh yes! Just like that." Gin catches my gaze, a hint of mischief in her eyes, a grin on her luscious lips. "Oh no! Blake, not there, that's the *wrong* hole!"

Fuck. I chuckle, trying to keep it light, when the fact is she's driving me wild.

Another loud moan. "Ah! That's so good. Fuck my ass like you own it, big boy!"

I groan and bite down on my lip. Where does she come up with this shit? At the same time, her dirty mouth, and the images she's conjuring with it, make me wish we were doing this for real. I can't wait to have her screaming my name while I fuck all of her beautiful holes.

Fuck, lust has never driven me this insane before. I've never wanted someone—

Ginevra tentatively places one small palm against my flexed abs, and her touch sends a shiver through me. Slowly, keeping up her fake moans and gasps, she drags her hand downward exploring each rise and valley of my six-pack. Lower, lower... Until she grazes my straining cock. It twitches at her touch and I suck in a sharp breath.

Our gazes lock. The curiosity and vulnerability I see in her eyes has transfixed me. Tentatively, she wraps her tiny hand around my cock. The way she does it makes me certain she's never touched a man before. How can that be true?

Fuck, just that light caress is almost enough to set me off. Then her hand falls away. I immediately miss her touch.

Gin wails, breaking that intense moment between us. "I'm coming! Fill my asshole with your cum, big boy! I want it dripping out of me all day long."

Fucking hell. One day I'm going to grant her wish. I'll fill her so full of cum it's going to drip down her thighs.

To end our game, I groan and give the headboard one

last shove. Then I drop my forehead to hers, and press my lips to the tip of her nose. She's silently laughing so hard tears stream down her cheeks.

"Good job." Now I have to get away from her before I do something stupid like sink my cock into her warm pussy. Or kiss that pretty, filthy mouth.

Dragging on a pair of slacks and a T-shirt, I step into the hallway to confront my step-mother.

As soon as she sees me, she snarls, "You're disgusting."

"I'm not the one loitering in the hallway listening to a man fuck his girlfriend." I lean casually against the wall. "Pervert."

She ignores my jibe. "I don't believe you have a girlfriend. I can only assume that's your girl *de jour* in there that you're trying to pass off as your—"

"She's my fiancée. I proposed to her over the weekend and she said *yes*."

Crimson climbs up Yve's neck and disappears under her caked on makeup. She sneers. "What a little harlot. She's certainly not after your money, because she won't be getting any."

"That's why I like her. She's not a gold-digging bitch like you. She loves me for myself." The lies roll off my tongue.

Yve pins me with a frigid stare. "You know my terms, so she better really be in love with you. One year, Blake, that's how long you'll have to wait for your inheritance now that you've decided to marry that woman instead of my darling Lexa."

"I'll survive," I drawl, already tired of this conversation. "Why are you here?"

"Have you set up a meeting with the seller yet? Or is Liam's inheritance going to go to Lexa? Word on the street is that Eion Bane's moving in fast. If you're going to secure that land for us then you better stop fucking around—literally—and get on with it."

"I'm meeting with him a week from today. It's already set." Fuck, this woman pisses me off.

"That better not be too late." She glares and turns on her heel. "You know what's at stake if you fail."

I wait until the click of her heels disappears out my front door, then heave an irritated sigh. Like that conversation couldn't wait a couple more hours until I was at the office? Yve's always liked pushing into other people's personal space, that hasn't changed. I hope this time she regretted it.

The only thing I regret is having fake sex with my fake fiancée. I can't wait until the day Ginevra's legally bound to me—I'll enjoy every inch of her.

CHAPTER 18

Ginevra

After the morning's excitement, I fall into a restless sleep and have naughty dreams starring Blake. When I finally wake up, drenched in sweat, my pussy pulsing with need, he's already left for work. So I decide to take care of myself in the shower. These handheld shower heads really are amazing.

Except once isn't enough. I build myself up a second time, remembering how I touched his cock—briefly, but still. I had to end our charade after that because I was so close to begging him to take me for real. To hell with the show, at that moment I wanted his hands and mouth on me, his cock inside my body.

And I was sober. Dead sober.

Only now do I realize that I didn't panic when he climbed on top of me this morning. Nervous, yes, but not riddled with anxiety. He could have touched me and I would have been fine—more than fine, I would have welcomed his attention.

My imagination wanders to the feel of his strong

body on top of mine, taking me, claiming me, and I shatter with a low moan as steaming water runs down my body.

Why did we decide to wait until marriage? We could be having sex now. Sex has no bearing on our fake relationship, it's just lust, physical pleasure. A release that we obviously both need.

For the first time in my life, I *want* a man to touch me. My intuition tells me that sex with Blake will be like nothing I've ever experienced before. I want that.

Turning off the water, I step out of the shower and get ready for the day. I'm relaxed and energized at the same time. Today's going to be a good day, I can feel it. Maybe Kyla and I will tackle a new recipe. One of these mornings, I want to wake up early enough to go with her to the markets where she buys her supplies. I know she goes early to get the best offerings.

I'm taming my blond curls into more manageable waves when my phone chimes. The sound reminds me that I still need to talk to my sisters. I've been avoiding them for far too long.

I swipe to see the text message and my stomach drops. Dread wraps around my insides like a snake around its prey. It's from Oliver, my ex.

OLIVER

I hope you haven't forgotten about me, babe. I think of you all the time. I like to think of you just like this...

The next message is a short video clip that auto plays. Bile rises in my throat. For a couple of seconds my gaze is glued to the screen as I watch Oliver give the camera a thumbs-up. Then he moves out of the way, revealing what's on the bed behind him—my bruised, naked body, tied and gagged as I scream for help.

My vision blurs with tears, and my phone slips from my numb fingers, clattering as it falls on the vanity top. Flashes of memory invade my mind until I cover my head with my arms and scream. Except no sound comes out. The images continue to bombard me no matter how determined I am to keep them at bay. Whatever Oliver gave me that night only heightened my senses so that I felt every nerve ending of pain, and worse, I remember it all. Every dreadful moment.

My stomach roils and I barely make it to the bathroom in time, vomiting in the sink.

No matter how safe I feel with Blake, my past will always be around to haunt me, it seems. Uncle Lorenzo's dead, but Oliver took his place. Who will it be next? Someone, I'm sure, because I can't seem to escape these types of men. They find me. They'll always find me. As soon as Blake and I divorce, and I'm no longer under his protection, another abuser will lure me in.

Or maybe I've been blind. Maybe Blake is one of them and he hasn't shown his true colors yet. But he will. They always do eventually. Oliver did.

When it comes to men, I'm the worst judge of character. I *know* I can't trust myself.

What if Blake hurts me like they did?

He will. I know he will.

My temples throb with a splitting headache. I can't let myself spiral like this. I need happy Gin today, and there's only one way to get her to come out. Vodka.

 Blake

Yve's been more of a pain in the ass then usual today, so I say fuck it and head home early, which is out of character for me. My workaholic reputation's sure to suffer from this decision. Not like I care—fuck it. My singular focus on the ride home is the alluring woman I left in my bed this morning.

I find Gin lounging by the rooftop pool. My mouth goes dry as I take her in. That thin scrap of fabric can hardly be called a swimsuit.

My gaze travels the area. If anyone sees her voluptuous body this scantily clad, I'll have no choice but to pluck out their eyeballs. Finding no one in the vicinity, I return my attention to her and prowl closer.

She shields her eyes against the bright summer sunlight. "Oh, it's you," she says cheerily.

"Obviously." Involuntarily, I rake my gaze over her hourglass curves. "The time has come. We'll be officially announcing our engagement at your sister's wedding this weekend."

"Whatever you say." She beams at me with the fakest smile I've ever seen. I'm getting better at determining her moods, and right now she's not as happy as she appears. The difference between fake-happy Gin, and genuinely-happy Gin is like night and day. One is a dark rain cloud on an otherwise clear day, completely out of place, and the other is like the sun itself shining down in all its glory.

"Whatever I say, huh?" I point toward the house. "Then get your ass inside and put on some real clothes before someone else sees you up here."

Her expression sobers. However, the wicked glint in her eyes should be enough forewarning. Reaching behind her back, she tugs on the string and her entire top falls in her lap, putting her luscious breasts on full display. My palms itch with the desire to cup them. They would make a nice handful.

Then, like a cat, she stretches, all the while keeping her gaze trained on me. Defiance radiates from her in waves.

Ginevra Pontrelli is a brat. She knows it. I know it.

What she doesn't know, yet, is that brats get punished.

Dropping into the chair beside hers, I drag her across my lap. Her surprised squeak warms my insides, egging me on.

"Disobedient girls get punished, Gin." I smack her scantily clad ass. Once. I want to see how she'll react. She might not be ready for this side of me yet—or ever. Not all women share my cravings, my fantasies.

She jerks in my hold, then grows still. I slap her other butt cheek, then smooth the burn away with my rough palm. Her breath hitches, but she doesn't try to get away. Her silence speaks volumes... if I'm reading her correctly.

I spank her more thoroughly, each strike measured, and followed up with kneading her hot, reddening flesh. She squirms beneath my touch.

"I've warned you before," I growl. "Good girls get rewarded and naughty girls get spanked. You've been a naughty girl lounging up here where others might see your gorgeous body. This body's mine. No one else's. But you don't seem to understand that yet."

My hand dips between her thighs, finding the swimsuit material soaked from her wetness. Tentatively, I slip two fingers beneath the fabric. She's so fucking slippery, so wet and ready. My dick swells, growing hard against her stomach. But I don't push her further, not yet, not until I know if she's going to clam up, or worse—spiral.

So far, I haven't figured out what exactly triggers her into a panic attack.

She rocks her body in my lap, grinding against my erection and chasing my fingers with her cunt. She arches her back and I slide one finger into her tight pussy, then the other. I've tasted her—once—which is not nearly enough to satiate my appetite. She moans as I finger-fuck her perfect pink cunt.

Then she surprises me by reaching beneath her and unfastening my trousers. Gin wraps her fingers around my thick cock, matching my rhythm, and I groan. *Fuck yes*. I need this. My hips jerk, demanding more. She squeezes me tighter and my eyes roll back in my head.

I leave her greedy pussy and smack her ass again. And again. Each of her small gasps drives me wild.

When I sink my fingers back into her, she's dripping wet. She shudders out a moan.

My little magpie likes to be spanked. *Good girl. Perfect girl.*

When my thumb finds her clit, I barely touch her before she orgasms. Her entire body tenses up, then shakes as she comes on my hand. She's hardly come down from her high when she adjusts on my lap, taking my cock into her hot, wet mouth.

Fuck me. I groan as she sucks me down, choking herself on my length. Another wave of pleasure rolls through her and her pussy clenches my fingers like a vise.

Fuck. She just came again from sucking on my dick.

It's enough to send me over the edge. I grunt, shooting ropes of cum down her throat as my hand tangles in her hair.

I pull her up and crush my lips to hers. Plunging my tongue into her mouth, I taste myself, as well as... vodka. Vanilla vodka. *Shit.* I should have known she was too eager, but... this morning she touched me and she wasn't drunk. I thought maybe... I obviously thought wrong.

Sitting back, I take her by the arms and put some distance between us. I can't tell if her eyes are glassy from lust or alcohol. I'm too pissed off to try to make the distinction.

"You're drunk," I accuse.

Her expression shutters. "No I'm not."

"You've been drinking. I can taste it. I can smell it too."

"Just a couple of drinks... earlier."

"It's two in the afternoon."

"So?"

"So. Earlier would have been in the morning." I eye her. "Are you an alcoholic?"

"Why are you so obsessed with how much and when I drink booze?" She squirms, trying to get off my lap, but I keep her in place. I'm not done with her yet.

"I've told you before, I won't touch you when you're drunk." Finally, I let her go.

She stands up, covering her tits with her hands. "I already told you I'm not drunk."

"And I think you're a liar," I snarl.

"Fuck you!" She chokes on a sob as she runs into the house.

Angrily, I tuck my dick away and glower at the swimming pool like it's the water's fault that everything just went to shit.

I should go after her. Apologize.

No, I shouldn't.

I should.

Damn it. I stand up so forcefully that the chair legs scrape against the patio as it slides backwards. With measured steps, I go look for her inside.

Why *do* I care if she's intoxicated or not? This thing between us is temporary, so why should I give a fuck about the details? Her pussy should be more important to me than her state of mind. Yet... when I take her body, I want all of her to know it's me she's with, without a doubt. I want every part of her involved when I fuck her—her body, her mind, even her goddamn soul.

Pure possessiveness courses through my blood, it clenches my chest and settles in my gut.

Ginevra's *mine*. I won't share her with anyone or

anything—not even that damn vanilla vodka. Nor the ghosts of her past. I want all of her for myself.

"Gin, are you in here?" I open her closet door. Her discarded bathing suit rests on the floor. So she was here. Where did she go?

"Mr. Baron," Fleur, my housekeeper, appears in the doorway. "Miss Ginevra left. She took a Lyft, just now."

"*Shit.*" I bolt from the closet and make my way out the front door in record time, but I'm too late to see which direction she went.

No matter, I'll catch up to her soon enough. This isn't the first time she's done this disappearing act and I did what I had to do in response. Grabbing my phone from my pocket, I pull up the information from the tracking device I planted in her purse. For good measure, I had one sewn into all of her purses. She owns quite a few and she never goes out without one.

I watch the dot move across the screen—a map of New York City. When it stops I zoom in to find the address of her location.

Got you, little magpie.

When I pull the car up to the address, I'm more than a bit confused. It's a building full of storage units. You need a code to get in, so after I park I have to wait for someone to exit and catch the door before it closes.

Inside there are three levels of long concrete and

steel corridors with units on either side. I start on the main level and work my way up until I find a half open roll-up door. The first two I came across were clearly people moving boxes in and out. But this one's closed except for about a foot of space at the bottom. Light and soft music spill into the hallway.

This must be her secret den. Does she bring men here?

The very idea has me burning with rage. If she has a man in there, I'll fucking kill him and ask questions later. Her little ten by ten will become a murder scene. I did warn her not to cheat.

I grip the bottom of the door and shove it up. The metal on metal roars as it glides open, then suddenly stops with a bang and a shudder. What I find inside is not at all what I expected. It looks like a teenager vomited all over this space.

Gin sits, wide-eyed, on a plush pink bean-bag surrounded by stuffed animals, sticker-adorned furniture, and boy band posters attached to the metal walls with duct tape.

What in the actual fuck?

"What are you doing here?" She stares at me, panicked.

"I followed you," I say absently, taking in every bit of this scene. "What is this place? Besides hell on earth," I mutter.

Gin stands up, holding a long stuffed snake around her shoulders like it's a fur wrap. "This isn't hell on earth. This is my place." She offers me a watery smile.

My gaze snaps to her. "What do you mean?"

A blush creeps up her neck and she glances down,

clearly embarrassed. "When I was thirteen, my parents decided it was time for me to grow up and have an adult bedroom, so this is where they put all of my stuff." She softly adds, "I come here when I'm feeling sad."

I assess the storage unit again, with a fresh perspective. This is Gin's childhood. Every piece of it is crammed in here. Every piece is a part of her and her past.

The back of my neck prickles with anger. This isn't right. These things shouldn't be locked up away from her if she still wants them. And she obviously takes comfort in having all of this stuff around or she'd get rid of it.

Nostalgia's a stronger motivator than most people realize. Some of us crave our connection to the past. Some of us will do anything to hold onto it.

Tomorrow I'll have all of this moved into the house. One of the guest rooms should be large enough to hold it all without being cramped like this small space. Ginevra shouldn't be coming to a storage unit in order to feel happiness. She should have that in her own home.

"Can you please leave," she mumbles, clinging to her stuffed snake. She looks so young, so innocent right now that guilt slithers through my gut. Less than an hour ago I did naughty things to this woman who is really just a girl.

I nod. "As you wish."

The relief I feel in knowing that she hasn't been running off to see a lover is palpable. I'd have been less surprised by that than this, but now I don't have to murder anyone in cold blood. At least not tonight.

As wrong as it may be, Ginevra's mine, and I want all of her, even her childhood dreams, in my home.

Ginevra

Champagne bubbles burst in my mouth. I'm wearing a sleek, couture bridesmaid dress that Arianna chose for her wedding. She and Dimitri seem so happy together, obsessed with each other, and I envy them. She deserves this hard won happily ever after with her husband.

That's one of the reasons I've been putting off telling my family about Blake. I don't want to overshadow my sister's happy day with my own drama. Arianna deserves the perfect wedding—which she had earlier—and now the most wonderful reception to celebrate with her family and friends.

Beside me, my cousin Ravenna's telling Ilaria some funny story. I giggle along with them, a bit too loudly, and they both give me questioning looks. I wave them off and grab another glass of bubbly from a passing server. I plan to drink my weight of this stuff before the evening's through. Blake and his judgmental attitude can go to hell.

The hairs on the nape of my neck rise as awareness zips across my skin. I turn to find Blake's gaze boring into me and quickly glance away. I told him to give me some space tonight since I haven't told my sisters about us yet. I just need a little more time. Tonight's not the night. Tomorrow. I'll tell them tomorrow.

He's not happy about that.

He's also not happy about the fact that I'm not wearing my engagement ring tonight. It's far too conspicuous. That huge diamond would only encourage questions.

Honestly though, the man's been driving me crazy all week. First he fingers me by the pool while I suck him off, then he shoves me away and accuses me of being drunk—when I wasn't. That hurt. Not to mention how embarrassed I felt.

Then he followed me to my storage unit, causing me further humiliation. The next day all of my things were moved from storage into the guest room across the hall from our bedroom. Which is the sweetest damn thing he could have done. But I'm getting whiplash from his hot and cold behavior. It's beginning to remind me of my ex. So his sweet, thoughtful actions are tainted by my past experiences with men.

Blake never apologized for tossing me aside after he was done with me at the pool. So I haven't forgiven him.

He can't just hurt me like that, make me feel used—and accuse me of being a liar—and then do some grand gesture and think everything is forgiven. It's not okay.

Most of all, I hate how my feelings are getting all tangled up in him. This is supposed to be *fake*, so why are my feelings so real?

Our attraction to each other is undeniable, so why can't we just have some fun together? I wish the rules and boundaries between us were more defined. Instead, I feel like I'm trying to figure this fake relationship out as we go along, and every time I turn around he has some new rule to follow, or a new condition he's put in place. At the same time, the lines blur and we keep pushing the boundaries we both agreed to.

What I'm purposely avoiding thinking about right now is how he spanked me and I liked it. How the pain turned me on.

I don't like pain.

That's not me.

I'm so confused.

"Would you like to dance?" a slightly Russian-accented voice speaks beside me. I turn, coming face-to-face with a handsome young man. Given his accent, my guess is he's part of Dimitri's bratva. It would be rude to turn him down.

"Sure. I'd love to." I drop my champagne flute on a tray and follow him onto the dance floor. The song's a fun, poppy, upbeat number. As I sway my hips, that sensation of being watched intensifies ten-fold. Turning my head, I find Blake's gaze laser focused on me. His scowl's so powerful it could make grass wither and die.

I try to ignore him and have fun with my dance partner. He's not the boss of me. But it's nearly impossible to ignore a man like Blake Baron. Even from across the room his presence demands my attention.

I glance at him again and his eyes narrow. That's the only warning I get before he charges toward me and takes me by the arm. The Russian boy immediately backs off, and I don't blame him, Blake's on the warpath.

He hauls me through the crowded room, then climbs the steps to the stage, interrupting my sister's wedding reception. All eyes are on us. A lead weight drops in my stomach as embarrassment colors my cheeks.

Oh God, what is he going to do?

"Sorry to interrupt," Blake says in a calm tone, sounding anything but apologetic. "We have an announcement on this happy occasion." He hauls me closer to him. "Let me introduce you to my future wife. Ginevra Pontrelli."

Instead of applause, we're met with stunned silence. Horror rips through me, and I know the emotion's written all over my face. He knows I'm not ready for this yet. How dare he force this on me?

Blake's hand curls around the back of my neck and his mouth captures mine. His kiss is possessive, claiming, leaving no doubt in anyone's mind that we're together. I'm frozen, my brain scrambled by his touch. When he finally ends the kiss, I draw in a ragged breath and try to get my bearings.

From his trousers pocket he pulls out my diamond engagement ring. "You forgot this at home, so I brought it for you." Taking my hand in his, he slowly slips the ring onto my finger. A predatory, possessive smile curves his lips, and the world around me tilts.

This game we're playing just got real. There's no going back now. I'm tied to this man until he gets what he wants, until our agreement is fulfilled, and he finally decides to toss me away.

A vise closes around my lungs and suddenly I can't breathe.

I knew I was in over my head.

I'm his pawn and he can do whatever he wants with me, he just proved that.

Blake laces his fingers through mine and leads us off stage. As soon as my feet hit the floor, Arianna, Sophia, and my cousin Ravenna are on me. I can't avoid them any longer.

"You know what to do," Blake murmurs in my ear before letting me go and disappearing into the crowd. My jaw drops in outrage.

Of course he'd leave me to deal with this on my own. *Asshole.*

My sisters each loop their arm through one of mine and practically haul me out of the main ballroom. Ravenna follows us, her expression worried. They take me to Arianna's private suite of rooms. The door clicks shut behind us and they circle me, waiting.

Sophia, my oldest sister, blurts, "What in the hell is going on, Gin?"

I cringe under their scrutiny. I'm supposed to lie to them, feed them the story that Blake wants, but I can't. Especially now, when all three of them are staring me down. They know me too well. I can't deceive them the way I can other people—and I don't really want to either.

Swallowing hard, I move toward the sofa and sit down. They follow, still staring at me with a mixture of concern and expectancy.

I throw up my hands. "All right! I stole from him and he's blackmailing me into being his fake wife for the next year."

"Oh, Gin." The pity's clear in Arianna's voice. "We were afraid it was something like that. You've been avoiding us for weeks. We knew something was wrong."

Ravenna whistles low. "However, stealing from one of the most powerful men in the city wasn't exactly our guess of what happened."

"Gin, how could you?" Arianna's accusing tone has me rolling my eyes.

I shrug. "It was a spur of the moment kind of thing. Plus, I didn't think I'd get *caught.*"

Sophia sighs, the heaviness of that sound draws my attention to her. "Well, you were caught and now you have to deal with the consequences." Her brow pinches. "Is he hurting you in any way, or are you all right?"

"I'm okay."

"I'm glad to hear that," she says. "He's Roman's best friend, so I've spent some time around him, but they've had a falling out recently and I don't know the cause of it. I thought Blake might be hurting you."

I shake my head and force a smile. "No. Our situation is complicated, but he's not cruel. Rude, yes. Abusive, no." I slouch in my seat. "One thing though... none of you are supposed to know the truth. If he finds out, he might call this whole thing off and press charges against me. So just pretend like I convinced you all that I'm in love with Blake and we're having a whirlwind affair. The wedding's in August by the way."

Sophia and Arianna exchange a loaded glance. Ravenna covers my folded hands with hers.

"Does this wedding have a date?" Sophia asks.

"Not yet. I haven't done any planning for it. I don't know where to start." Coming clean to my sisters and cousin helps to settle my nerves. A weight is lifted from my shoulders.

Arianna offers me a genuine grin. "I do know where to start. Let me help plan your wedding. That should convince Mr. Baron that we're buying your love story."

I perk up at that. "Really? You'd do that for me?"

The look my sisters share is one I know well—exasperation. But in all honesty, Arianna and I have never had an easy relationship. She's always chiding me about something.

"Of course! We do love you, you know." Arianna straightens her already perfect posture. "You might be trouble incarnate, but you're also our baby sister. We'll do anything for you when you're in trouble. All you have to do is ask."

My eyes burn and I have to swallow past the lump in my throat before I can speak again. "Thank you. I love you, too."

Ravenna squeezes my hands. "Everything will be all right."

The vise around my chest loosens. My sisters and cousin are the most amazing people I know and I'm so grateful for them.

"We get to plan a wedding!" Arianna's gaze lights up.

"A fake wedding," I remind her.

"Fake relationship," she points out. "The wedding will be real."

"Good point."

CHAPTER 21

Blake

"Mr. Zaleski's busy at the moment, but he'll see you as soon as he can." The receptionist points to the seats against the far wall. "You can wait there, Mr. Baron. I'll let him know you've arrived." She recoils under my glower.

I'm not used to being kept *waiting*, especially when I have an appointment with a client. Mr. Zaleski knows who I am, is he playing games? Testing the waters? I desperately need his prime slice of Manhattan property. If this was any other deal or potential client, I'd leave and make a new appointment after being sure he understands that I don't like to be kept waiting—for anyone. For any reason.

A couple of minutes tick by as I lean against a wall, my gaze locked on his office door. My scowl deepens when that door finally opens and none other than *Eion fucking Bane* emerges.

We're the same age. We went to the same university, where I graduated at the top of my class by a single point over him. To say our rivalry in college was ruthless would be an understatement. It was made worse by two of his brothers, Alistair who was two years ahead of us, and Malachy a year behind. It was Roman and me against the Bane brothers.

Now that we're adults it's a different type of war we wage. I've tried to take down their entire family, but they're one of the few untouchable empires. Plus, Roman and I agree that one of the younger Banes, Niall, is an okay fellow. So, we have a sort of truce with him.

"Baron," Eion Bane drawls as he approaches. His light brown hair is as perfectly styled as his tailored suit. I hate that his family and I use the same tailor. Can't the Banes find their own people to patronize?

"Bane, what an unpleasant surprise." I straighten to my full height, coming eye-to-eye with Eion. "I heard we were after the same slice of real estate."

"You might be after it, I've got it in the bag." His smile pisses me off.

"I wouldn't be so confident if I were you." The stakes are high for me, and Eion will undoubtedly underestimate the lengths I'm willing to go to in order for my brother to inherit. He's always underestimated me, that's how I graduated top of my class and he didn't.

He steps around me. "This one I am confident about because there's no other option. Mr. Zaleski will be selling to me. That's a fact."

"Don't get ahead of yourself, Bane. He hasn't heard my offer yet." I bare my teeth at him—it's not a smile—and head toward Zaleski's office.

Not only did this fucker keep me waiting, but he was

entertaining Eion Bane while he did it. Two strikes against him. If this were any other deal, I'd walk away.

I inhale a deep breath and square my shoulders before tugging the door open. I need to be calm. Killing Zaleski's a bad idea, or at least a counterproductive one. But he's not making a very good first impression and I haven't even met him yet.

The office is as sterile as the reception area. A large glass desk positioned near the floor to ceiling windows dominates the space, two chairs in front of it, a bar cart to one side. On the opposite wall is a seating area with a sleek, modern sofa and coffee table. This room screams *I have no personality, just a lot of money.*

"Mr. Baron, pleased to meet you." The man who approaches me is in his late twenties with short black hair and gullible green eyes. He's an open book dressed in a business suit.

Prey.

No wonder Eion's so confident he has this deal in the bag. I nearly laugh out loud.

Instead, I shake Mr. Zaleski's hand and drop into one of the two chairs opposite him. "Whatever Eion Bane's offering you, I'll double it." It's a ridiculous opening offer, but I prefer to get this over with as soon as possible.

Zaleski's eyes bulge. He recovers quickly enough from the shock and runs a hand through his hair. "I appreciate the offer."

But...

"But it's not only about the money," he continues. "I'm in charge of my family's rather large estate and we don't sell our land on a whim. I need to know your development plans, and they need to be written into the contract, if I decide to sell to you."

"I see." I don't see. What my company decides to do with the land is our business. Apparently he doesn't see it that way. Isn't that *special*?

In one sweeping glance, I size him up. He's young and out to prove himself as a responsible businessman. He's also going to be a pain in the ass. Clients like him have to be wined and dined, they enjoy the *get to know each other* phase, then there's always more than the price of the sale. There's extra little favors and sometimes a mutually beneficial ongoing relationship—but not always.

Sometimes they have an accident. Oops.

This is why Liam needs to step in and take over Titan Enterprises after graduation. I don't have the patience for this shit. I was never meant to make business deals in a boardroom.

He clears his throat, seeming somewhat uncomfortable. "Do you have a plan for the property?"

"Of course. That's a perfect location for luxury condos."

"Oh." He frowns. "You see Mr. Bane wants to build a five-star hotel. I like his vision."

You would, you simpleton.

"People want to live there, not visit and leave. Plus this city's in dire need of more housing, even multi-million dollar condos. Just think of the building's tenants. Your family's property will become the homes of celebrities and superstars. It'll have top-notch security and architectural design. At Titan Enterprises we pride ourselves on both luxury and practicality."

"Hm. You make some good points. I'll have to think about which way I'd like to go." He steeples his fingers, leaning his elbows on the desk.

"I'd like to show you some detailed plans, say... over dinner at *Spades*?" One of the most exclusive restaurants in town is sure to lure him in. All I need is his attention, and he'll soon come around to taking my offer.

Zaleski's gaze snaps to mine, his intrigue plain on his face. "If you can get us a reservation, then how about tomorrow night?"

"Consider it done. See you there at seven." I stand, extending my hand for him to shake. "This is the beginning of a long and prosperous relationship, Mr. Zaleski."

"Please, call me Oz."

"Oz?" I arch a brow.

"It's what my friends call me because of my initials *O* and Z. Oliver Zaleski. Oz."

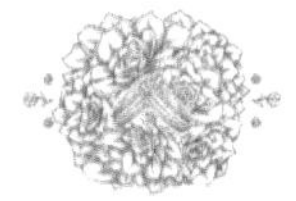

Loud female voices are the first thing I hear when I open my front door, followed by giggles. Avoiding them, I make a beeline for my home office.

Arianna's voice filters down the hallway. "We wouldn't want your wedding to end up like Sophia's bachelorette party."

I think it's both Ravenna and Sophia who say, "Make good choices, Gin."

"That party was epic, until... you know." Gin is the loudest of them all.

More giggling follows.

I manage to make it to the peace and quiet of my office undetected. My refuge. Until my gaze snags on the numerous paint chips hanging on the wall.

Since her sister's wedding last weekend, and our engagement announcement, Gin's finally resigned to her fate. Embracing it even.

Yesterday she told me that if she's going to live here for over a year then we need to paint the rooms. Apparently the neutral brown the interior designer chose is *boring*. That was her exact word: Boring. According to her, this place should have *happier* colors.

At least she agreed that we'd choose the palette together, and since it's my house, I have ultimate veto power.

I loosen my tie to get more comfortable, gazing at the assortment of blues, greens, and yellows stickered to my wall. When I moved her into my house I didn't realize we'd be doing so many *couples* things together. Dinners, family events, and now... choosing paint colors.

My computer monitor glows, waking up, and I check my email after having ignored it during my meeting with Oz and on the ride home. What a ridiculous name, does he think he's a wizard?

A new email pops up, from Yve, and I open it with a grimace. My gaze skims the text, moving quickly over the absurd message.

What the actual fuck?

It's a wedding invitation to Lexa's nuptials. Who the fuck..? She's marrying Franklin Cecil. My memory takes a few seconds to put a face to the name. When I finally do, my skin burns with rage. This has Yve's handiwork written all over it.

That millionaire asshole is at least two decades older than *I* am. He also used to be one of Yve's lovers. Now he's marrying her daughter.

That's sick. Twisted.

My phone rings and I pick it up. "Baron," I bark at the caller.

"Blake, darling. I hope you received the invitation to Lexa's wedding. It's in two weeks and attendance is mandatory. We set sail on the fifth. Be sure to bring your lovely fiancée." She hangs up before I can get in a word.

I study the invitation closely. Fuck me. We're flying to Miami then taking a yacht to a private island near Puerto Rico. That's going to be at least five days stuck on a ship with my family. Hell on earth. Then another couple of days on the island. A full week. Kill me now.

I'd rather sleep on a bed of broken glass than make this trip. But Yve isn't giving me a choice. If I refuse, who knows what kind of shit she'll pull. Plus, I need to be there, don't I? I'm not leaving Liam alone for a week with our step-monster. And Lexa... I need to figure out what's going on with her. Does she want to marry Franklin? Doubtful.

Gin will have to endure all of this too. It's the perfect opportunity to introduce her to my family, but I won't let her walk onto that boat unprepared. It's time my fiancée learns all about my fucked up family and the type of drama that's bound to unfold.

Ginevra

"Let's get down to business." Arianna flips open her laptop, fingers poised over the keyboard. "Where do you want to get married? Finding the venue is often the most difficult part of planning any wedding, especially on short notice. Do you want to stay in the city or is there somewhere else in the world you envision getting married?"

She's treating this like it's a real wedding, which warms my insides and sends butterflies through my stomach.

I think about her question. Staying in New York would be easier for everyone, but... that also means my ex could get to me. I don't know what he'll do when he finds out I'm getting married. My guess is that he won't like it, he might even try to interfere.

"I want to get married in Europe." An ocean between me and Oliver might be enough distance.

"Let's have a look..." Arianna types on her computer

as Sophia, Ravenna, and I lean in. "We have Belmond Hotel Caruso in Ravello, Italy."

The enormous white castle by the sea is absolutely stunning, but I shake my head. I'm not sure what I'm looking for, but I'll know it when I see it.

"How about Châteaux Vaux-le-Vicomte in France. This garden inspired the ones at Versailles." It's beyond beautiful, and luxurious, but again I shake my head and Arianna moves on. "The Savoy Hotel in London?"

The venue has an old world charm that draws me in instantly. Deep wood paneling, beautiful wallpaper, and a cozy yet rich quality to it that I adore.

"That's... it! That's the place." I glance at Arianna. "Do you think we can get in? It's the end of May already. August is only a couple months away."

"I'll have to call them and find out. But you're right, it will take a miracle. Did you like any of the other venues as a backup plan?"

"I could go with the one in Italy. That castle's gorgeous." But my fingers are crossed for London.

"I'll put them both on the list. I think you're going for old world vibes so I'll keep searching and see what else I find."

Grinning wide, I hug Arianna. "You're the best sister ever!"

"Hey, what about me?" Sophia playfully smacks my shoulder.

"Second best?" I laugh at her fake pout.

"Ladies." Blake's standing in the doorway to the sitting room. My breath hitches at the way his frame fills the space, and he looks good enough to eat in that navy blue suit. He's so damn attractive that it's not fair. "May I have a word with you, Ginevra?"

My stupid heart skips a beat every time he says my name, even though I'm not over being mad at him for calling me a liar. Or how he dragged me in front of my entire family and announced our engagement, when I specifically told him I wasn't ready. Though I should have expected that. Blake Baron is not a patient man. When he says he's going to do something—like announce our upcoming nuptials at my sister's wedding—you better believe it. Lesson learned.

So far, the aftermath has turned out just fine. If anything, forcing my hand has brought me closer to my sisters and cousin. So I don't really have any complaints.

"Sure." I follow him out of the room. "What's up?"

His jaw muscles work, he's annoyed, but I swear I haven't done anything wrong recently. "My sister Lexa is getting married in two weeks. Our presence is mandatory. We'll be gone for about six days."

"Oh. Where are we going?"

"To hell."

"Um..." I nibble on my bottom lip, confused. Surely he doesn't mean that literally, does he?

"To the West Indies. By yacht. We'll be trapped on a boat, then on an island, with my family for days on end. I'm not sure how to prepare you for such an experience, but I'll do my best." He lifts his hand to sweep a strand of my hair behind my ear and I step back, breaking the contact.

I don't like how Blake thinks he can do and say whatever he likes without consequence. His lack of respect for me...*hurts*. I wish there was a way to show him that I'm more than just a puppet for him to use as he sees fit. I have feelings too.

"You're still angry with me." It's a statement, not a question.

My lips twist as I consider my emotions. "You called me a liar when I wasn't lying."

A strained silence falls in the space between us. We gaze at each other, searching. Does he ever feel remorse? Will he admit to being in the wrong? I doubt it.

His reputation as *The Black Baron*, a monster in the night, isn't just a façade, that's who he truly is deep inside. Ruthless, unyielding, and remorseless. The scary thing is, I'm sure I don't even know the half of what he's capable of doing.

But living with him these past few weeks, I know that Blake's a man who has no chill. He wears danger like he wears his suits—perfectly tailored to him. He's a man who's used to getting what he wants no matter the damage he leaves in his path.

He speaks so quietly I barely hear him. "I'm sorry."

What? My mouth falls open but no sound comes out. Did I hear him right?

"Did you just *apologize* to me?" My voice cracks.

He waves dismissively. "There's a first time for everything, magpie, but don't get used to it. I'm sure it was a fluke."

I can't help the grin that spreads across my face. He scowls, which only makes my smile widen. He apologized to me because he hurt my feelings, and he meant it. He can downplay it all he wants, but I know he's really sorry. He'd never, ever utter those words if they weren't genuine.

I'm so blown away that the remainder of my pain and anger pops like a balloon. "You're forgiven."

He grumbles something unintelligible and closes the distance between us. This time I don't move as he tucks one of my stray curls behind my ear. His fingertips lightly brush against my skin, sending little shockwaves through my entire body. My lips part and he glances at them before stepping away.

"I need to get back to my office."

"Okay." The word comes out all breathy. This man doesn't even need to kiss me to make me weak in the knees. He's dangerous, rude, yet sweet at times, and I absolutely *cannot* fall for him.

No matter how much he makes my stomach flutter.

Or how I'm beginning to crave his touch.

I should hate him for blackmailing me, but... at this point, I don't. What began as a forced arrangement has morphed into a blessing in disguise. I'm happier here than I've ever been before. I don't hate him for blackmailing me, or for destroying the Marino family. I don't think I can hate this man for anything. That just shows how broken I really am. Unfixable.

Deeply, undeniably in trouble.

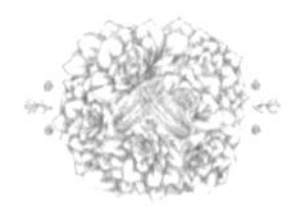

The next week goes by in a blur of activity. While Blake's busy at work, I spend every minute of my days either planning our wedding with Arianna or cooking with Kyla. I never knew life could be so full, I haven't visited my childhood things in all this time. They remain in that guest room, waiting, close by if I want them.

Most nights Blake doesn't come home until I'm already asleep and it feels like we've barely seen each other. Which is probably for the best. I can't think straight when he's around. All of this wedding planning has filled my head with unrealistic dreams of romance. Dangerous thoughts that I shouldn't be humoring, but I can't help it. This will be the very first time I'll get married. Why shouldn't it be everything I want it to be—except for the groom, of course. I shouldn't want him. I can't want him.

My phone buzzes and I pick it up. "Hey, Arianna."

"We got it!"

"Which venue?" I hold my breath, fingers crossed.

Kyla stops what she's whisking and stares at me expectantly.

"London!"

I squeal, and mouth *London* to Kyla. We do a little happy dance in the kitchen before she goes back to whisking.

I'm so excited, I can hardly handle it. "That's great! How did you do it? Oh, and what's the date?"

"We only secured it because they had a cancellation. Some heiress ran off with the groom's older brother, so we took their spot on July 19th. I'm getting invitations printed up and sent out today."

My stomach swoops and dives. Oh my God, in less than two months I'm getting married. This is really happening.

"Thank you so much, Arianna. I could not have done any of this without you."

"You're welcome. Now don't do anything too crazy when you leave town tomorrow for the West Indies. Have fun, but not too much fun. I'll only call if something extremely important comes up."

"Me? Do something crazy?" I scoff and Arianna groans before hanging up. Strangely, I haven't felt the need to act out lately. Not since after that first night I moved in with Blake. Which makes me believe that my need for raging parties and drunken debauchery stemmed from rebellion—against my parents. Against anyone who tries to control me. Though Blake's type of control isn't so different from my parents, I can't quite put a finger on it. He doesn't set me off the way they did.

Now... I don't know. I think I've changed. I feel like I'm growing up, maybe growing into a whole new person, and I think I like who I'm becoming. Glancing around the kitchen, a smile tugs at my lips, I certainly like being here. It feels like home.

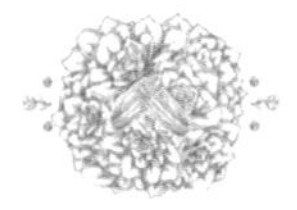

I'm sitting in the living room, reading the latest gossip in the *Big Apple Buzz* on my phone, when Blake comes home. He sets his briefcase down, and I launch into a rant. "Can you believe what these so-called reporters are saying about your sister's wedding? They call her a gold-digger. Worse, they say her mother and her future husband used to be lovers—that they might still be lovers. They even—"

"That part is true."

I gape at him. "*What?* Your step-mother's marrying her own daughter to one of her former lovers?" I can't believe it. That's... *disgusting*. Isn't it?

Blake nods, loosening his tie and removing his suit jacket. "I told you they're twisted. I don't think Yve and Franklin are together anymore, but he was around a lot right after my father died. They've been close ever since."

I pull a face. That's just wrong. "They mention us in here too."

"Oh? What do they say about us?"

"That I'm a gold-digging socialite who snagged the most eligible bachelor in New York."

"Well they're right, you did snag the most eligible bachelor in the city." He flashes me a rare grin.

I huff a laugh. "Of course you'd say that." I set down my phone. "That's enough of that, if your ego gets any bigger you won't be able to fit through the door."

A genuine smile briefly appears on his face, but it barely reaches his tired eyes. I didn't realize until now how dark the circles are beneath his eyes and how his skin's grown pale.

"You look like shit."

He laughs. "A fair evaluation. I feel like shit."

Getting to my feet, I pour him two fingers of whiskey from the bar and hand it to him. "Come. Sit down."

He's so tired that he doesn't even comment on me bossing him around, and he does as he's told, settling onto the sofa where I direct him. Rounding the piece of furniture, I stand behind him and ease my thumbs into the tight muscles of his neck. He groans. His head falls to his chest as I work out his kinks.

"When's the last time you had a proper massage?" I ask.

"Never."

"Why?"

"I don't like people touching me."

I pause, my hands hovering above his skin.

"Keep going," he grunts. "That feels fucking amazing."

Giddiness ripples through my chest and I double-down on working my magic on him. He doesn't like *other* people touching him, but he likes it when *I* do. I shouldn't be so happy about that, but I am. It makes me feel special. Feeling special to a man like Blake is addictive, and dangerous.

My fingers move from his neck to his broad shoulders which are equally as knotted up. He holds a lot of tension in this area. While I've never given anybody a massage before, I've had enough of them to generally know what I'm doing. Sure enough, he slowly begins to relax. Once I have him like putty in my hands, I rake my fingers through his thick blond hair, it really is as soft as it looks. As I massage his scalp, he moans.

"This is the sweetest thing anyone's ever done for me," he murmurs, eyes closed.

Satisfaction pulses beneath my skin. Releasing him, I walk around until I'm standing between his legs. From the front, I circle my thumbs on his temples, then ease his tight jaw muscles. He watches me through his dark blond lashes.

Setting his drink aside, he wraps his large hands around my waist and tugs me closer, until I land in his lap. I stare into his bright blue eyes, the intensity in them has my stomach fluttering and my heart swaying. Then he lowers his lips to mine. The move is slow, deliberate, as is his kiss. His mouth moves against mine languidly. This kiss is different from others, he's taking his time. I open for him and his tongue sensuously tangles with mine.

A fire builds between my legs. I want so much more of what he has to offer, but I'm afraid of falling too deep under his spell.

"Mm," he hums. "You taste so sweet, magpie. In fact, you might be too sweet for a man like me."

Ginevra

Yve stands up at the dinner table, glass raised. "I'd like to welcome you all aboard. We'll be cruising together for the next three days, then we'll arrive at the private island where this happy couple will be married on the beach at sunset." She smiles, but it doesn't reach her eyes. "To the happy couple, Lexa and Franklin." Everyone echoes her toast and we all drink.

When she goes to sit back down, I swear Franklin, who's seated beside her, grabs her ass. Yve glances at him, then leans slightly forward in her seat and his eyes roll back in his head. I really don't want to know what's going on under that side of the table.

Meanwhile, Lexa stares at her barely touched food, seemingly lost in thought. She is my age, with straight blond hair and cornflower blue eyes set in a heart-shaped face. Where I'm all curves, she's small and slim. Lexa has this pixie-like energy about her, she's beautiful in an ethereal kind of way.

I find it strange that Lexa's maid of honor, and only

bridal party member because they're keeping the wedding intimate, is Franklin's twenty-five year old daughter Samantha. Lexa and Sam don't really seem to know each other that well, so why's she her maid of honor?

Then there's Guy, Franklin's best man. Those two must be good friends because they keep laughing about inside jokes that go right over everyone else's heads. Personally, both those guys give me the creeps.

Thankfully, I'm seated between Blake and his brother Liam. Liam spends most of his time on his phone, which he hides under the table, barely paying attention to anyone. What a strange, disjointed family.

Franklin grunts and shudders, drawing my attention. Did Yve just jack him off? Gross. He winks at me, and my dinner threatens to come back up. Quickly, I drop my gaze. The last thing I want to do is draw that man's attention. Huh, maybe my sense of self-preservation is finally kicking in?

Blake did his best to warn me about his family, but there's a huge difference between hearing about them and experiencing them in person. He's kept me close to his side all day and now I understand why. Even now, his arm rests across the back of my chair. It's possessive, a barrier and shield against those around us. He'd prefer I wasn't here—to protect me from his family. Since I have to be here, we should make the best of it.

Yve dabs her lips with the napkin and clears her throat. "After Lexa's nuptials, I'm making it my mission to find Liam a beautiful bride. Maybe even... Samantha?"

Sam chokes on her wine, but Liam seems unfazed.

"I'm already seeing someone," he states, not bothering to look up from his phone. He's playing an app game.

"Oh? Who's the lucky girl?" Yve presses. When he doesn't respond, she barks, "Liam?"

He finally glances up. "My boyfriend's name is Maks."

Silence descends on the table. You could hear a pin drop. I hide my smirk behind my wine glass. Did they really not know Liam's gay? Arianna told me all about the drama between him and Maks, her bratva husband's second in command. Liam's all kinds of mixed up in that world, which Maks apparently hates because he wants to protect him.

"Well," Yve's voice has an edge to it. "There are places I could send you to fix your affliction. They have proven methods that could cure you."

I gasp, shocked she'd say such a thing. Her attention darts to me, assessing, then shifts back to Liam. He glares at her for a moment before he shrugs, going back to his game. I can only imagine what it must have been like to grow up with a step-mother like that. I don't like my father very much at times, but I'd choose him any day over Yve.

Blake's been awfully quiet, so I glance at him. He's watching his step-mother with a deadly glint in his eyes. For the first time, I wonder why he doesn't make her disappear, like he has to so many other powerful people. She must be holding something over him. But what could it possibly be?

Suppressing a soft chuckle, I inwardly shake my head at myself. The list of potential blackmail items Yve could have on Blake is probably endless. He's far from squeaky clean. If I wanted dirt on him, I could probably search his house and come up with something. Though I have no doubt he's excellent at hiding his crimes. He must have slipped up at some point, doesn't everyone?

After dinner and dessert we all have a nightcap in the lounge. The yacht is truly magnificent. It's basically a floating mansion with full-on suites for bedrooms and all the amenities you could want. Plus staff. Despite some of the company, I'm enjoying myself.

With Blake tailing me, I have a seat next to Liam. "I heard you just graduated. Congratulations."

"Thanks." He sips his scotch, making me think of a younger version of Blake. They have the same coloring, but Liam's much easier going than his older brother. "I'd be much more excited to join the company if it didn't mean working under... that." He glances at Yve.

Blake grunts his agreement. "You won't have to for long. One year, that's all. Then the CEO position at Titan Enterprises goes to you."

"Nepotism." I cough. Blake glares at me and I chuckle.

Liam laughs. "Nepotism is alive and well in the Baron family. Pretty soon you won't even notice it, and by the time you and Blake have kids you'll be grateful for it."

Blake and I glance at each other, both of us caught off guard by Liam's comment.

"I-I'm sure you're right." I humor him. It feels odd that Liam doesn't know our relationship is fake. But why would he? Blake kept his promise to tell no one, not even those closest to him about us.

Liam sighs. "Though there are times when I want to toss it all away and go work with Maks."

"Work with Maks? Are you fucking insane?" Blake struggles to keep his voice low. "You're not joining the Russian Bratva."

"Duh." Liam rolls his eyes. "It was a joke, Blake. Calm down. I know how much you've sacrificed to make sure I eventually take the CEO position in the company our father built. I'm not going to throw that all away. I'm grateful."

Blake nods, his shoulders visibly relax.

Liam turns to me. "What about you, do you have any plans for college?"

"Hah. No. I've never been all that good at school. Not like my sisters." I shrug. "I'm sure I'll find something I want to do eventually. No rush, right?"

"Or you could stay home and take care of Blake's babies. I just hope they have your personality and not his." Liam laughs at his brother's sour expression.

My own skin heats to an uncomfortable degree. Having children with Blake has never crossed my mind because this is supposed to be a short-term relationship, but apparently everyone else has thought about it. They expect it. Of course they do, we're engaged to be married.

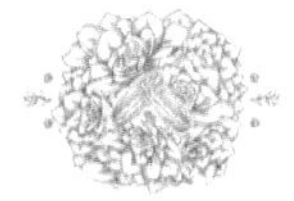

Over the next couple of days, Yve makes sure all the men and women have a chance to get to know each other. Which means structured time for us girls to hang out together. I've come to the conclusion that Lexa's miserable and I can't believe Blake's letting this wedding happen. Sam's not so bad and we have a lot in common, from our taste in music to our love of cooking shows. Though unlike me, she would never set foot in a kitchen. But Sam likes the TV drama.

Yve really is a manipulative harpy. I believe Blake held back when he told me stories about her.

We're sitting around the pool, sipping mimosas, when Yve says, "I don't understand how you put up with Blake. You must suffer terribly."

She's fishing, baiting me, and I know it. Now it's my job to convince her that Blake and I are madly in love with each other.

"Oh? What's so bad about my fiancé?" My use of that word makes her twitch, so I keep slipping it into conversations whenever I can.

"He's so mean. Rude all the time. Nothing is ever good enough for him. Plus he's anti-social, and you're the kind of girl who likes people." She waves dismissively, her gold charm bracelet catches the sun, glinting.

Hm. She's right on all counts. She knows her step-son pretty well.

"I happen to like Blake just the way he is. He's not all bad."

Yve's laugh grates on my nerves. "You don't have to lie to me, honey. He's a brute and we both know it."

"Honestly, I think that's what I like about him. He has this sophisticated caveman thing going on and I love it." My bright smile beams, without me having to force it. "Besides, once you get to know him, he's a real catch.

He's much more complex than he appears. The loyalty he shows his family speaks volumes, and he's perceptive, he always knows what I want before I do. He's amazing."

"I'm sure." Yve turns to Sam and strikes up a conversation. If anyone else blatantly blew me off like that, I'd be hurt or annoyed, but I don't expect anything less from this woman.

Politely excusing myself, I head inside. I've had enough tanning and awkward interactions for one day. And there's still our group dinner to look forward to. I inwardly groan. Can I have room service? No one will notice my absence, will they?

I've just stepped through the door when a hand grips my arm and I release a startled yelp. His spicy cologne hits me right before he pulls my back to his chest and he murmurs in my ear, "Sophisticated caveman, huh? I liked being called amazing much better."

"Are you always spying on me or is this a one-off?" I complain, while my heartbeat's drumming against my ribcage from his touch and the rush of his breath against the shell of my ear.

"Always. Don't ever forget it." He releases me, and I turn to face him. "You're such a good little liar that I almost believe what you said to Yve. Judging from her disgruntled expression, I think she does too."

"That's... that's good." What's not good is that at some point when I was speaking to Yve, I stopped lying. Blake is perceptive, attentive in his own way, and I do admire his loyalty and love for his siblings. When did this happen? When did I start sliding into this dangerous territory?

I pull myself out of my spiraling thoughts. "We need to talk. In private."

He nods and leads us to our bedroom suite, where I close the door behind us.

"You can't let Lexa marry that man." My hands rest on my hips. This is a hill I will die on. "She's miserable. I don't know her well at all—I mean we just met on this boat, and she barely talks, but I can tell she doesn't want this marriage. Why are you allowing this to happen? I know you care for her wellbeing."

"It's complicated."

"Enlighten me." I step toward him. "I'm this close to dragging her into one of those emergency rafts, and seeing how we fare at sea, rather than let her walk down that aisle."

He snorts.

"This isn't funny."

"No, it's not, but you are."

"I'm serious, Blake, I'll do it. Don't underestimate me."

"Wouldn't dream of it." He pulls out his phone. "Let's see what Lexa has to say."

A moment later, a knock sounds on our door and I let Lexa inside. She's so shy and demure, she reminds of my cousin Elena—Ravenna's twin sister—who lives in Italy. Except Elena wasn't always so closed off, something happened to her, and I don't know what. Maybe that's why I feel so strongly about protecting Blake's step-sister, who I hardly know at all.

Blake motions to Lexa. "My fiancée's concerned about your wellbeing and threatening to abscond with you, if her worries aren't laid to rest. Believe me, you wouldn't be the first thing she's stolen, so why don't you tell her your thoughts on your upcoming wedding."

Lexa turns wide eyes on me, hesitating before she speaks. "I need to do this, to marry Franklin. You don't understand, but this wedding is my way out. I'll finally be free of my mother."

"Can't Blake free you from your mother?" I ask, confused and desperate to understand. "What do you need? Money? A safe place to stay? I—we can help you."

She shakes her head. "No. I have to do this on my own. I can't get anyone else involved, especially family."

I glance at Blake, silently pleading for his help.

He shrugs. "I've already tried to offer her a way out. She won't take it." His gaze bores into her, and she swallows hard. I think she's hiding something, but what can it be? What is she not telling us?

"I don't understand. Why don't you just—you know —kill her?" I sound callous, but come on, the woman's ruining everybody's lives. Besides, I grew up in a mafia family, the idea of eliminating someone who's problematic isn't that big of a deal.

Lexa answers. "Because she has dirt on Blake."

"How do you know about that?" he demands.

"She bragged about it, of course. Liam and I both know she's blackmailing you."

I stare at both of them, stunned. What's with all the blackmail? Yve's blackmailing Blake, who is in turn blackmailing me. This is ridiculous, but I guess it's the only language we all know how to speak. Threats, lies, and twisted agreements—without those we'd never achieve what we're after.

Now, so much makes sense to me. Blake's hands are tied when it comes to Yve.

"What is she blackmailing him with?" I ask Lexa.

"Apparently she had him followed and caught him murdering someone on film. This was years ago, but she still brags about it, and how he'll never find the evidence." Lexa taps her bottom lip. "What is it she says... Oh yeah, how he'll never find it because it's too obvious."

Blake's gaze snaps to her. "She does? What does that mean?"

"It's probably embedded beneath her skin, who knows? You know what she's like, what lengths she'll go through."

"I do," Blake admits.

My mind races with the possibilities. Where would Yve hide that kind of evidence?

Blake's voice breaks through my thoughts. "Even if she has a copy on her, or someplace obvious, it won't be the only one. Damn it." He rakes his fingers through his hair.

Lexa shoots him a sympathetic smile. "I didn't think to mention it before because it's really not helpful information. It's been years, Blake, you're never going to find the recordings. We all just have to keep playing her games."

He heaves a sigh, the lines between his brows deepen.

"Well, since Yve's bent on making your lives hell," I murmur, "what do you say about having a bachelorette party tonight?"

Lexa's expression lights up for the first time. "Really?"

"Really." When life gets shitty, there's one thing that can make everything better for a while. A damn good party.

CHAPTER 24

Blake

A couple hours after dinner concludes, Gin, Lexa, and Sam are dancing on top of a table to a Taylor Swift song, while Liam showers them in champagne. They started this party off with tequila shots and Ginevra telling Yve to *shut up* when she protested and tried to get Lexa away. The stunned look on Yve's face will live on in my memory forever.

The girls closed ranks around Lexa, and once Yve realized she was outnumbered, she took Franklin and skulked off into the shadows. Her hooks are obviously firmly planted into him. They've been carrying on like lovers this entire trip, right under Lexa's nose. So why the fuck does my step-sister want to go through with this wedding? There's something she's not telling me. She's hiding something, and I want to know what it is.

I sit in a club chair, Guy across from me, and drink my scotch. We don't talk—Guy's almost as anti-social as I am, which makes him fine company—preferring to watch the younger people have their fun.

The way Gin not only stood up to my step-mother, but has also taken Lexa under her wing does something funny to my chest. I can't put a name to the sensation because I don't believe I've felt it before today.

It could be gratitude.

Pride? Maybe I'm proud of my fiancée?

I'm not sure what I'm feeling, but I've determined it's nothing bad. Quite the contrary.

"You're a lucky man."

My attention snaps to Guy, and the light sensation in my chest evaporates. He's staring at Gin, watching her hips move as she dances on the table. I don't like it. I hate the way other men gaze at my fiancée.

"Keep your eyes to yourself, Guy, or I'll pluck them out and feed them to you." My threatening tone leaves no room for misinterpretation.

His gaze lands on me, the blood drains from his face and he gives a curt nod. "I... need to make a call anyway. Excuse me." He leaves the room, and my pounding heart calms.

I spend the remainder of the evening watching Gin, Samantha, Lexa, and Liam party, while nursing my scotch. I doubt I was ever that carefree, even in my early twenties. Life had already forced me to grow up quickly. With a step-mother's manipulations to navigate, a father to fight with over everything, and Liam to take care of, there wasn't time for much silliness.

Watching Ginevra let go and have fun, seeing her live, so innocent and carefree, constricts my heart. She's turning out to be nothing like I expected. Which begs the question: was I wrong about my assumptions of her? She's far more naive and vulnerable and sweeter than I thought she'd be. That girl has a heart of gold hidden beneath that sassy, sexy kitten façade, doesn't she?

By blackmailing her into this arrangement, I thought I'd be punishing a heartless, conniving, gold-digger, someone like my step-mother. But Gin is nothing like Yve. They're polar opposites in every way that counts.

I should end this, call off our deal and let Gin go. She deserves someone better than me. But I can't and won't free her, and not just because my inheritance is on the line. Now that I have Ginevra within my grasp, who, in all honesty, I've been sneaking glances at for the past two years, I want to make her mine. I want to possess her body and soul, to twist her innocence into something sinful, to devour her sweet nature like ripe fruit.

Every night when I come to bed, she's already asleep and I leave before she wakes up. Gin has no idea the agony she puts me through every single morning and night. The feel of her soft body against mine, her warmth, the way my cock strains, desperate to have her, yet I deny myself that pleasure. Every single day, I resist. But I'm done holding myself back.

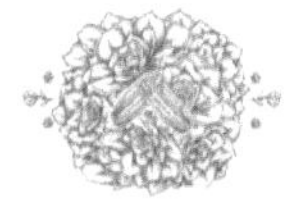

"I didn't know you could fly!" Ginevra gasps as we take off. My gaze slides to her, triple-checking that she's securely fastened in the helicopter's passenger seat, then we gain altitude.

The yacht docked early this morning and I had our things brought to our villa. The rest of my plan for today was hatched late last night while Gin enjoyed Lexa's bachelorette party. We have the entire day to ourselves and this helicopter ride around the islands is only the beginning.

"Hold on," I teasingly warn her. "I'm a little rusty." Tilting the helicopter, I maneuver us over the ocean's glittery blue-green waters, and Gin squeals with excitement. Her laughter sends liquid heat through my abdomen. I love making her smile.

For the next two hours we fly over expansive waters, sandy beaches, and tropical hills. From above, we see all the wonders these islands have to offer. None of it is as beautiful as the wonder sparkling in Gin's eyes.

I land on a wide expanse of deserted beach, then help Ginevra out of her seat. Taking her hand, I lead us around a jutting rock to a quiet cove where a lone table and two chairs sit under a cabana. Various rugs and carpets cover the ground, and a hearty lunch, complete with champagne, awaits us.

"Oh my god, Blake, what have you—? How did this get here?" Gin sits on the chair opposite of me, grinning like this is the most magical moment of her life. I have to admit the setup crew did an excellent job.

"You wanted a boat ride on a lake. Which I couldn't give you." I open the champagne and pour us each a glass. "I hope that this lunch on a beach might make up for it. If we stay long enough, we'll catch the sunset."

"Do we have anywhere else we need to be this evening?" She sips from her glass, then starts uncovering the numerous dishes of little sandwiches, shrimp cocktail and caviar on ice, and of course an assortment of desserts.

"We don't need to be anywhere but here, magpie, so

eat up and enjoy yourself." For a moment, I simply sit back and watch her nibble on a piece of fresh fruit. My gaze focuses on the sweep of her pink tongue as she licks her lips, then down to the smooth column of her neck when she swallows. I've never enjoyed watching a woman eat before. There's something extremely sensuous about it.

Of course, if anyone told me a few months ago that I'd arrange for a romantic lunch on a beach just to see a woman happy, I'd have scoffed at them. Then probably have shot them for being so fucking ridiculous. Yet here I am. Here we are, together, enjoying each other's company for an entire day.

"Why aren't you married?" Gin's question startles me, and I blink at her for a second before answering.

"Marriage is overrated at best. Most of the time it's simply a terrible, soul-sucking arrangement between two naive individuals. Why would I ever want that?"

Gin sucks cocktail sauce off of a piece of shrimp and my cock stiffens, expanding in my trousers. She's so fucking sexy with her small sounds of contentment and that innocent look in her chocolate brown eyes. Fuck, I want to corrupt every inch of her.

"My sisters seem happily married," she points out.

I nod in agreement. "They are both lucky. But do keep in mind that this is Roman's second marriage. I remember his first wife and the hell she put him through. In my youth, I witnessed my father's two gold-digging wives before Yve, who's the worst of them all, but it was Roman's marriage that made me vow to never marry. That woman destroyed him."

"But Sophia put him back together."

"True. Lucky bastard." I down my champagne. "But they are the exception."

"So once our charade is over, you'll go back to being a bachelor for life?"

"That's my plan."

"Sounds lonely to me." Gin pops a caviar dolloped cracker into her mouth, chews, and swallows. "I'd like to marry and have children someday. I like the idea of sharing my life with someone who loves me."

My mind paints a vivid picture of Ginevra in the arms of another man, them smiling at each other as a mini version of her plays nearby. The man sweeps a blond curl behind her ear. Crimson quickly paints over the mental image as rage and jealousy roil in my gut. No man should touch her like that except me.

As if to prove the point to myself, I reach across the table and glide my fingers through her hair, tucking the strands behind her ear. She glances at me and our gazes lock. My hand slides to the back of her neck and I tug her to me, my lips crashing down on hers. She tastes divine. I don't know if I'll ever get enough of her. But she's only temporarily mine to have, so I'd best indulge. I'm a glutton for this woman.

I take my time devouring her mouth, my tongue sliding against hers in a languid dance. Her small hands brace against my shoulders. I'm about to pull her into my lap so I can feel the rest of her, when thunder rumbles in the distance.

We break apart, gazing up at the darkening sky, just as the heavens open up on us. The shade awning won't survive for long. Shit, I hadn't planned for a storm.

Gin takes my hand, then we're running across the

sand to what I realize is a small cave in the cliff face. We're drenched by the time we get there, but for some reason I'm not pissed off about it, because we're laughing. I tuck her beneath my arm as we watch the storm from under shelter. It should pass soon.

"That came out of nowhere!" Gin wrings out her hair. "I'm a mess."

I glance down at her. "You are. You're a beautiful mess."

Her gaze searches mine, I'm not sure what she's looking for, but I guess she finds something she likes because she reaches up and crushes her lips to mine. I lift her up, her legs wrap around my waist, and I press her back to the cave's smooth wall. Our kiss grows frantic, desperate, a silent plea for more. With one hand I grip her ass, and the other I wrap around her neck, my thumb on her fluttering pulse point.

"I want to fuck you, our agreement be damned. Tell me you want that too, Gin." My raw voice speaks of my desperation.

She releases a shaky breath, then nods. "I want that too. B-but I have to tell you something first."

"What is it?" My thumb draws circles on her silky smooth neck. "Tell me."

"I... I'm not as experienced as you think. In fact, I don't even know if I'm any good in bed." She glances away.

"Look at me, magpie. Use your words. You can tell me anything."

Her gaze reluctantly drifts back to mine. Self-doubt and vulnerability shine through her eyes, and I'm nearly overwhelmed by my need to protect and possess her, all at the same time.

"Okay." She licks her lips. "I don't fully remember any of my sexual experiences because I've always been very drunk. When I'm trashed is the only time that I can handle someone touching me. If I'm not drunk, being touched makes me feel sick to my stomach, and I panic. M-my ex used to get angry with me when we tried to..." She's shaking in my arms and I'm sure it's not from the cold or her memories.

I ignore the part about her ex—for now. Later I'll be sure to hunt him down and make him pay for how he treated Gin.

"But I touched you. I touch you all the time."

"I know. You're... different. I don't know why it feels different with you, but it does. I want you to touch me, Blake, but I'm also afraid." Her confession wrenches my heart. "I don't even know if I like sex."

I tangle my fingers in her hair, pulling her into a soft kiss. "Believe me, you'll like sex. Give yourself to me and I'll take care of you, baby girl." I can tell by the look in her eyes that she wants to trust me, but she's scared. "I promise to make it good for you. I'll treat you like it's your first time, okay?"

"D-do you promise not to hurt me?" She asks in a small voice that shreds my heart. Why the fuck would she ask that question? Unless...

"Did someone hurt you? Besides the ghost?"

Her gaze drops to my chest.

"Gin," her name comes out in a warning tone. "Who hurt you?"

She shakes her head, closing her eyes, and obviously

refuses to answer me. One day I'll get all the secrets out of this gorgeous, broken woman.

"I'd never hurt you unless you wanted me to." My words bring her attention back to me.

"Why would I want you to hurt me?"

"You liked it when I spanked you. Didn't that hurt?"

"I guess so. But... you weren't being cruel. That was a pleasurable kind of pain."

"Exactly."

Her cheeks grow pink. "Oh."

"Since we're on the topic of confessions, you should know that I don't only want to fuck you, Gin, I want to worship your body. I want to possess every inch of you, mark you as mine, and steal every shred of your sweet innocence until all you crave is me and my dark desires. If you let me have you, I'll ruin you for any other man. Do you understand?"

"Yes." She swallows hard. "I want you. Please." Gripping my hair, she claims my mouth in a passionate kiss.

I warned her. She had the chance to get away and she didn't, which means now she's mine. *All mine.*

CHAPTER 25

"Ruin me," the plea falls from my lips between kisses. He growls in approval, grinding his hard cock against my aching center. He must have thought his warning would push me away, but all I've ever wanted is more of him, to see beneath his mask.

"Not here," he says. "I won't take you like a beast against this rock wall."

"I want it here. Please, I don't want to have to deal with your family right now. I don't want to go back to the main island yet."

His blue eyes darken with desire, and something more sinister that I can't quite name. "As you wish."

He sets me on my feet, then disappears into the rain for several minutes. It's just enough time for me to begin to spiral. What am I doing? What if I freak out as soon as we start taking our clothes off? The embarrassment hardly seems worth the effort. I hug myself, screaming inside my head. I hate being so fucked up.

But when he asked who hurt me, I couldn't tell him. I don't want him to know my story–how other men have treated me–I don't want him to look at me like I'm damaged.

I'm fine being a slut, a tramp, a whore in the eyes of society, but I refuse to be labeled a victim. I never want anyone to know the truth.

Blake returns with a giant blanket, which I realize is the table cloth, and a few pillows that aren't completely sodden. He's dripping wet, his button down plastered to his muscular chest, and my mouth goes dry. He's so handsome that he's hard to look at sometimes. Heat pools between my legs and I know that I'm going to give this a try. For the first time in my life, I want this. I want him like I've never yearned for anything before.

He spreads the large blanket on the ground and tosses down the pillows. Running his palms over his wet hair, he smooths it back. Then his gaze lands on me.

"Come here, magpie." He beckons me closer. I nearly fall into his arms, my body pressed to his, I fumble with his shirt buttons. "Here, let me help you." He grabs the two sides of his shirt and gives it one violent tug. The buttons go flying. He shrugs out of the wet garment, tossing it aside. I caress his warm skin, tempted to lick the rain drops from his abs.

He pulls me in for a heated kiss, while his deft hands strip away my clothes, until I'm standing in my lace underwear. He purposefully falls onto the plush tablecloth, turned blanket, and I land on top of him. His lips leave mine to venture further south, kissing my throat, my shoulders, the tops of my breasts. Rolling until we've switched places, he keeps his eyes on mine as he sucks down on the inside of my breast. My back arches and I moan, knowing he's leaving his first mark on me.

His tongue darts out, licking the hickey before he moves lower trailing his lips over my stomach. At my hip he pauses, biting down hard enough that I gasp. The sensation of his body over mine, his hands and lips on my flesh feel foreign but amazing. When he drops his mouth to my panties, and starts teasing my clit through the thin fabric, I moan.

"I want you to beg for it, baby girl." His hot breath sends trembles through me.

"Please," I say. "I'm ready, please."

He chuckles, his fingers toying with the edge of my panties. When he dips them beneath. Finding my pussy hot and wet, he lets out a rumbly groan against my clit. *Oh fuck.*

Sucking down on my sensitive bundle of nerves, he slips two fingers into me and my entire body shudders at the sensation. He stretches me, slowly moving in and out of my wetness, and my eyes roll back in my head. This... oh my god. He curls his fingers, pumping them, and I shatter into a million pieces of ecstasy. The orgasm comes on so suddenly that I struggle to catch my breath.

Blake slides off my panties, then unclasps my bra, lying me bare before his hungry eyes. His gaze slides across my skin like a lover's caress as he drinks me in. Goosebumps erupt over my flesh, my nipples pebble, and I've never felt more seen, and vulnerable, in my entire life.

"Sweet girl," he murmurs, before he sucks one nipple into his mouth. He rolls the peak between his teeth and I scream, my back arches and my fingers fist into his hair. "That's my girl. Come for me again."

He sucks down on my other nipple as he fingers my dripping cunt. I ride his hand. Heat and pressure build low in my stomach, sparks glitter across my vision, and flutters erupt in my core.

"Blake," I scream his name as I fall apart again. Wave after crashing wave of searing hot bliss shoots through me.

He doesn't give me a chance to recover this time. In a second his trousers are off and he aligns his cock with my entrance. Keeping his eyes on me, he slowly pushes inside, stretching me with each thick inch. I open my legs wider to fully take him. Just when I think I'm at my limit, he bottoms out, a soft groan falling from his lips.

"You're so fucking perfect, magpie. Look how good you're taking my cock, and fuck, you feel even better than I imagined." His eyelids flutter closed for a second. "I know you're on birth control so I'm going to fill your pretty pussy with my cum. But first you're going to come on my dick."

I whimper. Having him on me, and in me, makes my head spin. His rich scent invades my nose, adding to the sensory overload. Then he begins to move his hips in slow, deep thrusts and my brain short circuits. I hold onto his broad shoulders as his body moves within mine. I've never felt anything like this before. It's so, so good.

I shiver beneath him and he pauses. "Are you okay, baby?"

I nod.

"Use your words, Gin. How are you feeling?"

"I-I'm fine. Good." I try to clear my head, but it's a

useless attempt. "I never knew it could feel like this. It's so good." I choke on a sob.

"Fuck." Blake angles up on his forearms to get a better look at me. "Is this too much?"

"No! Don't stop, I need more."

"I'm not going to fuck you while you cry. I'm twisted, but I'm not that fucked up."

I give him a watery smile and try to explain. "These are happy tears. I'm a little overwhelmed, but I'm okay. Please, give me more. I need more. I need you."

He pistons his hips, giving me so much more that the sensations go from overwhelming to out of this world. Clinging to him, I gradually adjust, until I'm meeting each of his thrusts and moaning his name.

Blake varies his speed and depth. He'll fuck me hard and fast, only to still deep inside my pussy, then continue in measured, slow thrusts, every muscle in his body straining. We're both covered in sweat, our skin flushed. Our tongues tangle when he takes me slowly, these kisses raw and honest, then I cling to his chest when he ravages my body.

"Please," I beg. "Please, let me come." Any rational thought left my brain long ago. All I know is that I need this release, I can't take it any more.

He slips his hand between us, his thumb finding my clit, and I explode around him. My pussy clamps down on his cock like a vise as I scream and scream. He curses, his hips pumping quicker, deeper, harder until he follows me over the edge. His guttural cry echoes through the cave.

I'm not sure if I passed out or fell asleep, but I wake up to Blake wiping tears from my cheeks.

"Did I hurt you?" he asks, clear concern in his blazing blue eyes.

"No." I cry harder, unable to stop. Why am I sobbing? Then I realize... "I'm so sorry. I just never thought that I could have this."

It's true. I thought I was too broken to enjoy intimacy with another person and actually enjoy it. He's given me a priceless gift. One that I'm not sure how I can ever repay.

Blake draws me into his arms, holding me close as I cry into his chest. "Of course you can have this, baby. Beautiful girl, this is only the beginning of what you can have. I can't wait to show you more, for you to discover all the things that you like, there's a whole new world open to you."

"I'm sorry, I'm ruining the moment."

"No, you're not. This moment's perfect." He rubs soothing circles on my back, lulling me into relaxation and a brief nap. When I wake up, laying in his arms, the sun sinks low on the horizon, painting a perfect blend of pastels across the sky.

In silence, taking comfort in the feeling of him, I watch the sun disappear. This has been one of the most intense, but also best days of my life. Maybe *the* best day of my life. I have Blake to thank for this. All I need to figure out is how to thank him.

"Come. We should get back to the villa." He quickly dresses, then bundles me up in the blanket and carries me to the helicopter. I'm so exhausted, both physically and emotionally, that I doubt I can stand right now, much less walk. How does he seem to know that?

It's a quick flight back and no one's around to bother

us as we settle into our own villa and order room service for dinner.

That night Blake makes love to me again and again. I can't think of how else to describe what his body is doing to mine, because this isn't fucking, it's too deep, too tender. He treats me like I'm the most precious thing he's ever held. Of all the men in the world, how is it that I feel safest in the arms of this ruthless villain? More than safe. Prized, admired, and cherished.

He soothes my damaged heart, fills it with possibility and hope. My heart doesn't care that I can't fall in love with him. He might be gentle and caring with me, but he's not the type of man who would ever love me in return.

A heart as cold and dead as his can never be revived. I'm not foolish enough to believe that I'm the one to melt him, to shine a light into his dark soul until he discovers love. That will never happen.

It's in my best interest to distance myself from him, but I'm afraid it's far too late for that. He's going to rip out my tender organ and hack it to pieces. There's nothing I can do about that anymore, because what I feel for him is no longer fake.

CHAPTER 26

Blake

Ginevra is fucking perfection. Her body was made for me, I'm absolutely sure of that now. I told her I'd ruin her for other men, but fuck if she isn't ruining me for other women. How will I ever find another creature this divine?

Her soft curves rest against me as she sleeps. It's late morning, but we were awake on and off all night because we couldn't get enough of each other. I still crave another taste of her this morning.

What is this woman doing to me?

I ate up every single one of her gasps and shivers last night. If I didn't know better, I would have assumed she was a virgin from the way her body responded to me the first time. She's so tight, and cutely awkward in her inexperience. Yesterday in that cave was a trial in restraint. I wanted nothing more than to lose myself in her, fuck her into the sand, but I gave my word to treat her gently, and I did.

She was so exhausted afterward that she let me carry

her to our villa, settle her into a hot bath, and then feed her in bed. I never knew tending to a woman could be so...fulfilling.

But that's the thing with Gin, she constantly has me surprising myself. She makes me act against my nature—except that everything I do feels natural with her. No one else, only with my little magpie.

Someone starts pounding on my door. "Wedding brunch starts in twenty minutes. Don't be late!" Yve.

Fuck, she's annoying.

For the first time in my life, all I want to do is stay in bed, with Gin. But if we're going to witness my sister's shit-show of a wedding this afternoon, we'd better get up and ready.

"Sweetheart," I softly murmur, waking Gin. "It's time to get up. We have to be at brunch in twenty minutes."

"Twenty minutes?" she sleepily murmurs. Then she shoots up, landing on her feet beside the bed. "Oh my god, I have to get ready!"

I chuckle as she races into the bathroom to shower, erasing our combined scents from her body.

After the ceremony, I'm dragging her back here for another round. I might have to extend our stay because I'm nowhere near done with this woman.

Somehow, Gin manages to shower, dry her hair, put on makeup, and be dressed by the time brunch is served in the courtyard. We make our appearance at the very last minute. Yve narrows her gaze on us, but thankfully, doesn't say a damn word. Once everyone has a plate, we eat in silence for a few minutes.

I glance at Lexa. She's shoving the food around on

her plate like she's not hungry. Her soon-to-be husband sits much too close to Yve.

Across from us, Guy eye-fucks Samantha, who not so subtly flips him off. Liam doesn't even notice because he's too busy with his phone. I inwardly sigh. Today's shaping up to be fucking lovely—a damn waste of all of our time.

After brunch, the girls will be at the spa for a few hours, then Lexa has to get ready for her wedding this afternoon. I manage to catch her before she leaves the table and draw her aside.

"Don't do this." I keep my voice low so we're not overheard. "You're not marrying that swine."

She folds her arms. "This is my choice, Blake. I'm not going to argue with you about this on my wedding day."

"Wedding day?" I scoff. "This whole event is a goddamn sham. The man you're supposed to be marrying has barely looked at you. He won't make a good husband. If he isn't doing so right now, he will cheat on you with your own mother. Christ, won't you listen to me!" Frustration burns through me because I know Lexa won't change her mind. Stubborn girl.

"Everything will be fine." She pats my arm and offers a sad smile. "What I'm about to do is in everyone's best interest. Just... please forgive me." Lexa leaves me staring after her as she catches up with Gin and Samantha.

Forgive her for what? For being a goddamn fool?

Fine. Since she's giving me no other option, Franklin Cecil can have her, but not for long. When I return home, I'm going to destroy him. I just need to figure out how to do it without Yve coming after me. Would she put me in prison for obliterating her friend's life? There's only one way to find out. Though I doubt it. If I'm locked up, then it's game over for her too because she won't have me to toy with any longer.

I need to find that dirt she has on me. Searching for it again just moved to the top of my priority list.

Lexa's a beautiful bride. I can't believe she's marrying that asshole Franklin. I should put a stop to this. I'm tempted to do just that as she appears at the end of the aisle, prepared to make her way to the altar alone. The string quartet starts to play a wedding march and she takes a step forward.

I glance around for inspiration on how to ruin the ceremony. The quickest, surest way to put an end to this would be to kill the groom. Or the officiant. I'm not especially picky. The only reason I waited until the last minute is because I thought Lexa would see reason, eventually, and put a stop to this herself. Fucking hell.

A helicopter appears over the hill, effectively drowning out the music and whipping sand into our faces. At first, I think it's the press coming for an inside scoop on the wedding. Those fucking vultures wouldn't bat an eye at stooping so low.

Except when I look up, my gaze collides with that last man I expect to see. Eion *fucking* Bane. He's swapped his tailored suit for tactical gear, and he slides down a rope, landing right in the middle of the aisle. Lexa runs to him.

I don't believe this. What the actual fuck is happening?

The fucker wraps his arms around her, then tosses me the most devilish smirk right before they're lifted into the air. Lexa loses a shoe when Yve makes a grab for her. All I can do is stare in disbelief amid Yve's shrieks and Franklin's flurry of obscenities. Everyone else seems as shocked as I am.

Eion fucking Bane just stole my sister away from her wedding.

"Well, I didn't see that coming." Gin chuckles. "That's one way to leave the groom at the altar. You go, girl!"

I look at her like she's lost her mind. "Do you have any idea who that was?"

She stares back at me. "No."

"Eion Bane. CEO of Bane Development Group, and my biggest business rival. Lexa knows not to go anywhere near the Bane Brothers. I'm going to fucking kill him. Come on. We're going home." I grab Gin's hand and head toward the resort's main building.

"We can't just leave. What about all of our stuff?"

"I'll have someone collect it and deliver it to our home. Right now, I need to charter a jet to get us the hell off this island."

CHAPTER 27

Blake

"Mr. Bane will see you now." The receptionist tips her head toward the double door as I glower at her for making me wait. There's nothing worse than being made to wait to see a member of the fucking Bane family. I'm sure Eion enjoyed the hell out me loitering in his lobby. *Fucker.*

I charge into his office and snarl, "Where the fuck is my sister?"

Since we returned home last night, I haven't been able to find a trace of Lexa anywhere. She's all but vanished and this piece of shit is responsible. The only reason I didn't come in here with guns blazing is because Lexa went to him, she fled into his arms, I saw that with my own eyes. If I had even the slightest suspicion that Eion kidnapped my sister, he'd already be sitting in my interrogation room.

"She's safe." He leans back behind his desk, sipping a coffee.

"She better be safe or I'll rip you to pieces." I sneer.

Eion bares his teeth, it's not a smile. "She's safer than she was with you. I'm not the one who was about to let my own sister shackle herself to that creep. I'd never let anyone touch her, especially not Franklin Cecil. That fucker can rot in hell."

"Lexa isn't yours to take care of." Placing my palms on his desk, I lean forward. "Where is my sister?"

"I can't give you that information."

"Oh, you will." I cock my head. "How is pretty little Bridget doing? I heard she started her own interior design business after college. I might have to call her up."

"Keep your filthy hands off my baby sister, Baron. I'm warning you, don't fuck with my family." Eion seethes.

"Then take your own advice and don't fuck with mine. Where's Lexa?"

We glare at each other for what seems like an eternity, neither of us backing down. It's like university all over again.

"She'll call you when she's ready to talk," he says, finally breaking eye contact. "Until then, I can't give you any details other than that she's safe and well hidden from her mother."

"Bane, I'm warning—"

"She called me for help. I'm sure I was her last resort, she only did it out of desperation. She said she didn't have anyone else to turn to because involving you or your brother would complicate your family dynamic. So, she reached outside of her family for help. *She* called *me*."

I stare at him, furious and pained that Lexa didn't put her trust in me. I would have gotten her out of there, to hell with Yve and her schemes. But Lexa wouldn't bring down Yve's ire on me. She was protecting all of us by calling Eion. Still, knowing that I can't protect my own siblings devastates me.

Lexa asked for my forgiveness. Now I know why.

Blowing out a breath, I straighten. "Tell her I'm not angry with her. She needs to call me."

"I'll deliver your message."

I nod. "Good."

My business concluded, for now, I turn to leave his office. He stops me by saying, "Don't touch Franklin Cecil. He's mine."

I spin around to face Eion. "Like hell he is."

Eion rises from his chair, standing eye to eye with me and I read the determination in his gaze. "Franklin thought he could touch Lexa. He's a dead man."

"Lexa isn't yours to avenge."

"She will be."

"Over my dead body."

"If you insist, Baron. In the meantime, I'm going to tear Franklin apart piece by piece and you can read all about it in the papers. I'm sure the *Big Apple Buzz* won't stop reporting on it for weeks. That tabloid can never resist when I throw them a nice juicy story."

"Fine, you can have Franklin, but release Lexa when she's ready to come home. She can come live with me to get away from Yve."

"I'm not a fucking monster, Baron. I'd never hold Lexa against her will. As soon as she has her shit together she'll leave, like she always does."

"What do you mean?" I pin him with a glare. Has

Lexa turned to him for help before? How do I not know about this?

"When she calls, I drop everything for her."

Like hell he does.

"How do you two even know each other?"

A grin touches his lips. "That's one secret I'll never divulge."

"Fuck you, Bane."

"Right back at you, Baron."

Turning on my heel, I get the fuck out of his office. I can't stand to be in his presence for a moment longer than necessary. At least Lexa's safe. I hate the fact that I know Eion Bane well enough to know his word is solid. If he says she's okay, then that's the truth. He's a virtuous fuck in that regard.

Late that night, I'm in my home office scrolling through the dark web's job postings—nothing of interest—and sifting through what my little birdies have to say. The priority list of information includes a photo of Yve and Franklin fucking, I could have done without seeing that, as well as a flurry of gossip about Lexa's wedding gone awry.

So much for having the ceremony at an undisclosed location. Someone on that island followed all of us quite closely, and the rumors and photos have spread like wildfire.

There's even a picture of me with Ginevra, along

with a theory that she has, in fact, finally snagged the most eligible bachelor in New York State. Apparently our demeanor with each other is far too intimate to be fake.

I smile at that assumption.

I'm always amused when my birdies end up sending me gossip about myself. This happens because not every source knows that it's me they are reporting to. All they know is that if they submit information, they get bitcoin. Everything about the process is anonymous.

Hell, I've heard rumors that my form sends the information to the *Big Apple Buzz*. False, of course. I'd never help those lowlife so-called reporters with anything, especially not when it comes to divulging tidbits from my precious stash of secrets.

CHAPTER 28

Ginevra

"Happy birthday, baby," Blake murmurs in my ear, and I groan, smashing the pillow to the side of my head. "Don't hide from me. I'm waking you up to give you your first birthday gift."

Gift? Did he say gift? I squint... seeing only darkness. Not a shred of light illuminates our bedroom.

"What time is it?" I roll onto my back.

Blake stands beside the bed, his outline visible as my eyes adjust to the dimness. He's fully dressed, though he kicks off his shoes and loosens his tie. "It's four in the morning. I can't wait any longer to start celebrating your birthday."

"Blake," I whine, torn between going back to sleep and curious about why he's so impatient. Most of this week he's been coming to bed with me, instead of staying up until the early morning hours, except for tonight. He said he had work to catch up on, so I went to bed, knowing he'd join me later. But he's always careful not to wake me up when he finally turns in.

I squeak in surprise when his body weight dips the bed and he extends my arms above my head, fastening them together with what I believe is his silk tie. Suddenly, I'm fully alert, my heart rate spiking.

"What are you doing?" I test the restraints, finding them secure. "Blake, what is this?"

"Shh." He lights a candle on the bedside table and a warm glow washes over us. "Do you trust me, magpie? Will you give your control over to me so I can show you everything I can give you?"

"M-my control?"

"Did I stutter? Yes, your control." His blue eyes bore into me. I shake my head. He didn't stutter, I'm just repeating what he said as a stalling tactic as I try to wrap my brain around why he's tied me to the headboard, and not panic.

"I..." My words trail off as he caresses the edge of my breast and my heart pounds harder against my ribcage.

"What's wrong?"

I'm breathing in short, shallow puffs of air, my vision darkening at the corners. I tug again, trying to free my wrists this time as blazing panic threatens to pull me under.

"Shit. Stop, you'll hurt yourself." Blake makes quick work of the restraints, then takes my hands in his and massages my sore wrists. "What just happened, Gin? Talk to me."

I shake my head, my entire body trembling with adrenaline.

"Please, talk to me."

"I-I can't." I squeeze my eyes closed and focus on my breathing, willing myself to calm down. "I'm sorry." My voice is barely above a whisper, but he hears me and pulls me against his chest. His strong arms wrap around my shivering frame and I sigh, the dread leaving as quickly as it came.

"Don't be sorry. There's nothing to be sorry for, ever." He rubs circles on my back. "I'm sorry for frightening you. You were okay yesterday morning when I held your arms above your head and fucked you, so I thought restraining you with my tie would be fine. Obviously, I was wrong."

I inhale his masculine scent, feeling terrible about overreacting. If only I told him about... what happened, then he'd understand. But I can't bring myself to say anything about it. It's too embarrassing. I'm too ashamed. The past needs to stay right where it is, in my past. Though times like this I wonder if it ever won't come to haunt me.

What if... what if I can change things, make a different future for myself?

"Blake?"

"Yes?"

I tentatively reach for his silk tie and hold it out to him. "Tie me up."

"No. I won't—"

"Please. You took me by surprise before and it freaked me out, but I'm ready now. I want this, please." I want him to do this to me. He's Blake, not Oliver, and there's a world of difference between these two men. I know that now.

He studies me for several long moments, his bright blue gaze seeming to dive beneath my skin, laying my soul, and all of my secrets, bare to him. If only it was that easy to let him in, to allow him to see all of me, but it's not. Even if I want it to be sometimes.

"Take away my control," I tell him. "Show me."

His eyes scan my face one more time. "If you want me to stop, just say so. Understand?"

I nod.

"Use your words, Gin."

"I understand."

"Good girl." He takes the tie from me and loops it around my wrists, tight enough to hold them together, but not as secure as before. "Now I'm going to blindfold you."

Oh god. What have I gotten myself into?

I swallow hard, and he narrows his assessing gaze on me. "Okay," I murmur and nod. He reaches toward me, securing the blindfold in place, and plunging me into darkness. I release a shuddering breath.

"I'll never hurt you, Gin, you know that." His deep, silky voice chases away my demons. "Now lie back and let me taste you. Here, let me guide you." His large hands ease me back onto the mattress. "Let go, baby girl, I've got you."

Without being able to see or reach for him, I let my other senses take over. His palms smooth up my thighs, parting my legs, his hot breath teases my bare pussy. He nibbles at the soft flesh between my legs, leaving his mark on my inner thigh before dragging his tongue to my clit. I whimper as he circles it. The partial sensory deprivation heightens his every touch.

"That's my girl," he says when I moan, arching my back in a silent plea for more. "Just let go, and I promise to make you feel good on your birthday. Do you trust me?"

"Yes," I pant.

Blake teases my clit, tongues my sensitive flesh, and has me squirming with need, building closer and closer to release. I desperately want more, need more, to tip me over the edge.

"Please," I beg. I can't see him, but I can picture the smirk on his gorgeous face as he pushes two fingers into my throbbing cunt.

"Such a hungry pussy, so greedy for anything I give it. Fuck, baby, can you feel how wet you are for me?"

I let out an incoherent noise and rock my hips, riding his fingers. There's moisture against my thighs. He removes his hand, ignoring my protest, only to drag his wet fingers lower and circle my asshole. I startle at the sensation, the word *stop* on the tip of my tongue, but then he nudges my ass at the same time as his tongue flicks across my clit, and I explode.

The most intense orgasm of my life wracks my body and unravels my mind. Fireworks spark behind my eyelids.

I feel Blake shift, then he's hovering on top of me, his body heat warming my flushed, sweaty skin. He lines himself up with my entrance and pushes in. My pussy stretches to accommodate him, and I gasp, the sensation more intense than usual.

"You have no idea how long I've wanted to fuck every single one of your beautiful, delicious holes, magpie." He rocks his hips, driving into me. "That includes this one."

His hand slides down my ass and he inserts a finger.

Oh my god. To my astonishment, I don't panic. If anything, with his cock inside me, it feels good.

"I want to feel your muscles tighten and clench around my cock and fingers when you come." He pinches my nipple, earning himself another of my breathy moans. His lips press to mine, his tongue demanding entrance, and I open for him. He tongue-fucks my mouth in time to his cock and fingers.

The mixed sensations are too much. He's every-where, filling me up in every way that he can. His raw, brutal possessiveness has me screaming his name as I fall to pieces, completely giving in to him not only with my body, but with my mind.

"That's it, sweetheart, come for me. Such a good fucking girl, just like that. *Fuck.*"

His hips jerk with his release and liquid heat spreads through my insides. When he's finished, he stills, buried deep, and removes my blindfold.

"Hello, beautiful." He drops a sweet kiss to my fore-head, my nose, my lips. "Was that too much or did you enjoy it?"

I swallow past the lump in my throat and smile shyly at him. "I enjoyed it."

Which surprises me, and makes me somewhat uncomfortable too. I didn't think I could stand anything anal since... what happened with my ex. Obviously that's not the case. I came–twice.

But what does that say about me? That he can touch me like that and I like it? Am I finally overcoming my trauma or am I more fucked up than I realized? Broken beyond repair.

"Oh my god, remind me to tell Kyla this is the best Belgian waffle I've ever had." I moan around my last forkful of the fluffy, crispy goodness, sad that my plate's now empty. Blake chuckles and drops the last quarter of his waffle in front of me, which I immediately devour.

We spent the morning alternating between sex and sleep, and I sure worked up an appetite. Breakfast in bed was an excellent indulgence.

As soon as I'm finished eating, Blake takes away my dish and replaces it with a small gift wrapped box.

"Happy twenty-first birthday. This is the first of many today."

I'm so giddy that my hands shake. The genuine grin I offer him has his lips curving up at the corners. I love seeing him smile. He should do that more often.

Shredding the paper, I remove the lid from the box and peer inside, finding a sparkly object. I gently take it out and hold it in my hand. My chest squeezes at the same time as my stomach flutters. I immediately recognize the figurine encrusted with black, blue, and green diamonds. The magpie.

"You..." My brows pinch with confusion. "This is a Baron family heirloom. I almost stole this from you, why are you giving it to me now?"

"Because I see the way your gaze seeks it out when we're in the hallway, and how your eyes light up every time you see it. Nothing escapes my notice. You long for this little magpie figurine, so I decided that it should be yours." He reaches for my hand and closes my fingers around the piece. He's right, I hadn't even noticed that I always stare at it when we walk along that hallway, but I do. I've loved this figurine since the first time I spotted it. It's so sparkly, it makes me happy.

"Thank you." Thickness clogs my throat. "I love it. Really love it!"

This time, his smile reaches his glittering eyes. The way that expression transforms his face from handsome to breathtaking, literally stops the air in my lungs. His birthday is in November and I'm going to make sure it's as wonderful as today's been so far.

"I can't give you just one magpie though," he says, climbing out of bed and pulling on a pair of slacks. My gaze appreciatively roams over his bare chest and shoulders.

"Why? What do you mean by that?"

"One magpie represents sorrow. That simply won't do. Come with me. Don't worry, we're not leaving the house. Not yet."

I'm not sure what he's talking about, but curiosity spurs me on. I wrap myself in a silk robe and take his offered hand. He leads me through the house to the garage. What can he possibly be hiding in here?

Blake tosses me a key fob. "Click that button."

"Okay..." I do, and a car up ahead honks and lights up. Slowly, I approach the adorable, glimmery blue, two-seater vehicle. "Is what I'm looking for inside your car?"

"*Your* car," he corrects me. "I thought it was time you

had a little more freedom. This BMW Z4 should help you with that."

I gape at him. Is he for real? He bought me a car for my birthday? "You're joking!"

"No joke. Look at the license plate."

I glance down, reading the plate: MAGPIE. Holy shit. He bought me a car! I squeal and sprint to it, running my palm over the blue almost metallic paint.

"Two magpies for joy."

I spin toward him. "What are you talking about?"

"It's nothing, just an old nursery rhyme that I can't seem to get out of my head these days."

"How does it go?"

He clears his throat.

"One for sorrow,
Two for mirth,
Three for a wedding,
Four for death,
Five for silver,
Six for gold,
Seven for a secret never to be told.
Eight for a wish,
Nine for a kiss,
Ten for a surprise you should be careful not to miss."

I giggle, never in a million years did I expect Blake to recite an old nursery rhyme meant for children, much less follow these old superstitions.

"So this car is my two for mirth?"

"Yes. I hope it brings you joy."

I fling my arms around his neck and pepper his chin and neck with kisses. "Thank you! You're the best."

"I know," he drawls, earning himself a roll of my

eyes. He smacks my ass in punishment, which leads to us having sex on the hood of my new car.

The rest of my birthday is like something out of a dream. We shower together, making each other come yet again before getting ready for the day. I get to drive my new car, turns out it's a convertible which I love on this warm summer day, to a mystery location. No matter how many times I beg Blake to tell me where we're going, he refuses.

I'm speechless when we pull into a crowded parking lot beside a massive concrete building. They check our names off a list at the door, then suddenly I'm in a film studio.

"You seem to like watching these, so I thought you might enjoy the live experience." Blake motions me to a seat. In front of us, the stage is set up like a kitchen. A backdrop displays the show's title and I excitedly bounce in my seat. This is one of my favorite cooking competition shows! We have front row seats to watch chefs make their creations.

I lean over and kiss him. The joy rushing through me feels like it's going to make me burst any moment, I can hardly contain it all.

For an hour, I watch the chefs at work while Blake stares at me. Every time I glance at him, he simply smiles. *Smiles.* Like he's happy. How crazy is that? Honestly, I could get used to this indulgent, generous, relaxed side of my fiancé.

After the show, we get to go backstage and meet the chefs. They humor me as I barrage them with questions, being kind enough to give me insider tips and tricks. I can't wait to chat with Kyla about everything I learned today. I'm sure she already knows most of these things, but she's someone I can talk to about cooking and her eyes don't glaze over when I get excited about the science involved.

"Oh my god, that was amazing," I tell Blake as we head back to my car. "This is the best birthday I've ever had."

He smirks. "It's not over yet."

"Really? What's next?"

"Well, unfortunately, I'm not allowed to keep you all to myself today." He slides into the passenger seat. I can hardly believe he's letting me drive again. He's always so in control of everything, but right now he's letting me be in charge, placing his trust in me. "Your sisters wouldn't allow it, they insisted on seeing you today. Arianna even threatened me with bodily harm if they didn't see you on your birthday. Do you know she has such a vicious streak?"

I laugh. "Yeah, don't let her prim and proper mannerisms fool you. She is married to a Bratva *pakhan*, after all."

"True. Anyway, we are expected at the De Luca estate this evening. Sophia insisted on hosting your birthday dinner. It's about an hour and a half drive from here and we're staying the night. Before you ask, our overnight bags are in the trunk. So let's see what your little magpie car can do on the highway, shall we?"

A thrill buzzes through me as I press the ignition. "Buckle up."

CHAPTER 29

Ginevra

Father comes into the kitchen of Sophia and Roman's mansion. Glancing around, I realize I'm alone and my stomach drops, especially when I note that determined gleam in his eyes. There's no getting away from him now, not while everyone else is in the other room, celebrating my birthday with drinks and cake now that dinner's over.

I slipped in here to admire their new oven. Now I'm regretting that decision.

"It seems like things are going good between you and Mr. Baron," he says, trapping me in the corner of the kitchen. "Only one more month until you have a gold band on your finger and he joins our family. I better not be disappointed in the end."

"How you feel in the end is not my problem," I snap.

His face reddens, eyes narrowed. "I'll be happy as long as you keep spreading your legs for him and he becomes my son-in-law. By association, that will make me the most powerful man on the East Coast."

"Blake's a person, not one of your pawns." I face off with my father, feeling much less intimidated and more sassy than usual with him. The truth is, he can't fucking touch me anymore. Now that I'm under Blake's protection.

"Every person is someone else's pawn, you stupid girl." He eyes me. "I didn't see your worth before, you're not like your sisters, but I guess everyone has a use."

"And what? My use is to snare Blake for you? If you think you'll ever be able to control him, you're wrong."

"Why don't you shut your stupid slut mouth and leave Mr. Baron to me, huh?"

I stare at him, used to this type of verbal abuse that he's spewed at me all my life. For the last twenty-one years I don't remember a time when my father was kind to me, or loving. He's always treated me differently from my two sisters.

"Why do you hate me so much?" I ask in a strangled voice. It's a question that has been on the tip of my tongue numerous times, but I never dared speak it aloud. Until now.

Father frowns, as if my question caught him off guard. He shakes his head and glances away, raking a hand through his short beard. Just when I figure he's not going to answer me, he speaks.

"Because you're not mine."

I snort. "Of course I'm yours, who else's would I be?"

"Shut up for once in your life and listen because I'll never talk about this again." He glares at me, and I snap my mouth closed. "You're not mine. Your father is dead— I killed him."

My lips part in shock, all kinds of possible scenarios

coming to mind. Was Mama unfaithful? I can't see that, not with the closeness of their marriage. So...

"He kidnapped and raped your mother because of a deal between us gone wrong. I fucking killed the bastard, but then you were born. I begged my wife to get rid of you, but she was convinced that you were my child and not his. As soon as you were born, I had a paternity test done and it told the horrible truth. You're a constant reminder of how I failed to protect my own wife, my family." His gaze shifts from haunted to loathing. He really does hate me for something that is way beyond my control.

I don't even know what to say. This revelation leaves me reeling, sick to my stomach now that I know where I come from. My skin crawls.

"To your mother, you're her daughter, she'll never see you any differently. But to me, you're the most vile little creature. When you were little, I thought I could forget the truth, to pretend you belonged to me, but you're the spitting image of him. I should have gotten rid of you when you were a baby."

I blink back tears, I'm not sure if they're from devastating sadness or anger. Maybe both.

The kitchen door clicks shut and we both turn, finding Blake standing in the doorway. How long has he been there? How much did he overhear?

He sneers at the man I thought was my father. "I should get rid of you right now for being the worst father any child could have. How can you blame her, when she's completely innocent? You're a coward, Pontrelli, for letting your guilt ruin her life. She deserves so much better than you."

My heart flip-flops at Blake's words.

"This is none of your business, Mr. Baron."

"I beg to differ. Everything and anything involving Ginevra is my business. You're supposed to be the most important man in her life and you've devastatingly let her down. I won't make the same mistake."

Father points at me, seething. "She's tainted. Even you must be able to see she's not good for—"

Blake moves so quickly, neither of us has time to react. He punches my father, sending him sprawling to the kitchen floor, where he stays down, blood seeping from his nose and mouth.

"I warned you not to speak like that about my fiancée." Blake shakes out his hand, clenching and uncurling his fingers as he stares down at my papa. "Don't ever come near her again. She's no longer your responsibility, you piece of shit. You don't deserve her."

Blake steps over him, coming to my side. He pulls me into a tight embrace, then steers us out of the kitchen. "Let's go home, baby."

I nod my agreement. My emotions are a wreck, and the number of questions blasting through my mind are giving me a headache. This has been one crazy birthday —both good and bad.

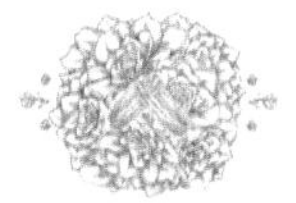

"Did either of you know?" I'm on a group call with my sisters because this conversation is too complicated for text messages, and it can't wait to meet face-to-face. What my father said to me has been haunting my every waking minute.

"Of course we didn't know," Sophia says. "I mean, you look different than me and Arianna, but genetics can be funny like that. I never would have guessed you weren't Papa's daughter."

"Not that it makes any difference," Arianna cuts in. "You're our sister, always have been and always will be. Papa was cruel to tell you the truth."

He probably did mean to hurt me with the truth, but at least now I know. His actions throughout my entire life all make sense now. Not only do I remind him of what happened to my mother, but I'm also a reminder of how he failed to protect her. Which is a blow to his ego every time he looks at me.

"We love you, Gin. Nothing will ever change that." Sophia's tone is adamant.

Arianna adds, "It doesn't matter that you're technically our half-sister. So don't give it another thought. Okay?"

"Okay. I love you both too."

"Are you going to talk with Mama about it?" Sophia asks.

I consider her question. Should I? I need to give it some more thought, so I just answer, "Maybe. I'll let you both know if I do. In the meantime, let's not bring it up. This is our secret."

"Our lips are sealed," Arianna says. "If you ever want to talk more about it, just let us know. We're here for you, Gin."

"Thank you." I appreciate my sisters so damn much.

Tonight I sit on Blake's lap while he scrolls through a dark web chatroom and feeds me chocolates he ordered from Paris. A satisfied rumble sounds in his chest every time my lips wrap around his fingers. Since we returned from Lexa's no-go wedding, and my strange birthday celebration, this has been our life, and it's been divine.

Lexa finally called Blake last week. He immediately launched into a tirade about her and Eion Bane, which went over about as well as I expected. She hung up on him and hasn't called again since. I know he still worries about her, but he needs to chill the fuck out if he wants Lexa to talk to him.

Him chilling is easier said than done. He's always wound so tight, unless it's just the two of us together. Like right now.

"So, this is the secret to your reputation as the *Big, Bad Black Baron* that has everyone shaking in their boots." I suck on a piece of chocolate as he sorts through snippets of gossip from a ton of different anonymous sources who he calls his *little birdies*. "Isn't this like cheating or something?"

"I pay for this information. That's hardly cheating," he rumbles. "It's not my fault that no one else has this wonderful program to make sense of all the information out there."

"Is there anything useful today?"

"Not really. Nothing about Yve, or the blackmail material she has on me—not yet. But it will come eventually. Someone will see something, and then everything else will click into place. That's how this works."

"Fascinating." It really is. I glance at Blake, he's fascinating too. I never would have suspected him of being a computer nerd, but he can go on and on about data and programming, the same way I can about cooking techniques. He's truly passionate about this computer stuff. It's adorable.

I shift on his lap. "What about your inheritance?"

"What about it?"

"What is it? One of the nights on the yacht, Liam told me that you haven't gotten yours yet. I'm curious about what it is."

Blake stiffens, suddenly uncomfortable, but I don't understand why.

"I'm sorry, you don't have to–"

"It's why I'm fake marrying you. Yve won't give me my inheritance until I've taken a wife, and I must remain married for one year."

Oh. So that's the reason behind our ruse.

"You seem to have everything you could possibly want, so why fake marry me? What do you have left to gain?"

Blake clears his throat and shoots me a quick glance. "In all honesty, it's of little value."

"Now I'm even more intrigued. Tell me."

"This is pathetic, but don't laugh at me."

"I promise, I won't laugh."

He sighs, running his fingers through already tousled hair. "My mother died when she gave birth to Liam.

Before that, she and I were close, very close. You could even say I was a mama's boy. Following her death, my father quickly remarried—twice. Both times to scheming gold-diggers who hated me and my little brother. I despised my father for subjecting us to those cruel women. Then along came Yve. She manipulated him into giving her everything in the end."

My heart aches for him and his terrible childhood.

Without looking at me, he continues like he's desperate to get his story out. "When I went away to boarding school one year, Yve collected up everything I had left of my mother and hid it. All of the photos, her journals, everything I'd kept to remind me of her was suddenly just gone. Yve and I have been enemies ever since. But that's what I'm doing this for, to get my mother's things back."

"Oh my god, Blake, that's—it's—"

"Pathetic, I know. I'm hardly the sentimental type of man."

"I was going to say heart-rending." Looping my arms around his neck, I kiss him, long and deep. The more I discover about this man, the more I want him. Now I'm more inspired than ever to be the best fake wife he'll ever have. That bitch can't win.

I pull away from him, putting a slice of distance between us. "Thank you for telling me."

He warily eyes me. "You're sworn to secrecy. If that got out, it'd ruin my reputation."

"My lips are sealed."

"They better be." He leans in for another kiss. "Speaking of important things, Friday night we're having a dinner guest. I've already given the menu to Kyla. I want you to be my charming, sweet hostess that night. It's a work thing, and I really need to win this acquisition. A lot is hanging on it."

"Like what? Can I know, or is it a secret?"

He adjusts me on his lap and turns off his computer, giving me his full attention. "You should know, so that you understand the stakes. It's more of Yve's bullshit. Our guest is selling a piece of property and he's deciding between two buyers: Me and Eion Bane."

"So that's why you hate Mr. Bane so much," I muse.

"One of many reasons. Anyway, we need the seller to choose me. Yve is threatening to disinherit Liam if I lose this deal. She'll take away the position that's waiting for him and potentially give Titan Enterprises to Lexa, or who knows, whatever she decides on a whim." He picks up his scotch glass and scowls into it.

"So this dinner is meant to win over the seller? I'm guessing you want him to like us more than he likes Eion Bane, is that right?"

Blake nods. "Exactly."

"Then let me have at him. I'll win him for you."

"I hoped you would say that. Be your radiant self and he'll fall at your feet, magpie." He softly kisses my lips. "Let's get to bed, it's late."

Friday evening rolls around and I'm wearing a blue silk dress the color of Blake's eyes. My blond curls form an artfully messy updo that exposes my neck. Every time I look in the mirror, my ex-father's words come back to haunt me. "You're the spitting image of him."

A rapist.

I shake away the thought. No good will come from dwelling on it. I'd never bring this up with my mother. I wouldn't do that to her, so I may as well lay it to rest. The man I'm genetically related to is dead anyway.

I'm finishing up my makeup when Blake enters my dressing room. My mouth goes dry as I take him in. That tailored navy suit emphasizes his broad shoulders and trim waist, not to mention his impressive height. His blond hair is perfectly arranged and he smells heavenly.

"This is for you." He stands behind me, draping a sapphire and diamond necklace across my collar bone, then fastens it at the back of my neck. The jewelry is stunning. "Beautiful," he murmurs, dropping a kiss on top of my head.

"What's the occasion?" I ask, feeling like I'm missing something important.

The corners of his mouth quirk. "No occasion. I just saw this in Maçon's new collection and it struck me as a magpie-worthy piece. It goes with your dress, so why not give it to you now?"

I stare at him in the mirror, once again shocked into silence by how precious he makes me feel. If I didn't know any better, I'd think I'm always on his mind, that he spends his time daydreaming about me. But that can't be true. He's much too busy. Then he does a thing like this, so innocent, yet heartwarming, and completely out of the blue.

I could fall in love with this man. My heart clenches. Why is that thought so painful?

"I'll see you downstairs. Our guest should be here soon." He slips from my room, leaving me staring after him.

Am I falling in love? Butterflies flutter in my stomach and my skin warms. I catch myself smiling in the mirror, my expression completely smitten. Oh god, this isn't good. I can't fall for my fake fiancé no matter how unexpectedly wonderful he is.

Pulling myself together, I finish my makeup, trail my fingers over the stunning necklace I'm wearing and slip on my heels. Now, I'm ready to woo our dinner guest until he signs that property away to Blake and Titan Enterprises. I like Liam, he deserves to keep his inheritance. Furthermore, Yve is a cunning bitch who needs to be taken down a notch or two.

As I make my way downstairs, masculine voices reach my ears, signaling that our guest has already arrived. They're in the sitting room, probably having a drink before dinner.

I make my way toward the doorway, a welcoming grin plastered to my lips, and step into the room. My smile falters. My heart stops. I freeze, my mind blank with terror.

No. It can't be him. How is he in my house? What is he doing here?

Blake turns to face me, a fresh drink in his hand. "Ginevra, I'd like you to meet Oliver Zaleski. He goes by Oz. Oz, this is my fiancée, Ginevra Pontrelli."

I quickly shake off my shock, though fear lodges itself deep beneath my skin as I gaze into Oliver's sparkling green eyes. He's amused—which is never a good thing.

"N-nice to meet you, Oz." I stumble over my words at first.

"The pleasure's all mine." He extends his hand—to my horror—as I'm forced to shake it. Otherwise Blake will realize something's wrong, then question me, and I can't tell him what happened. That secret I've buried deep down, and it will never see the light of day, so help me God.

As soon as my hand slips into Oliver's a shiver runs up my spine, nausea churns my stomach, and I quickly pull away.

Blake notices my abrupt movements, a frown tugs at his full mouth. I ignore the unspoken question in his eyes and paste a smile back on my face. I have to pretend to be charming, to win over Oliver, when all I want to do is run and hide. How did I get myself into this situation?

It will all be fine.

Everything is fine. I repeat that mantra in my head over and over.

Oliver isn't letting on that we know each other, so I won't either. I can do this. He's not Oliver, he's Oz—a nickname I never heard him use while we were dating. But the truth is, I never knew the man standing before me, and I certainly don't know him now.

"So, Oz, my fiancé tells me you're in real estate." I gesture for him to sit on the sofa and take the chair across from him. Blake folds himself into the chair next to mine.

Oliver's eyes flash with malice when I mention my fiancé. He doesn't like that I'm engaged to another man. Dread coils tighter around my guts.

I'm fine. Everything will be fine.

"Actually, I'm simply selling off a piece of my family's estate. I recently came into my inheritance, and I'm doing my best to ensure everything is well-managed. The money from this sale will do wonders for some investment opportunities that have come up." He flashes me a grin. I used to love that boyish expression, but now it makes me sick.

It occurs to me that Oliver isn't surprised to find me here, which means he knew walking into this that Blake and I are engaged. What is he playing at? Will he sell the property to Blake, knowing that he's my fiancé, or is he here to torment me under the guise of this business deal? With Oliver, I never know what's going on in his head.

The gong sounds, summoning us to dinner, and saving me from having to make small talk with my ex in front of my fake fiancé. *Fuck my life.*

Blake settles at the head of the table, leaving Oliver and I to sit across from each other. How am I supposed to eat while looking at him? While he's watching me with that malevolent gleam in his eyes?

Kyla, and our housekeeper Fleur, serve us dinner then disappear into the kitchen. Lucky them. I'd do anything to join them right now.

Blake and Oliver chit-chat about sports and the stock market for a while, which gives me a few minutes to calm my frayed nerves. The meal Kyla created for us this evening is delicious, yet I barely taste it as I chew another bite and swallow. My throat's painfully tight. My mouth dry, no matter how much wine I sip.

About a half hour in, Blake's phone rings. He fishes it from his pocket, frowns at the screen, and excuses himself. Panic threatens to engulf me when he leaves the room, leaving me alone with Oliver.

No, no, no, don't leave me here.

As soon as Blake's footsteps fade away, Oliver leans forward, elbows braced on the table. "Ginny, it's been so long since we last saw each other. I've missed you, babe."

My food threatens to come back up. "Why are you here?"

"I have business with your *fiancé.*" He grimaces. "But did you really think I was going to let you go? The fact that you're engaged changes nothing, it means nothing to me. You're mine and you always will be, no matter how many other men you fuck, you stupid whore.

"I always knew you were a fucking gold-digger. Were my millions not enough for you? You had to go after that *billionaire* instead? You know, he's just using you as a fuck toy. As soon as he's had his fill of your cunt, he'll toss you on the street, and guess who'll be there to pick you up? *Me.*" He jabs a thumb at his chest. "I'll scoop you up off the pavement and take you home where you belong. Then we can pick up where we left off."

Bile rises in my throat. That whole scenario chills me to the core. What will happen when Blake and I are through? My father will cut me off, he hates me, but surely I can turn to my sisters. Anyone but Oliver. I can't let him get his hands on me again. I won't survive it a second time.

Oliver chuckles at my silence. "Maybe I won't have to wait that long to have you again. I could always write a clause into the sales contract where I get you once a week. Or maybe every other weekend. Do you think Blake would go for that, Ginny? Is he that desperate to have my property?"

Oh god. I'm going to be sick.

What Oliver doesn't know is that Blake is beyond desperate for that property, so much depends on their deal going through. Would Blake sign away my freedom, my body, to this psychopath? I want to believe he'd never do such a thing, but he did blackmail me, and his reputation shows he has very few scruples. But he's dedicated to his siblings, especially Liam. I don't know where I stand when it's a choice between me or his brother. I have a feeling I'm on the losing side.

"I can't wait to fuck every one of your holes again, Ginny, and this time I'm going to make you bleed. You're a naughty girl for running away from me, for climbing into Baron's bed, and bad girls get punished, don't they? You think I hurt you last time? You haven't seen anything yet."

I don't answer him, I can barely breathe. My hands tremble beneath the table as I mindlessly destroy the cloth napkin in my lap.

CHAPTER 30

Blake

I've been waiting for Lexa to call me back for over a week, too bad her timing is terrible. Even so, I don't dare to let the unknown number she's calling from go to voicemail. We need to talk.

"I'm not moving in with you, Blake, that's final." For such a little pixie, she sure is stubborn, unmovable as a mountain when she wants to be.

I grind my teeth together, but hold my tongue. We don't need a repeat of the last time she called and hung up. "Fine. But I am sending you money. I don't want you owing Eion Bane a single fucking penny, Lexa. Got it?"

She huffs. "Fine." Then her tone softens, "I'm okay, I promise. I can't explain anything to you right now, and I'm sorry about that. Just please do whatever you can to make sure my mother doesn't find me."

"I don't even know where you are, how is she supposed to find you?"

"I'm hoping she can't. That's why I can't tell you where I am either. Everything I'm doing is to keep you and Liam safe, I swear. You're both my family and I love you. I'm sure you'll try to track my call, so I'm going to go now. Good night." She hangs up and I mutter a curse. Of course I'm trying to track her location. She knows me too well.

Disgruntled, I head back to the dining room and my pompous, irritating guest. He's done nothing but blow his own horn all evening. Any subject he knows everything about, he's a fucking expert. I roll my eyes. He's on my last nerve, but until this deal goes through, I have to pretend I don't want to murder him.

Plus, I don't like the way he looks at Gin. There's something off about it that I can't quite put my finger on.

As soon as I enter the room, I notice the thick, charged atmosphere. Gin's pale face paired with Oz's smug expression sets my teeth on edge. What have they been doing while I was gone?

I take my seat, and Oz immediately launches into more business chit-chat. "...all that to say, we have a deal."

That catches my attention. "A deal?"

"Yes." Oz leans back in his seat and puffs out his chest. "I've made my decision. I'm going with your company. Your vision, and Titan Enterprises, are the best fit for my property. I'll have the contract drawn up in the next few weeks." His gaze flits briefly to a quiet, distant Gin. "Congratulations on your upcoming nuptials. We'll finalize the details once you're back from your honeymoon."

A wave of relief crashes over me. This is the first step toward securing Liam's inheritance and place at the company. But I'm not counting on this victory until we've signed on the line and the paperwork's been filed. Then I'll celebrate.

"Agreed," I state.

"I'm sure we have a long and mutually beneficial relationship ahead of us." Oz grins at me, and I resist the urge to punch him.

"I'm sure we do."

He stands. "My lawyers will be in touch."

"Aren't you staying for dessert," I grind out, only because it's polite and I'm still pretending to be a good host. This deal isn't done until it's done, after all.

"You know, I think I'll skip dessert this time. Rain check." Oz shakes my hand. "Thank you for a lovely evening."

He tips his chin to Ginevra, and she gives him the fakest smile I've ever seen on her lush lips. I've been so preoccupied with Oz all evening that I haven't noticed how tense and uneasy she seems. What the hell is going on?

I walk him to the door, impatient about getting him out of my house. Once he's finally gone, I return to Gin, finding her in her dressing room with a bottle of vanilla vodka in her hand. She only drinks that stuff when she's distraught. She takes a shot and stares into the vanity mirror.

"Are you unwell?" I ask, approaching her.

"A little. I'll be fine."

"What's wrong? Talk to me." I move closer. "Did he do something to you when I was gone?"

Her wide, fearful eyes find mine in the mirror, and that look punches me in the gut. Something is very wrong. I kneel before her, taking her hands in mine.

She glances away. "I'm fine."

"You're obviously not fine. What did he do?"

"Nothing."

"Why won't you tell me the truth?" I plead, trying to get her to look at me, but she won't.

"I just... c-can't." Her voice breaks.

"All right. What do you need from me?" I lean in and kiss her, but she doesn't kiss me back. I don't want to cause her any more distress, so I pull away and stand up. "I'm going to draw you a bath."

She nods, taking another swig of vodka.

I go into the ensuite and fill the tub with water, adding bubbles and bath salts. While the water runs, I pull up my house cameras on my phone, reviewing the recording of what happened in the dining room while I was on the phone with Lexa. There's no sound, so all I see is Oz speaking to Gin and her growing more and more distressed.

Rage grows like a cancer in my chest. As soon as that paperwork is filed, I'm going to have words with Oz.

What I don't understand is why Gin refuses to tell me what happened. She knows I'll protect her, right? I'll do anything for her.

Unless... What if she won't tell me because she's playing me for a fool? Jealousy and suspicion tangle in my gut.

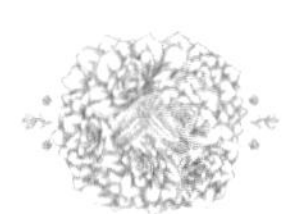

Unable to sleep that night, I leave a softly snoring Gin in my bed and tiptoe to my office. Suspicion eats at me and I need to lay it to rest. Firing up my computer, I search for any link between Gin and Oz.

In no time at all, I have all the information I need staring back at me on my screen. *He's* the ex-boyfriend. The fucking *ex*. Shit.

She'd said she was seeing someone and they broke up shortly before our... arrangement. I've had so much going on since then that looking into her ex-boyfriend, who was supposed to be out of the picture, was way down on my priority list. That was stupid of me, I should have looked into this sooner.

They know each other, they dated for several months, so why act like they're strangers at dinner? What are they hiding? Are they secretly still lovers?

I spear my fingers through my hair and tug on the ends. Ginevra and her secrets are going to drive me insane. Is she really the sweet, abused young woman she seems to be, or is she a master manipulator playing me for a fool? Hell, her and Oz could be in on this together.

Now I'm just being fucking paranoid. Right?

I can't figure out their angle, if there even is one. But one thing's for certain, they're both keeping secrets—and they're both lying to me. Why?

Ginevra

Blake seems to have let everything go concerning the dinner with Oliver. For the last two weeks he hasn't brought it up at all. Which is a relief because I can't tell him about my past with Oliver, it's too embarrassing, too shameful.

Blake treats me like a princess, like I'm precious to him, and I don't want that to change. I don't want him to see how broken I am, or know about the ways I've been used. He'd probably be disgusted. I can't risk that, it would break my heart.

Sometimes I even wonder if I got what happened with Oliver all wrong in my mind, like what if the way I remember it isn't really what happened? What if I did give consent and just don't recall that detail?

I push the intrusive thought from my head. I'm not in Paris the week before my wedding to dwell on my ex-boyfriend. I'm here to shop before we head to London for the ceremony in two days. This is my bachelorette party.

We walk along the street, ducking into one boutique

after another. Our mostly invisible security team surrounds us. Sophia and Ravenna stroll ahead, they've been practically inseparable this whole trip and it's good to see them so close. Arianna's constantly typing on her phone, working while on vacation. My cousin Elena, Ravenna's twin sister, lingers at my side, her gaze darting around nervously.

I reach for her arm. "Are you okay? You seem... anxious."

"I'm fine." She licks her lips, her gaze finding mine. "I haven't been out of the house in months and being here is a little overwhelming. So many people and noises."

"We're well protected. If it's too much, you can always return to the hotel. You're not obligated to spend every minute out with us." I offer her a reassuring smile to cover up my worry.

No one knows what exactly happened to Elena three years ago, but ever since that trauma she's been living with relatives in Italy. Apparently as a recluse.

"It's okay," she says. "I probably should get out more."

"Maybe I can come visit you sometime and we can live it up all over Italy."

"I'd like that."

"Really?"

Elena shrugs. "Honestly, I don't know, but I'd love your company. Right now I feel like I'm not really living. Each day blends into the next." She runs her fingers over a rack of silk scarves. "If I keep going like this, one day I'll wake up and find that my entire life has passed me by, and that scares me."

God, I didn't realize how bad she's gotten. Is no one taking care of her, checking in on her?

I glance at my sisters and Ravenna who are all happily married and living their own lives. Maybe they don't have time to see what's really going on with Elena. She must be so lonely.

I face her and say, "After my wedding and honeymoon, I'll come stay with you for a while, okay? We're not going to let your life pass you by. Promise."

A rare smile appears on her lips. "Okay."

"Now let's go annoy Arianna, she's been glued to her phone all day."

Elena shakes her head, but follows me as I steal my sister's phone right out of her hands.

"Hey!" Arianna protests, coming after me. "Gin, give it back this instant!"

I toss it to Elena, who catches it, but quickly hands it over to a flustered Arianna. I don't know why messing with her never grows old, but it doesn't.

"You're a menace to society," she mutters, and I laugh.

"But you love me anyway, admit it."

She rolls her eyes, resuming to work on her phone. "I'll never admit that."

"Please?" I give her my best puppy dog eyes and she cracks.

"Fine. I love you, but you're still a menace."

Sophia rounds a display and finds us. "Are you two bickering again?"

"No," Arianna and I say in unison to our older sister, then bust out laughing.

Our sibling dynamics are so ingrained from spending

our entire lives together, that it's an odd realization that they're actually my half-sisters. And my cousins... I'm actually not blood related to them at all because they're Papa's brother's children. But I don't really care. Even if they aren't my blood, I choose them as my family.

Why am I so nervous? It's the big day. I'm wearing a divine Skye Adair wedding gown from her newest collection, and as far as I can tell everything is going perfectly—at least that's what Arianna's been telling me all morning. But my nerves are frayed. I'm having the wedding jitters for a marriage that will ultimately be fake. All of a sudden this seems like a very bad idea.

I mean, what are we doing with our lives? Fake or not, we'll be legally bound for a year and that seems like the kind of thing that stays with a person for the rest of their life. One day soon, I'll be an *ex*-wife. That doesn't settle so well with me.

I release a long, steady breath and stare at my reflection in the full-length mirror. The dress is the most beautiful thing I've ever seen, hugging my curves but still elegant and bridal. A sparkly tiara nestles in my blond updo, a few well-placed curls tickle my neck and shoulders.

This is what a princess looks like, or maybe even a queen. Certainly not a blackmailed mafia don's daughter, who recently found out she's not only illegitimate, but a child of rape. Which could also be why I'm nervous today. While I've learned the truth, Papa and I agreed to continue playing our parts for the sake of the family, to keep the peace, so he'll be walking me down the aisle. Blake hated the idea at first, but when I told him it's what I really want, he gave in.

I know Papa can't wait to get rid of me. If only my marriage to Blake had longevity. It doesn't, and I need to come to terms with that. Once we divorce, I'll be out on my own. Even if I was welcome to return home, I wouldn't, not now that I know the truth about my parentage.

I'm fine.

Everything will be fine.

A light knock sounds on the bridal suite door before it opens. Papa enters, his demeanor less aggravated than usual. "Are you ready?"

It's time. I knew it would be soon, as Arianna came in a while ago and swept everyone out of my room so they could find their seats.

"I'm ready." Willing my heartbeat to slow down, I arrange the veil over my face, then turn to the man who helped raise me.

"One more thing, Mr. Baron gave me this to give to you." He reaches into his pocket and hands me a small gold box. Opening it, I find a hair pin decorated with a diamond bird. A magpie. I stare at it for a long moment.

What was that poem about magpies?

One for sorrow,

Two for joy,

Three for a wedding...

An unexpected smile tugs at my lips. This side of

Blake is the one that I adore most. He gave me two magpies for my birthday—the figurine and my car—now a third for our wedding day. So maybe... maybe this day means more to him than I realized? A fluttery sensation comes to life in my chest.

I glance up at my father. "Can you put this in my hair? I can't see the back to position it." I hold my breath, expecting him to refuse.

Instead, he motions me toward him and takes the pin from its box. Carefully lifting my veil, he sticks the pin securely in my hair then helps rearrange the lace.

He offers his arm and I take it. Clearing his throat he says, "You look very nice."

My brows arch in surprise. I don't remember the last time he gave me a compliment, even a backhanded one—which this isn't.

"Um. Thank you."

He bobs his head once, curt, then we're heading to the chapel. Someone signals that we're coming and the wedding song begins to play. My heart flutters and a chill rushes up my spine, prickling my scalp in its wake. I must actually tremble because Papa shoots me a somewhat concerned glance. Each step feels like there's a lead weight attached to my foot.

My gaze latches onto Blake where he stands on the dais, stunningly handsome in an immaculate tuxedo. His expression gives nothing away, but I swear there's a softness around his sapphire eyes.

That's when it hits me. The realization that I've fallen for him. That's why this wedding feels so wrong. I'm in love with the man I'm marrying when our relationship is supposed to be fake.

I thought I'd been in love before, but now I realize that's not true. I've never felt this... lost, floaty, achingly emotional about another person before. I want to make him the happiest man alive.

Oh God, this is a disaster waiting to happen. I'm one year away from having my heart crushed, blasted to smithereens, all because I've done the one thing that I wasn't supposed to do and fallen in love with this wicked devil who stands before me. A year married to him will only make our eventual divorce that much more devastating.

The ceremony goes by in a blur of repeating phrases and crippling doubt. Then Blake's sweeping me into his arms and his soul-shattering kiss makes the entire world fall away. His family and mine fade from existence as his lips move against mine, his tongue seeking entrance. I open to him, reveling in the feeling of him against me.

All too soon, it's over.

I return to reality in a shower of cheers and applause. This day is supposed to be one of celebration. If only my heart beat with joy instead of dread.

No, I can't slip into the darkness, it's not where I want to be. I can be optimistic about this. What if Blake changes his mind? What if he can fall in love with me too? It's possible. Isn't it?

CHAPTER 32

Blake

She's mine. My wife. The realization hits me like a runaway freight train. Even my suspicion of her motivations, and her deceptive behavior, doesn't overshadow the burning possessiveness scorching my veins.

Half an hour, that's as far as I make it through our reception before whisking Gin away to our honeymoon suite. I may not be entirely happy with her right now, for keeping secrets, but I can't wait to take Mrs. Baron to bed. She's just become my *wife* and this new reality completely consumes me. *She's mine.*

"This is rude, we can't just leave all of our guests—"

"Yes we can." I pull her into our suite, kicking the door closed behind us. Then my lips are on hers, desperate and demanding. She's mine for a year and I'm going to make the most of it each and every day.

If she is fucking Oz, I'll have to remove him from existence, and that will solve that problem.

I lift her into my arms bridal style and carry her to

the bedroom, peppering her with kisses. She clings to me, both of us lost in the moment, and we fall onto the bed.

"You need a safe word."

Her eyelids flutter open. "I do?"

"Yes. I'm not going to risk you hurting yourself again. You're my wife and I'm going to show you exactly what that means. So what is your word?"

"Um... cupcake?"

I stare down at her. "Cupcake? Why cupcake?"

"Because I like cupcakes." She shrugs.

She's so fucking sweet. I kiss the tip of her nose. My adorable, secretive little magpie. "Fine. Cupcake it is. Remember that. Now, I'm going to tie you up."

She licks her lips, and nods.

I strip her out of the silky wedding gown until she's only wearing a white satin bra and thong with her heels. She looks like an angel—I'm about to make her look like a fallen angel, sinful and satiated. I take one of my silk ties and secure it around her wrists, then loop it into small knots all the way to her elbows, binding her arms together. Rolling her onto her stomach, I sit on the bed and drag her pelvis across my lap. She wiggles her round ass.

"This is for being a naughty girl." I bring my palm down on her exposed butt cheek, once, twice, three times, hard enough to leave red marks. Her body jerks and she cries out, but she doesn't try to get away. I spank her again.

I know she's my kind of kinky girl when I slip my fingers between her thighs and find her dripping for me. She likes the pain and loves the pleasure.

I tan her backside until she's glowing red, her flesh

hot, and her cries have turned to moans. When I finally find her clit, she falls apart for me with a long groan and shaking limbs.

Why does she have to be so goddamn perfect?

Flipping her over, I let her rest for a moment on her back while I undress. My gaze eats her up, from her flushed cheeks, to those delicious curves, to her soaked panties.

Dropping to my knees—because that's what this woman does to me, even when I'm upset with her—I tongue fuck her through her damp underwear until she comes again. Then I slide the ruined material down her legs and toss it on my pile of clothes, so I can pocket it later. She usually doesn't wear panties so this is a rare chance to collect a pair for myself, saturated with her scent.

I climb up her body, holding my weight on my forearms, until we're face to face. She opens her thighs wide, lifting her hips in a silent plea for my cock. I oblige. Sinking in one inch at a time, it's a slow torture for both of us. I groan, and her eyelids fall shut.

"Eyes on me, baby girl, I want to see into every corner of your soul while I fuck you." Her hooded gaze finds mine. "Good girl."

Once I'm buried in her sweet, hot pussy, I pull almost all the way out before slamming in—taking, claiming her as mine. My mouth finds her soft shoulder and I suck on her skin, leaving my mark.

Holding eye contact, I fuck her with wild abandon. *My wife.* Every single thought of her as my wife drives me higher and higher.

"What's your name?" I pant.

"Gin."

"Your last name."

"Pon—Baron."

"Say it. Say your name."

"Ginevra Baron."

Fuck yes. "Say it again."

"Mrs. Baron." She moans as I piston my hips, driving her into the mattress.

"Who are you to me?"

"Your wife."

Damn right you are. "And who am I to you?"

"M-my husband." She groans. "I'm so close."

"Beg me for it, magpie. You know I love to hear you beg."

"Please, please make me come... husband."

Fucking hell. She'll be my ruin, that's for sure.

I adjust my angle, hitting her g-spot just right and she shatters, taking me with her as her pussy milks my cock.

Pulling out, I empty myself on her stomach and tits. She jolts at the unexpected warmth of cum coating her body. Before it dries, I write in it with my finger, spelling out: Mrs. Baron. If I could, I'd have that tattooed into her flesh. Now that I think about it, that is a possibility. Dimitri tattooed his name on his wife, so...

If only our time together didn't come to an end in a year. But after that, her contract is fulfilled. She has no reason not to sign the divorce papers and run as far from me as possible. Any woman in her right mind would do just that. I'm hardly husband material.

If there's one thing I know about myself, it's that I'm not lovable. Not in the slightest.

So, we'll live out this fantasy until we either ruin it or our time together comes to an end.

The property acquisition is almost a done deal. So much so that Yve has taken a step back and seems to be relatively content. By that I mean she didn't try to sabotage my wedding, or interrupt our short honeymoon while we've been in London. I'm not sure if negotiating the contract has been keeping her busy, or if there's another reason she's not her usual, vile self.

Either way, hopefully the sale will go through by the time we're back in New York and Liam will take his place within the company. All is looking up on that front.

Which brings my attention back to Gin. If she's hiding her connection to Oz, what else is she untruthful about? Have I misjudged her after all these months together? Or is she really that talented of an actress to show me a complete façade that I unwittingly fell for?

Maybe she really is the gold-digger I thought she was in the beginning. Her past trauma, her sweetness, the way she looks at me like I can save her from her demons, is any of it real?

The way her presence is a ray of sunshine in my world of darkness... is it all a lie? A carefully crafted story to get under my skin? Perhaps.

Two can play at this game though. I aim to tear apart my new wife until I can decipher reality from fiction. I need to understand her motivations. I'm going to figure out who she truly is. Starting now.

She comes out of the bathroom, cheeks flushed and hair wrapped in a towel. My heart stops for a moment. She's so fucking beautiful. Too bad she's a liar.

"I have something for you, magpie." I set the small, matte black box on the table. Her gaze lands on it and lights with excitement. I hate how much that brightness in her eyes warms my chest.

"For me? What is it?" She approaches and I reach out, snare her, and reel her into my lap. Even though she's lied to me, I want to feel her body against mine.

"Open it and find out." I can't resist licking up a droplet of water on her neck. Her soft moan goes straight to my cock and I'm hard for her in an instant. Maybe the sex is what's clouding my judgement. She's a siren and I've fallen victim to her sweet, deadly song.

She lifts the box into her small hands and removes the top. A sharp gasp falls from her parted lips as she picks up the thick black credit card. There's nothing on it except her new name stamped on the back. Ginevra Baron.

"This is..." My wife is speechless for once.

"Without a limit," I tell her.

"But we signed papers, a prenup to make sure I don't get a single penny from you. Why would you give me a limitless card?" She frowns up at me, and I smooth away the crease between her golden brows with my thumb.

"Because while we're divorcing in twelve months' time, right now you're my wife and you deserve to be treated as such, with all the perks included." What I'm not telling her is that this is a test. If she's a gold-digger she won't be able to resist the urge to spend as much as she can as quickly as possible.

Take me for all I'm worth, little magpie, and prove to me that I'm right about the worst version of you. As much as that pains me, I must know the truth.

"Oh," she says, her features caving, which is not the reaction I expected.

"What's wrong?"

"Nothing. This is very generous of you." She slides off my lap, taking the card with her, and continues getting dressed before packing up. By tonight we'll be back home.

CHAPTER 33

Ginevra

Sunday night we're at an art opening for one of Blake's business associates in Manhattan. Normally, I'd drown myself in the free flowing champagne and chat with the many acquaintances here, but I don't feel like indulging in either tonight. I haven't felt like myself since the wedding, which was made worse the other day when Blake confirmed that we'll divorce in a year, then gave me that black credit card.

My clutch feels heavier with the card taking up space. I should have left it at home. Actually, I should cut it up and burn it. Doesn't Blake understand that I don't want his money? I'll be in a tricky spot once we divorce, but I'm not going to take advantage of him, I know how much he despises gold-diggers, and my future financial issues are mine to sort out. Not his.

I don't want to give him the impression that I can be bought. I'm never going to use that card. Not ever.

The more crushing thought—that he'll never love me —I keep at bay. I can't face it right now.

Soft, seductive music filters through the dimly lit gallery. The only real illumination is on the artwork. The paintings are amazing, evocative, and on any other evening, I'd enjoy them. Instead, I loiter by Blake's side, getting introduced as his wife, then ignored as he discusses business.

After the fifth such occurrence, I excuse myself and go to the restroom. I never thought I'd say this but I'd rather be curled up at home watching one of my cooking shows than at this party. What is happening to me? Where has the old Gin gone? She knew how to have fun no matter what.

I regroup in the bathroom, layering on another coat of lipstick to pass the time. Several elegantly dressed women come and go before I decide to brave another hour of being Blake's arm candy. This kind of thing never used to bother me, but it does tonight.

As soon as I exit the restroom, a hand clamps around my throat tight enough to cut off my airflow, and drags me into a shadowy corner. Panic seizes me at the familiar, tainted scent of spicy vanilla, Oliver's custom cologne. I try to scream but there's no air in my lungs. He spins me to face him, my back to the wall.

"Ginny, I finally caught you alone. Shh, babe, don't make a sound or your husband will find you on your knees for me. I don't think that's the impression you want to give a man like him, is it?"

All I can do is shake my head. My eyes water. My throat burns.

Oliver steps closer, dominating my personal space, his solid grip tightens ever so slightly around my windpipe. "The contract is almost finished. I didn't put any clauses in there pertaining to you and me, but if you want me to sign the final draft then you'll be at my office on Monday morning. Be there at nine. Wear something sexy for me."

He grabs the back of my head and slams his mouth on mine. I try to protest, but I can't breathe. My fingers dig into his arms, silently fighting, begging him to release me, but he doesn't listen.

As soon as I'm on the brink of passing out, Oliver lets go.

"See you on Monday, Ginny. I don't think I need to tell you this, but if you don't show up I'll come find you. Baron always leaves the house early on the weekdays for work." With that threat, he blends into the crowd.

I cough and sputter, my head spinning as I try to get control of my breath and my pounding heart. A cold sweat breaks out across my skin, leaving me shivering in the dark corner.

"There you are." Blake's deep voice makes me freeze. "I was beginning to worry... Why is your lipstick smeared?" He steps closer. "You smell like cologne."

I panic. "S-someone pulled me into this corner, but now they're gone."

He scoffs, the sound makes me cringe. "Do you think I'm a fucking idiot? Who is he, Gin?"

"Who is who?"

"The man you're sneaking around with, cheating on me with. Tell me his name."

I gasp. "I'm not cheating on you. I'd *never* do that!"

"Liar. You look like you just got fucked," he spits out the harsh words. "Come. We're going home." He takes my hand and all but drags me from the venue. Fury rolls off of him in waves and the people in his path quickly step out of his way.

In the back of the car, he fumes, sitting as close to the opposite door as possible. I stay on my own side, seriously considering telling him everything, but the words won't leave the tip of my tongue. I'm shaking, but I'm not sure if it's from the fear of seeing Oliver tomorrow or the devastation of hurting Blake's feelings. Or maybe I'm angry at him for calling me a liar—again.

But that's what I am, right? A liar, if only by omission.

He deserves the truth, even if it will destroy us. One of the many reasons I don't want to tell him is because Blake's never looked at me like other men do, he's never treated me like nothing, like trash. Even when he first blackmailed me, I felt like he was looking at *me,* not some object. There was an intensity between us, we played and toyed with each other, and it was actually fun. For the first time in my life, I really felt *seen.* If he knew the truth then he'd see me as nothing more than a used toy.

I've been used and abused by so many men that somewhere along the way I started to embrace it, to accept that I deserved to be treated that way. It didn't matter whether I gave them consent or not. They acted like it wasn't my place to do so anyway.

Until Blake changed all of that. He made me realize that I was wrong, I don't deserve anything that's happened to me. But everything that I've been through makes me feel dirty and cheap.

He's the only man who's *ever* cared for me, who's ever talked to me and treated me like a human being. He found out that the slutty-girl reputation I created for myself was not the whole truth.

I had a choice to make back then, I could either be a victim or I could embrace a positive, empowered sexuality. I'd rather be known as the girl who enjoys sex whenever she wants it, than the girl who got sexually assaulted too many times to count.

I learned from a young age that no one ever believes the girl. So why bother?

But Blake saw past all of my brokenness, and he helped heal me. Now I really am the girl who enjoys sex and who knows she's worthy of pleasure—and maybe love.

I don't want to lose that. I can't stomach the thought of losing him.

I don't know what to do. My secret and lies are eating me alive. But if I confess everything, then he'll never look at me the same. He'll treat me differently. How could he not? I want to hide the worst version of myself forever—especially from him. It's too shameful.

I keep my lips sealed and the distance between us seems to expand further, as never ending as the universe.

Will I lose him by keeping my shame to myself?

I quietly scoff. We're getting a divorce in less than a year, so does any of it really matter?

Yes, it does. I want this fantasy for as long as it will last. So my lips have to remain sealed.

CHAPTER 34

Ginevra

The next morning I wake up and Blake's already gone for the day. I go through the motions of showering and getting dressed, considering my options. If I don't show up at Oliver's office, he'll find a way into this house, or worse. He's so unpredictable. In the past I wouldn't dare cross him, or do anything that might upset him. I always played along with his games.

But that Gin is dead. She died sometime in the last four months, I'm not entirely sure when because it was a slow, gradual demise. I didn't realize she was gone until this moment.

The new Gin isn't going to put herself at Oliver's mercy. She's stronger than that. Smarter than that now. She's not a victim anymore.

I tossed and turned all night going over the potential outcomes of my decisions. Even my dreams were haunted by what I should do. I've come to a conclusion. I'm going to tell Blake everything. As scary as that is, it's the right thing to do.

Yes, my decision is one-eighty from where I stood yesterday. If Oliver wasn't harassing me, I'd keep my mouth closed. Blake and I would live out our year together in peaceful bliss. But I can't go to Oliver's office, let him do... things to me, and then come home to my husband like nothing happened.

That would destroy me, and us.

My only option is to take away Oliver's power over me, and that means telling Blake everything.

Will he throw me out for keeping secrets? For lying to him? Maybe. It's a risk I'm going to take because another side of me wants to put my faith in him. To trust him enough to let him see all of me and believe that he might still want me afterwards.

There's a chance, right? At least I can hope and dream that there is. So, as soon as he comes home, we'll talk.

Unmotivated to do anything other than rehearse what I'm going to say to him, over and over, until I'm sure I have the right wording, I spend the day in my room. Kyla checks on me a couple of times, but I assure her that I'm fine, just busy with my own shit.

At a quarter past nine in the morning, my phone chimes. Just as I expected it's a ranting text from Oliver. When I don't reply, he keeps going, sending me threat after threat until I'm mentally and emotionally numb from the barrage. Checking out is the only way to deal with him when he gets like this.

To that end, I silence my phone and tuck it in a drawer. I won't let my fear of him dissuade me from what I need to do. From doing what's right.

Morning turns to afternoon, which fades to night. I

told our housekeeper, Fleur, to let me know when Blake comes home, but so far he's not here. I consider texting him, but I shy away from it.

Night bleeds into the early morning hours and still no sign of him. In an effort to ignore Oliver, I've spent hours going over everything that I need to tell Blake. I've worked myself up so much that I'm emotionally exhausted. I can't keep my eyes open for another moment.

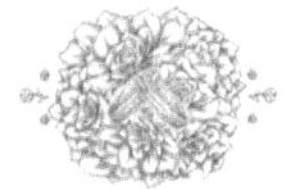

The incessant ringing of my phone wakes me, and I grab it out of the drawer where I tossed it yesterday. I glance at the notifications. There must be a hundred missed calls from my sisters. What on earth is going on?

My phone rings again and I answer Sophia's call. "What—?"

"Have you seen the article? In the *Big Apple Buzz*?"

"No..."

"Look at it now. But only if you want, it's very disturbing. Call me back." She hangs up and I open the gossip paper's app. The glaring headline has my stomach doing a nosedive.

WIFE CHEATS ON NOTORIOUS BLAKE BARON WITH MILLIONAIRE HEIR OLIVER ZALESKI

I scan the article, which is all lies and twisted truths,

scrolling all the way down to the video at the end. My mouth goes dry.

No, no, no. This can't be happening.

Against my better judgment, I push play.

Our privates are blurred but the video clearly shows Oliver railing me from behind while I'm tied up, my face contorted in pain—or pleasure—it's difficult to tell since there's no sound. But I remember that night with vivid clarity. The pain, my cries for him to stop only urging him on, and how helpless I felt that I couldn't get away, how I couldn't fight back.

He'd given me some kind of drug that kept me lucid but unable to control my body. Then he treated me like a puppet, arranging me how he wanted and tying me in place. Then he—

"Did you enjoy yourself?" Blake's steely tone draws my attention. He's standing in the doorway, arms folded, his features so impassive they could be carved of ice.

I lick my parched lips. "Did I enjoy what?"

"Screwing Oz. You sure look like you were having a good time in that video." His eyes flash with malice.

I'm stunned into silence. Bile rises in my throat. My stomach heaves, and I dart to the bathroom, barely making it to the sink before retching my guts out. I'm shaking, tears streaming down my face. How could he think such a thing?

Blake storms in after me. "You can stop with the act now, Gin. I know all about your relationship with Oz. Your *lover*." He spits the word at me.

"He's not my lover," I manage to get out before dry heaving into the sink. I didn't have much to eat yesterday.

"Then what the fuck do you call this?" Blake shoves his phone in my face, the video playing.

I bat it away with enough force that his phone flies across the room, skidding on the marble floor. "Do you really want to know what that's called?"

"Yes, I do!"

"It's called *rape!*"

Blake freezes, every muscle in his body tensing.

When he doesn't speak, I continue, "Take a c-closer look at that why don't you? I'm screaming for him to s-stop! But you don't believe me, do you? You think I'm a liar and a slut. That I'd cheat on you with my horrible ex because you're too insecure to realize I'd never, ever do such a thing. You have no idea what he did to me." My voice breaks on that last word. I sob, my legs giving out and I sag to the cold stone floor.

Suddenly Blake drops to his knees, then he's caging me in his arms, my face buried in his chest. I'm so mad at him, but I don't have the energy to fight him right now.

"Fuck. I'm so sorry. I'm a goddamn idiot. Of course I believe you, sweetheart."

He believes me. That's all it takes to break me wide open.

I ugly cry at his admission. He holds me tighter and I draw on his strength to get me through another anxiety attack. By going against Oliver's demand, I brought this on myself. Of course he'd leak that video to the press in order to punish me. Now the entire world thinks I'm an awful person. A cheater.

But I want Blake to know the truth. He deserves it.

Eventually, I hiccup, blow my nose on a tissue, and

lean against Blake's solid chest, his arms wrapped securely around me.

My first confession comes out flat. "My uncle started molesting me when I was nine."

He tenses around me, but doesn't say anything, giving me space to speak.

"I told my father but he ignored me, accused me of l-lying, so I never went to anyone about this kind of thing again. Not when I was eighteen and a guy raped me in a pool house, or any of it. Then—"

"You don't have to tell me this, magpie. You don't owe me any—"

"I need to tell you," I whisper like I'm already losing my voice. "I should have told you the truth from the beginning, but I was afraid."

"Afraid of what?" he murmurs close to my ear in a quiet, soothing tone.

"Afraid you'd hate me, that you'd look at me differently. That you wouldn't w-want to touch me ever again."

He pulls away only far enough to cup my cheeks and look me in the eye. His gaze burns with sincerity. "Oh, baby girl, nothing could ever make me not want you. You've become my world, Gin. I'll do anything to keep you happy and safe. I was a jealous fool, blinded by my own fears, and I'm so very sorry."

I nod. We'll see if that's true or not.

He says I've become his world, yet he has also reminded me that we're divorcing in a year. If I mean that much to him, then why would he throw away our relationship? I can't figure him out. Right now, I'm too tired to try.

Summoning my inner strength, I glance away, and continue my story, "Word got out about me and that guy, except instead of blaming him, everyone started calling me a *slut*. They said I deserved it, for the way I look, for the way I dress."

"You don't. No one deserves that," Blake cuts in, hugging me closer.

I inhale a shuddering breath. "I know, but after a while I guess I started to believe them, and I just let guys do whatever they wanted to me. I was already damaged goods so what difference did it make? I never said *yes*, but I didn't say *no* either. N-not until Oliver."

I swallow hard, my hands shaking again. The weighted silence that stretches between us tells me Blake has a lot to say, but he's keeping quiet to give me the space I need to get all of this out.

"I-I met Oliver at a party last year. At first he seemed suave, charming... a lot of fun. He seemed to actually like me, not just my body. But then he wanted to have sex and I just... I had to be intoxicated to go through with it. It didn't take him long to see the pattern and h-he got rough with me right before Christmas and we broke up. But he's so... cunning, and he convinced me to give him another chance so we started dating again after the New Year."

I was so stupid to fall prey to him. *So dumb.* "Again, everything was fine for a while—good even. Until his moods started getting darker and his actions more and more erratic. Th-that night he s-spiked my drink with something that m-made my limbs so heavy, but my h-head was clear. He t-took me to this basement that was all s-set up, like a p-porn set.

"The part of the v-video you saw was just the beginning. I... I lost count of how many times he r-raped me that night. I felt *everything*. The next day m-my entire body was o-one giant bruise, except for my face, he n-never touched my face.

"I couldn't tell anyone what had happened, I was too humiliated, and they w-wouldn't believe me anyway. Plus O-Oliver told me he'd l-leak the v-video if I said a word about it. I told my parents that I was s-sick for a week and s-stayed in my room to recover. The n-nightmares were the worst part of it, and the l-loneliness. After that, I broke up with him and he's been th-threatening me ever since."

I deeply inhale, having gotten the worst parts out of the way. My pulse thunders in my ears, nearly drowning out Blake's next words.

"Is that why you pretended to not know him at dinner?" Blake gently asks.

"I'm t-terrified of him," I admit. "I p-panicked and didn't know w-what else to do. He th-threatened me that night when you took that call, then a-again at the art opening. H-he told me to come to his office yesterday morning, but I didn't go. That's why the *Big Apple Buzz* published this article."

"The article should be gone by now. I called in a favor to have all traces of it removed before confronting you."

"Y-you did?" I glance up at him. While his tone's soft, I read the fury in the hard set of his jaw, the need for violence in his stormy eyes. He really does believe me. And so far, he's not treating me like I'm disgusting. It's like... like nothing's changed between us, even with the truth laid bare.

"Of course I did," he says. "I'll be personally paying a visit to the *Big Apple Buzz*'s CEO later today as well. It seems they've forgotten who they're fucking with."

"Right." A smile flashes across my face. "The big, bad Blake Baron."

"No. *Mrs. Baron*." He nuzzles my neck. "They can mess with me all they want, baby girl, but no one fucks with my wife. Even if I foolishly believed you cheated on me, I'd never allow those vipers to drag your name through the mud. You're mine, Mrs. Baron, and you deserve both privacy and respect."

My heart skips a beat. All the tension, and worry, bleeds from my body.

"What stopped you from going to his office?" he carefully asks.

Reality comes back to me like a frigid splash of water across my face. "I kn-knew that if I went, then this would n-never end. He'd continue to pull the strings. My only other option was to confess the truth to you and hope you'd f-forgive me, but you d-didn't come home yesterday."

"There's nothing to forgive. None of this is your fault, Gin. I'm serious. You're so brave for telling me everything." He strokes my hair, wrapping a curl around his finger, and I relax further into him. "Now that I know the truth, I'm going to kill Oz. Slowly. Painfully. He'll never hurt you again."

"Promise?"

"I promise with all my heart."

CHAPTER 35

Blake

"I'm sorry, sir, but Mr. Zaleski can't see you today. You need to make an appointment and come back another time." This secretary has no idea that she's playing with fire. But she's beginning to catch on. Her gaze nervously flits back and forth between me and Gin.

I didn't want to bring my wife to this encounter, but she insisted. I think she's attempting to face her fears, her abuser, in a relatively safe and controlled environment. With me by her side, I'll never let anyone touch her again.

The stupid fucker in that office should have run far, far away instead of hiding behind his secretary. That decision alone tells me how arrogant he is, and I can't wait to break him.

I pull out the knife I keep on me at all times. It's not impressive to look at, but I know how to use it. "You can either buzz open that door, or this is about to get bloody. If I have to come behind your desk and—"

Her skin pales and she pushes the button. Apparently threats of bodily harm are still effective. I'm sure she doesn't get paid enough to deal with this kind of shit.

"Now that wasn't so hard, was it?" I don't wait for an answer to my rhetorical question. My hand in Gin's, we enter Oz's office, where the smug fucker sits behind his desk, Italian leather loafers resting on top.

"What a pleasant surprise," he greets us, a wide grin on his lips. "To what do I owe the pleasure of this visit?"

"Shut the fuck up," I snarl at him.

Releasing Gin's hand, I round the desk and punch that smirk off Oz's face. The blow tips his chair backwards and he crashes to the floor with a satisfying thud. I've been wanting to do that for weeks.

I kick his stomach, knocking the air from his lungs. He blocks my next strike by curling into a ball.

Fucking pathetic.

"Please," he begs. "Stop."

"Get up and fight me like a man, you piece of shit!" With a swipe of my arm, I clear the top of his desk. Its contents rain down on him. Everything Gin told me about their time together, about everything that's happened to her, replays in my memory and it's all I can do to hold myself back from slitting his throat here and now.

How was I so blind when she hinted that her ex was abusive, that I didn't see it? Why didn't I look into it? I need to do better by her and stop being such a self-absorbed prick all the time.

"You can't hurt me," Oz wheezes. "I haven't signed the paperwork yet."

I seethe at him. "Then get up and sign it. Now."

Slowly, he gets to his feet, hugging his midsection and rubbing the bruise forming on the side of his jaw.

"No. As soon as I sign that you'll kill me, won't you? If you want that property, get the fuck out of my office. I'll sign it when I'm good and ready." Oz cocks his head. "Or are you going to play that bitch's white knight, and throw everything away for one stupid whore? Is she worth it?"

I freeze, my fingers curling into fists again. He doesn't know it, but he's forcing me to choose between my brother's future and avenging my wife. I'm between a rock and a hard place. *Fuck!*

Glancing over my shoulder, I take in Gin's stricken expression. Her gaze meets mine and the resignation, and hurt, I find in it twists my gut. Guilt settles like a stone in my stomach. She already knows the decision I have to make. And I already hate myself for it.

I turn back to Oz. "That deal will go through. Sign it."

"Given this turn of events, I'll be in touch to continue our negotiations. You don't think I'm stupid enough to sign that contract without any assurances, do you?" When he sees my expression, he says, "You don't have to answer that."

"Don't ever go near my wife again," I warn him. Defeat drags me down like riptide. I should be cutting pieces from his flesh, not giving in to his demands. How did this go so wrong?

I acted impulsively. That's how. For once in my life, I didn't wait and collect all the necessary information before striking, all because this is too personal. Now I'm fucking regretting my brashness.

Taking Gin's hand in mine, I storm out of his office. Frustration vibrates through my bones. That's not how that interaction was supposed to happen. Oz should be strapped to a chair, begging for his life while I flay him for every ounce of pain he caused Gin.

Instead, I'm standing in an elevator with her and unable to meet her eye.

"Are you going to make a deal with him?" she asks in a small voice.

I nod. "But this time, I won't be keeping my word. He'll pay, eventually. I'm sorry it can't be right now." When she doesn't say anything, I try to explain. "Liam's entire future's on the line with that deal."

"I know. I understand."

Finally, I glance at her. "You do?"

"Of course I do." Her words contrast the pain in her eyes. She can say she understands, that everything's all right, but I know it's not. She slips her hand out of mine.

I'm beginning to feel like I was put in an impossible position and I just made the wrong decision. Logically, I can get the paperwork signed, secure Liam's inheritance, and then go after Oz for what he did to Gin. That sequence of events checks out. It's a rational plan.

So why do I feel like I'm losing my wife?

CHAPTER 36

Ginevra

I understand perfectly. Blake will always choose his family over me, and that's okay, right? His love and devotion to his family is part of what makes him a good person, despite all of his flaws and lack of moral compass in all other aspects of life.

But I've come to realize that I don't want to be second, or third, tier down on his priority list. If I'm going to be in a relationship—even a fake one—I need to be number one. I won't settle for less. I don't deserve less than that.

Blake will never love me and that's also okay. He's done enough for me, more than I ever thought possible, so it's time for me to repay him however I can. To make everything even between us and end this charade. If I thought there was a chance Blake would fall for me in the next eleven months, I might hold out hope, but I see the light now. It's time to move on.

It's been two weeks since the disastrous confrontation in Oliver's office. In that time, I've been planning, setting things in motion that all lead me up to today.

Sitting at my vanity, I study the two objects in front of me. One's a small vial of a substance called syrup of ipecac, that when added to a person's drink will induce vomiting. It's fast-acting, but short-lived. Harmless, really. This little potion I got from Ravenna, after swearing her to secrecy. I could have asked one of my sisters, but I have a hard time letting them see my darker side, and I know Ravenna can keep a secret better than anyone. She hid her identity from her husband for weeks when she swapped places at the altar with her twin.

The other object is a mini flash drive. This I ordered online.

I have a confession to make... Ever since Lexa mentioned that Yve keeps the dirt she has on Blake close to her, I suspected it was on her charm bracelet. It's too blatantly obvious. Hiding in plain sight. No one would think Yve might put something that important so easily accessible. But she did, and I know her secret.

Guilt coils around my throat. Could I have stolen the bracelet and set Blake free before our wedding? Yes. I probably should have, too.

But hope stopped me. Hope is a dangerous thing at times. Especially when you're in love, especially when that love is unrequited.

Today I'm going to right that wrong.

My phone chimes with a new text.

LEXA

The meeting's set for noon at the location you wanted. Good luck.

GINEVRA

Thank you for doing this.

LEXA

Anything to help. <Devil emoji>

I finish my hair and makeup, then pack the rest of my suitcases. After I'm done with today's business, I have a flight to Milan, Italy, where I'll be staying with my cousin Elena until I can get my life sorted out.

When eleven rolls around, I take everything down to my car in the garage. Once I'm ready to go, I leave a goodbye note for Kyla in the kitchen, and one for Fleur in the foyer. They've both been so nice to me while I've lived here, and I wanted to thank them, just not in person because I can't risk either of them notifying Blake of my intentions.

The restaurant where I'm meeting Yve is almost an hour away with traffic. I arrive right on time, immediately spotting her security detail inside. As soon as she sees me, she frowns.

"What are you doing here? Where's Lexa?" she demands.

"She'll be here soon," I reassure her. Lexa won't, in fact, be here at all, but Yve doesn't need to know that yet. "Let's sit down."

"I don't want to sit down. I want my daughter."

"If you're on good behavior, I'll notify her to come in. Sit. Down."

She purses her lips, but settles back into her seat. She's already ordered a coffee, so I do the same. While the server partially blocks the view of us from Yve's bodyguard, I quickly spill the vial's contents into the cup. It's been a while since I've stolen anything, and I've never used sleight of hand to poison someone before. I guess there's a first time for everything, and this is for a good cause.

I mean, none of this could happen to a nicer person, right? The strangest part is, I'm not nervous at all. I thought I'd be an emotional live wire, but a strange, peaceful calm has settled over me since this morning.

"So, where has Lexa been hiding all this time?" Yve starts in. "You must know, since you two are so very close all of a sudden."

"Lexa will have to fill you in on what she's been up to. It's really not my place to say anything."

"Then stop wasting my time and call her," she snaps. Seeming to realize her mistake, she takes a sip from her cup as she calms down. "I will be perfectly courteous. Please tell my daughter to come inside."

I hold her gaze for several seconds. "Okay."

Retrieving my phone from inside my purse, I send Lexa a text, but it's not what Yve thinks.

GINEVRA

Here. It's going well.

LEXA

Good.

I glance up at Yve. "She'll be here in fifteen minutes."

Yve sighs, taking another sip of her coffee, and I do the same.

"When are you going to give Blake his inheritance?" I'm curious, and we don't have anything else to talk about to pass the time.

She eyes me. "I told him he has to be married for one year before he can have it."

"You really thought that would be impossible for him, didn't you?" I watch her take another sip, and resist the urge to tap my foot under the table. I thought this stuff was supposed to be fast-acting. How much longer is it going to take?

"Of course I did, otherwise I wouldn't have set marriage as the obstacle." Yve huffs. "Then you came along and ruined everything. That ogre worships the ground you walk on, so there's no hope of you two getting a divorce anytime soon."

Her comment catches me by surprise. Does he worship the ground I walk on? I don't see it. But apparently we successfully fooled everyone around us into thinking we're the perfect couple.

That thought makes me sad.

"Then why don't you give him his inheritance now and be done with it?" I urge.

"I don't know... I'm not ready to admit I may have lost this round. But—" Her eyes widen and she covers her mouth. "Excuse me."

Showtime. Yve launches herself toward the bathroom, her bodyguard sprints after her until she starts vomiting, then he rushes out of the women's room to stand watch at the door.

Arranging my features to reflect concern, I hurry in after her but her guard stops me.

"You can't go in."

"She needs my help. Who's going to hold back her hair while she throws up? You?"

He cringes, his pallor tinged green. "Go in."

I slip past him, finding Yve in one of the stalls. It's surreal seeing such a horrible woman, who seems untouchable most of the time, on her knees in a public bathroom.

Coming to her side, I deftly remove her charm bracelet, while saying, "Oh my god, are you all right?"

"Do I look all right, you imbecile?" She vomits again, and I quickly replace the flash drive on her chain with the empty replica.

"Here let me get your hair out of your face." As I fuss with her hair, she tries to wave me off, until she's sick again. With all of these distractions working in my favor, I fasten the bracelet back in place. She never notices a thing.

"Get away from me!" She shrieks, calling for her bodyguard, who is not keen on entering the restroom.

Backing away, I pocket the mini flash drive. "I hope you feel better soon."

I give the guard an apologetic glance and point to the door. "She's calling for you. Good luck." He reluctantly ducks inside.

At the table, I grab my purse and leave. Mission accomplished.

Soon this flash drive will be in Blake's hands, he'll be free to do whatever he wants with Yve, as she'll no longer have any power over him. He can pressure her, or even torture her, into telling him where she hid his mother's things. He can do whatever he wants. Yve's reign of terror is over.

CHAPTER 37

Blake

"Gin? I'm home!" I call out again, to a disturbingly quiet house. Where the hell is everyone? Granted it's late, so the staff are gone, but usually Gin is up and around to greet me when I arrive home from work. So where—?

I walk into our bedroom, noting the neatly made bed and the envelope sitting in the middle. My chest tightens as I pick it up, dread coiling around my ribcage. Ripping it open, I upend the content onto the duvet. A small, bejeweled flash drive, and a letter. I turn the flash drive over in my fingers as I read the note.

Dear Blake,

I'm pretty sure this is what you've been looking for. I took it off Yve's charm bracelet. I hope this helps you get out from under her thumb.

Since you've found this, that means you're

home from work and I'm not there. I've decided to spend some time with my cousin Elena in Italy. I don't know when I'll be back.

I hope you get everything you want for your brother and for yourself.

Best, Gin

Her letter doesn't settle well with me, there's far too much she's not saying between every single one of her words. Especially that last line. Guilt eats at me for choosing my brother over her. I just wish she understood that I've looked out for him for his entire life, it's part of who I am. I didn't mean to offend her, or make her feel less than, or anything like that.

But, obviously she does, because from what I can tell, she just left me. Maybe she just needs some time and space to herself. Or am I being dense again?

I weigh the flash drive in my hand. She can't be that mad at me since she just gave me the best gift ever. If this contains the blackmail material Yve has been holding over me all these years, then having this in my possession changes everything.

Pulling out my phone, I check the tracking app to locate Gin. She's telling the truth, the tracker places her over the Atlantic. I locate her flight number so I get notifications for when she lands, just to be sure everything went okay.

In my office, I wake up my laptop and insert the drive. There are only two video files on it. I let them play, confirming that *this* is what I've been searching for, for years. Yve really did have this on her every single day.

How did I not bother to look closer at her charm bracelet? It's so fucking obvious. Too obvious, that's the problem.

I bring up Niall Bane's contact and press the call button, putting it on speaker phone. He's the only decent Bane brother, the black sheep from the rest of that brood, and he owes me a favor.

"What do you want, Baron?" he answers.

I appreciate the way he cuts to the chase. "I'm sending you a couple of files. I need you to hack into Yve's computer, and her other devices, and find any duplicates of these."

Niall sighs. "I don't do that kind of work anymore."

"You do for me. Get off your good boy soapbox and get your hands dirty. I'll call us even after this."

That catches his attention. "Okay. I see the files you sent. I'll get back to you when it's done."

"Good." I hang up, leaning back in my office chair. My gaze lands on the paint chips hanging on the wall. We've narrowed it down to fifteen shades of blue. Progress.

Fuck, I hope Gin's not gone for too long. I already miss her.

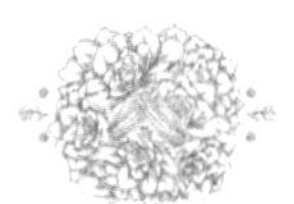

Everyone empties out of the elevator when they see me coming. I push the button for the executive floor and ride up alone. Early this morning Niall called to say that he found two backups of the incriminating evidence against me, and erased them both. Three copies is about the level of duplicates I expected Yve to keep. Now they're all gone. My trap is prepped and ready to spring.

I had to act quickly, in case Yve caught onto me, so this morning I contacted my acquaintance at the FBI and sent over some choice pieces of evidence of Yve's illegal doings. People she's paid to have offed, backroom business deals, the dirt I have on her will take someone years to dig through, so I just handed over the highlights.

The FBI will be at the office to pick Yve up within the hour, but I can't resist seeing the look on her face when she realizes our game is finally, thoroughly finished.

Exiting the elevator, I head straight for her office, but find it empty. Her secretary informs me she's in the boardroom with a client. I burst through the door and immediately halt in my tracks.

Yve's in here, alone with Oz, her client, who happens to have my step-monster on her knees as she sucks him off. That's a sight I could have lived the rest of my life without. Now it's seared into my retinas.

I sneer in disgust. Yve lurches to her feet, and Oz lazily tucks his dick away with a smirk. I can't wait to knock out his teeth. Finding him here is actually a boon. All of this nonsense ends today.

"Oz, it's time you signed the paperwork. I'm done fucking around with this."

"Oh, are you? Well," his gaze darts to Yve, "we have a different idea of how this is going to go down. It's nice of you to join us. Why don't you have a seat?"

I remain standing, but my attention shifts to Yve. What the fuck is she up to now?

She purses her over-stuffed lips and leans against the conference table, victory shining in her eyes. "Ozzie here told me all about your little scene at his office." She *tsks*. "The deal is off. You failed. Which means Liam won't be coming to work for Titan Enterprises. In fact, I'm making Ozzie the new CEO." A vicious grin appears on her face. "Oh, and you're *fired*."

My jaw clenches as I reel from this devastating turn of events. Then the reality of the situation dawns on me. *Ozzie. A nickname.*

"You two were in this together, weren't you?"

Yve laughs, the sound grating on my ears. "You finally figured it out. I have to say it was hilarious making you bend over backward to woo Ozzie, all those dinners and having to pretend as if you liked him. This was one of my best games yet. Wouldn't you agree?"

"It sure was fun." Oz snakes his arm around her waist, then glances at me. "You should have known you were never going to win this one. I mean how many times did I have to delay signing that contract for you to get the hint? You're not as smart as you think you are, Baron. You never even bothered to look for a connection between me and Yve. We've known each other for years."

"True. I'm good friends with Ozzie's mother." She entwines her fingers with his. "I've known him since he was a child, and had the honor of being his first when he turned sixteen."

Christ. I'd rather be buried alive with vipers than listen to this creepy shit. Step-monster, gold-digger, child molester, Yve continues to disgust me with her layers of depravity.

"Honestly, you two are boring me. So let's change the subject, shall we?" I fish the tiny, bejeweled flash drive out of my pocket and hold it up for them to see. "Cue panic."

Yve stares at it, then fumbles with her charm bracelet, her face pale. She laughs, relieved. "Mine is right here. But that was a cute joke, you had me for a second."

"It's not a joke. You bought this online, how easy do you think it was to order another one and swap it for the original? I found two video files on here, and once I knew what I was looking for, it was easy enough to have someone track down and erase all three copies. The shit you had on me... poof, gone."

Her features contort in rage as her skin becomes increasingly flushed. "How—?" Realization dawns. "That little *bitch*!"

I cluck my tongue. "Be careful how you talk about my wife."

"What's going on?" Oz asks, his gaze flicks back and forth between us. "What does this mean?"

"Nothing, it means absolutely nothing." Yve removes the drive from her bracelet and plugs it into the laptop sitting on the conference table. She clicks a few buttons, then a couple more, before straightening her spine and gazing across at me. "Well played, Mr. Baron. Well played."

We both know she's done. The game has been seen through to its completion. I've won.

"Babe, what just happened?" Oz is really getting on my nerves.

"We're finished. Blake's won."

"The fuck we are!" Oz spears his fingers through his dark hair.

Yve trains her gaze on me. "What do you want? What's your price to let us go free?"

Cool satisfaction runs in my veins as I take in her defeat. "You think you can buy me?"

"Everyone has a price. Even you."

"All right. Him. He's my price." I nod toward Oz. "I'm going to kill him slowly, painfully."

"Fine." Yve shoves Oz in front of her. "Take him. He's all yours."

"You bitch!" He turns, backhanding her so hard she crumples to the floor.

The door bursts open and several FBI agents enter the room, taking in the scene before them. They spot Yve and, hauling her to her feet, arrest her.

My gaze bores into Oz's. Now that Yve's taken into custody, there's no one here to hide behind. He's all mine.

As if reading my mind, his eyes widen and he blurts out, "You can't touch me."

I lift a brow, for once interested in what he has to say.

"You can't touch me because I know what happened to your father. I know how he died, and it wasn't an accident. Yve and I did it together."

Silence fills the room for a split second before Yve cries out, "You fucking idiot! Keep your goddamn mouth closed."

Oz snarls at her. "Fuck you, you back stabbing bitch. How does it feel?"

"I'm going to murder you, you little shit!" She charges at him, but the agents capture her again, cuffing her this time.

Oz holds out his hands, wrists together. "I'm confessing to murder. Arrest me." As the FBI agents do just that, he tosses a smirk my way. Slippery fucker. We both know now that he's in the system, I can't touch him, at least not easily.

Gin's vengeance will have to wait—again. *Goddamn it*. I can't fail my wife any more if I try. Worse, I now need to stay here and make sure neither of these two are granted bail. I have to keep a close eye on them until this is truly well and done. If they get out, Gin won't be safe.

Thank fuck she's all the way in Italy, out of harm's way.

Ginevra

Elena's been living with her second cousin's great aunt Antonia since she left New York three years ago. Parma's in the northern part of Italy, about sixty miles from Milan where I flew in. The city is chock full of art, architecture, and music, it's stunningly gorgeous and the people are so nice.

Aunt Antonia's of an advanced age. She spends most of her days and nights in her chair, while her caretaker tends to her needs. Most of the times I've seen her, she's been asleep. She looks so peaceful.

Elena really has been alone here. While she has beautiful surroundings, the loneliness must get to her after so many years. To think she spends most of her time inside, when that vibrant city is just out the door. That needs to change.

"I have an idea," I tell Elena.

She peeks up from the book she's been reading for like an hour. "What's that?"

"Pack your suitcase, we're going to get out of here for

a while." I've been here for less than a week, but the solitude is already driving me up the walls. There's too much quiet, too much time to think. Right now, I really don't want to have space for my thoughts.

"What? We can't just... *leave*."

"Why not?"

"Aunt Antonia needs me here."

"For what? You're not taking care of her, and she's never awake. I doubt she'll notice you're gone."

Elena closes her book. "You're right. But I don't have any money."

"I do." I've been trying to keep my disappointment and anger at bay, but the fact that I've been here for days and Blake hasn't texted once, hasn't called, nothing. It pisses me off. To realize that I mean so little to him, that I can fly to an entirely different continent and he just doesn't care at all? It hurts. Call me petty, but it's time for some revenge.

I pull out the matte black credit card from my purse. "This should get us to wherever we want to go."

Elena looks doubtful. "Isn't that Mr. Baron's card?"

"It has my name on it."

"I thought you two were done. Why would you spend his money?"

"Because he thinks I'm a gold-digger, so why not prove him right? Since all he cares about is money, then I want to hit him where it will count. He might not have noticed that I'm gone from his life, but I guarantee he'll pay attention once I knock a few zeros off his bank account balance."

Elena laughs, a rare smile on her lips. "You're scary sometimes. Remind me not to ever get on your bad side."

"So, are you in?"

"Yeah, let's do this. I'll pack my bag, but I don't have much."

"Sweet cousin, we're about to change that. Retail therapy is going to make both of us so much happier."

Her smile falls. "If you say so."

"Trust me."

"She's not going anywhere. Especially with you." The formidable Italian blocks Aunt Antonia's doorway. I'm not sure who called in this six foot five barbarian, but he's really getting on my nerves.

Hands resting on my waist, I pop my hip. "And *who* are you?"

He glares at me. "Maximo."

"Never heard of you." I pick up my purse. "But why don't you be helpful and take our suitcases to the taxi."

Elena giggles. Maximo looks offended, but also a little out of his depths. Besides being ridiculously tall, and broad, I'd guess he's in his late twenties. Jet black waves soften his angular features, the short beard helps too. But it's those stunning sea-green eyes that will forever make him memorable. Which is how I know I've never met this guy before.

He clears his throat and stands taller, as if that's even necessary. "I'm Maximo Pontrelli. Son of your father's cousin. I'm in charge of ensuring Elena's safety."

Ah, so he's family. Or at least, he's Elena's relative, since I'm not really a Pontrelli.

I glance at her. "Why didn't you tell me you had a jailor?"

"Because I've barely been anywhere. I've seen him like once a year when he visits Aunt Antonia for Christmas."

He clears his throat again. "I visit more often than that."

"Could have fooled me."

Oh, I like a snarky Elena. She doesn't come out nearly often enough.

I turn my attention back to him. "Fine. You can come with us as our security detail."

"I think not. I have more important responsibilities to attend to here."

"Sure you do, which is why you're here trying to stop two women from traveling around the country on vacation. Super important work." I hold up a palm to stop him from interrupting me. "Before you launch into more crap about Elena's safety, she won't be traveling as herself. *Duh*, how stupid would that be. Haven't you seen her fake identity? Passport and all. It's not like she wasn't just in Paris and London for my wedding."

Maximo eyes me, then glances at Elena. "Do you want to go?"

She nods.

"Okay. But you will take this and check in every morning." He hands her a cell phone. "That is secure. And it has a tracker. Keep it on you always."

Overprotective men. I swallow down a snarky comment. Elena takes it from him and tucks it in her bag.

"You will also give me a full itinerary of where you're going. I expect it to be on my phone by tonight."

"Fine." I grab my suitcase. "Can we go now? Our taxi's waiting."

He steps aside, then surprises me by taking both my and Elena's suitcases to the cab. Maybe there's a gentleman hidden beneath that rough exterior after all.

"Thank you."

"Stay out of trouble," he warns. "I know which daughter you are, the trouble-maker one."

"Well, it seems my reputation precedes me."

"I'm very serious."

I sigh. "I'll take care of Elena. I promise. We're going to have lots of fun—very carefully."

He rolls his eyes. "Go. Stay out of trouble. Anything goes wrong, then you call me."

"You got it. Bye."

He murmurs something under his breath, but I don't catch it because I'm already sliding into the taxi's backseat.

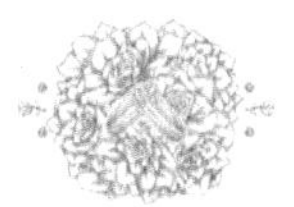

We spend the next two weeks sight-seeing during the days and partying in clubs and on private yachts at night, slowly working our way south along the eastern side of Italy. We stay in Venice, Bologna, and Bari, before getting to Messina and working our way up the western side.

Getting away from our lives, staying in luxury hotels,

and just being in the world has done us both good. Elena's less gloomy. And I... I'm still mad at Blake. Three weeks and still no word from him. Maybe he thinks he's doing the right thing by giving me space or some other ridiculous male rationale. Whatever. I don't care.

Except sometimes at night when I miss him so much it's physically painful. On those nights, I cry myself to sleep, but by morning I'm okay. I need to be more than okay, for Elena. My issues are nothing compared to hers, I'm sure of it, and this trip is just as much for her as it is for me.

We're taking the long route to Naples, driving along the coastal road, when I spot a sign that says *For Sale* in Italian. I veer off the road so suddenly that Elena shrieks.

"Sorry! But look!" I park in front of a sprawling mansion set right into the hillside overlooking the sea. "This is gorgeous. Let's take a look."

"Um, okay. At a house? Why?" Elena gets out of the car.

"I don't know yet. Just for fun?" I'm not sure what's caught my attention about this place, it's just a whim, an adventure.

After poking around the exterior of the vacant property and taking in the amazing views, I call the number on the for sale sign. The realtor shows up ten minutes later and tours the interior with us. As soon as I step into the stone floored living room with an entire wall of windows overlooking turquoise waters, my heart sings.

For the first time in weeks, I feel light and bubbly—happy. This is a state of being I yearn to capture forever.

"How much is it?" I ask the realtor.

She brings up the specifications on her tablet. "It's

listed at twelve point five. But the sellers are quite motivated as they've already moved into their new home."

"Twelve point five..?" I'm not familiar with housing costs.

"Million."

Twelve and a half million euros for this place? That's a lot of money. A huge chunk. Like lightning, an idea sparks to life.

"If the buyers can sign the paperwork today, I'll take it."

"That's...very fast, Mrs. Baron. These things take time, there's inspections and—"

"I'll make it an even thirteen million euros, if they'll sell today. Waive all of that other stuff, I don't need it."

"Oh. Okay." She looks at me like I've lost my mind, but I don't care. Then she's on her phone, speaking rapid-fire Italian.

Elena comes up to me. "Are you seriously *buying* this place?"

"Yep. I love it. It's gorgeous." I gesture at the modern, updated kitchen, and all the other amenities. "Besides, we need to move you out of Aunt Antonia's place. This is perfect. We can live here together."

Elena side-eyes me. "You're doing this for us?"

"Yes. And... maybe Blake will finally notice when his account drops by about thirteen and a half million dollars."

She snorts. "I'm guessing he'll notice all right. You're crazy."

I grin. Hell hath no fury like a woman scorned... or ignored by her husband.

CHAPTER 39

Blake

"Sir, are you saying that you'd like to let the charge go through?" The credit card representative sounds shocked. "It's thirteen and a half *million* dollars."

"I heard you the first time. Now, listen to me. Let. The. Charge. Go. Through. My wife is clearly revenge spending her way through Italy, so keep the card active and approve all of her purchases."

"Yes, sir."

I hang up, annoyed at being practically harassed by the card company with how many times they've called over the past two weeks. Everything Gin's purchased so far has been pretty predictable: Clothing, shoes, purses, luxury hotel rooms, dinner at some of the best restaurants in the region.

However, a house? That's a new one.

I pull up her location on my phone. As long as she has her luggage with her, I always know where she is. Right now she's outside of Positano, south of Naples, right on the coast. Apparently my magpie found something that sparkles.

I can't wait to see her again. I've been giving her space to do as she pleases—to hate me—while I've been stuck in New York dealing with my step-monster's arrest. I need to see this through to the end before I can go after my wife. If that's even what she wants, for me to chase after her.

I haven't heard from her, so I'm guessing I'm supposed to make the first move. *Soon, magpie, soon.*

Oz came clean about everything, confessing in detail how he and Yve murdered my father and took control of the Baron family estate. They've forged, blackmailed, and bribed their way to where they were, before I collapsed their empire. My strike opened the floodgates. The number of people who've surfaced to complain and inform on Yve and Oz is astounding.

If only all of this business wasn't taking so long. I originally planned to let Gin have her space for a couple of weeks, but I'm not going to be free of this for at least another week or two. Which might be fine. Either I'll chase after her, or she'll come back when she's done fuming. Won't she?

Why are women so difficult to figure out? I wish I could read her mind. That would be helpful. But alas, I cannot.

The following week, the card company doesn't bother me at all, but I regularly check my account to see that my wife is spending her way through Naples, Rome, and Florence with her cousin. In addition to the tracking device in her luggage, I also have eyes on the ground just in case she's ever in trouble. That's how I know she's traveling with Elena, and that Elena also has a tail courtesy of her second cousin Maximo Pontrelli. He's apparently a man who takes his responsibilities seriously.

With Yve's downfall, there's been upheaval at Titan Enterprises that I've been dealing with, in addition to fast tracking Yve's case. Liam has smoothly stepped into his board position and taken the company's reins. He's a natural born leader. I'm so proud of him.

My phone rings. "Baron, here."

"Mr. Baron, it's time, Yve Baron has taken a deal and plead guilty."

Resounding relief sweeps through me and I let out a whoosh of breath. *Finally.* The number of palms I've had to line, with an astounding amount of money, to make this go through smoothly and quickly is now paying off.

"I'll be there in an hour." Hanging up, I meet my driver out front and we head to the courthouse. It's time to finish this and let justice be served.

I could have tortured and killed Yve myself, but for years I've been daydreaming of her spending the rest of her life in prison. Death seems too quick and merciful for a viper like her, I wanted a longer sentence, for her to suffer for years instead of days.

After I go through security, I'm escorted to a small room on the second floor where Yve waits. I made sure the judge refused to set bail so she's been stewing in a jail cell for almost a month. Stripped of her usual superficial glamour, she appears older and frailer than her forty-five years of age. I can hardly believe almost twenty years of battling with this woman is finally coming to an end.

"Don't look so smug," she snaps as I sit down opposite of her.

"I can't help it," I drawl.

Yve glowers, but she's lost some of her spark. If she can't handle a few weeks in jail, prison will be hell on earth for her. Since she's relatively young, she'll be incarcerated for a very, very long time.

She took the deal I offered, signing everything over to me, under threat of me exposing even more of her crimes. She wants a reduced prison sentence–compared to what it could be–and I want to get to my wife, it's a win-win.

Our lawyers get straight to it, presenting me with the power of attorney paperwork that puts the entirety of the Baron estate under my control. Yve signs it all as quickly as she can, while glaring daggers at me. My signature follows hers and the deal is done.

Now she gets to serve out her sentence, and I get what should have always been mine.

"Where are my mother's things?" I ask her. "Where did you hide them?"

She settles back in her chair and crosses her arms. "That's the one thing that you can't force me to give up. Now that I'm in here, you can't touch me, not really. So you can kiss your mother's things goodbye because I'll never tell you where they are."

My jaw works. She's right, I can't torture the information out of her now that she's in custody. I should have thought about that before. *Damnit.* It's too late now.

"I'll find it." I stand up, ready to leave and never see her conniving face again. "I'm taking possession of your charm bracelet, I'm sure there's a clue on there."

"Twenty-five years is going to pass in the blink of an eye. When I'm out early on good behavior, I'm going to kill you, your brother, and your wife. Mark my words."

"I wouldn't be making threats in your position, unless you want another few years added to your sentence."

She clamps her mouth shut, and I exit the room. Thank fuck that's over. With her and Oz locked away, I'm free to go get my wife.

My private jet takes me to Parma, Italy. It seems Gin and Elena have returned to the city, done with their adventure. I hope my wife is ready to come back to New York with me. I have so much to say to her about us, and about our future. A month apart has given me a lot of time to think and there's no way in hell I'm letting Ginevra slip through my fingers. I might be falling in love with my fake wife. Though nothing about *us* is fake anymore.

She's my wife, for as long as we both shall live. I'm a fool for not realizing it sooner.

I knock on a colorful front door in a crowded neighborhood, double-checking that I have Elena's address right.

The door opens a crack, Elena's shy face coming into view. "May I help you?"

"It's me, Blake Baron. Gin's husband. Is she here?" I know damn well she's here because of the location pinging on my phone.

Instead of inviting me in, Elena slips out and closes

the door behind her. "She left. Her plane took off about an hour ago."

"What do you mean? I know for a fact her suitcases are inside."

She nods. "They are... She took a carry on and caught a flight back to New York. She didn't take much because she's not planning to stay there for long. It's a quick trip to say goodbye to her family and friends."

My pulse spikes and my thoughts race. *To say goodbye?* Without thinking, I blurt, "I don't understand."

Elena sighs, like I'm thick in the head. "She's moving here, to Italy. Permanently."

"Are you serious?"

"Yes. She even bought a house. Didn't you know that?"

I did, but I thought it was just a stunt she was pulling. How could I have totally misjudged that, her, everything?

She glances up and down the street, then at me. "I know what happened between you two, about the blackmail and everything. If you care about her at all, you'll let her go. She's so sweet and full of life. She's too good for a horrible man like you, Mr. Baron. Let her out of your twisted arrangement. She doesn't deserve to be forced to be with you."

Her words twist their way into my heart like corkscrews. What did Gin tell Elena about me? Does she really think I'm horrible? Perhaps I'm being selfish by coming after her and insisting we stay together. I promised myself I'd do better by her, but obviously I'm failing.

Then I distinctly recall Gin calling me *terrible, horri-*

ble, unfair. She hasn't complained much recently, but perhaps she's simply resigned to her fate, to my demands.

What does my wife really want?

"Right..." I step away from her, in a kind of daze as I make it back to my jet and prepare to head home.

Elena's right, Gin does deserve better. In truth, I'd forgotten about how I'd blackmailed Gin, that seems like forever ago. But it obviously hasn't slipped her mind. Is she really only my wife because of the threats I've hung over her head all this time? What will she do if given an actual choice?

I rake my fingers through my hair, my gut wrenching. Fuck. I let this go too far without realizing it. I used her, with the intention of ending our marriage, of tossing her away when I no longer needed her. What kind of fucking monster does something like that?

Me. I do. It's all I've done my whole life, so why would Gin be any different? But she is. I actually care about her feelings, her happiness. For the first time in my life I want to consider another person's perspective and emotions. I want to put them above my own. Is that love? Is that what it means to love someone?

Up to this point, I've treated her no better than any of the other men who've used and abused her for their own pleasure, for their own gain.

I'm actually worse than them because I did what they couldn't do—I trapped her. Snared her into a legally binding contract after giving her no choice. Fuck, I really am a terrible person.

How did this get so out of hand? Was it the amount of time we spent together after I moved her into my house? I'm sure the massage, her cooking for me, and all the other sweet, thoughtful gestures blurred the lines. By the time we arrived in the West Indies our business deal had completely fizzled—more like it had been obliterated by a tsunami. And our wedding... that was the single most real experience I've ever had with another person.

Since then, I kept repeating the same bullshit to her about our arrangement and how we'll divorce in a year. Because those things were safe to say. What wasn't safe to speak aloud were things like... *I want you. I love you.*

My body told her, but my lips never did. I was too much of a coward.

What do I do to fix this? How do I make her see that she's not tied to me unless she wants to be?

When the jet finally takes off, I'm still racking my brain for a solution. This shouldn't be so difficult. Often the easiest solution is the best option.

I know. I'll take Elena's advice and set her free. I'll give her a choice. I'll divorce her.

Then she can make up her own mind about whether or not she wants to be together. It will be a new start. A clean slate.

Pulling out my laptop, I set my thoughts down in an email. This is the most selfless thing I've ever done in my life. I'm setting her wishes above my own. Giving her a choice when all I really want to do is sweep her into my arms, kiss her breathless, and never let her go again. In fact, what I'm about to do goes against every fiber of my being, every impulse I have. But Gin deserves a better version of me than the one she's experienced so far.

This is it. This is selfless, caring Blake Baron. A new me.

He's a fucking mess, but he better know what he's doing. If he fucks this up for me, I'll kill him.

CHAPTER 40

Ginevra

"*What the fuck?*" I say way too loudly, earning myself glares from the other first class passengers. "Sorry." But seriously, what the actual fuck?

I scroll through Blake's email, the first contact I've had from him in a month, reading and re-reading it again.

He's divorcing me via email?

In equal parts, I want to scream and cry. I also want to throw my phone across the plane, but that would only get me more unwanted attention. I don't need to be escorted off this flight in handcuffs once we land.

Blake *fucking* Baron is breaking up with me via email! I know he's an emotionless, insensitive prick, but this is a new low, even for him. I mean, I thought that I saw a deeper side of him, one that did care, that could feel, one that someday might fall in love with me.

I was so wrong.

I had my doubts about how much he cared for me, but this... this shows me that everything I thought we had was one-sided. I gave my heart to a man who can never, ever love me in return.

My gaze skims the email one last time.

Outrage boils my blood. I have to turn off my phone before I do something stupid like email him back, or worse, text him my thoughts. I practically handed him his freedom from Yve and the first thing he does is divorce me? Wow. Apparently, he can't wait to get away from me and start his new life.

To think I missed him so damn much these past four weeks. By the time we got back to Parma, I couldn't wait to return to New York and see him. To rekindle our connection and see if he wanted to move to Italy together. I've fallen in love with the country and told Elena that someday I want to live there, maybe someday soon.

I came back because Blake and I need to talk, to clear the air, so everything might be all right. As much as I didn't want to, I forgave him for hurting me somewhere between Naples and Rome. I was being selfish. Of course Blake should put his family first. That's normal, right? Healthy even?

The entire situation just shows how messed up and naive I am about healthy family dynamics. Who am I to demand the number one spot in his considerations? I'm only his wife.

Well, not anymore. Soon I'll be the ex-Mrs. Baron.

How was I so wrong about everything? I thought he at least cared about me a little. Maybe I was blinded by my own infatuation. By my own unrequited love for him.

Has he been happy, relieved to have me out of his life

this entire time I spent in Italy? Is that why he never contacted me?

I guess this answers all of my questions. We have nothing to say to each other. If he wants a divorce, I'll sign the papers and set him free. I'm going to say goodbye to my family, then move to Italy—alone.

When the plane lands at LaGuardia, I disembark with my carry-on, grab a cab and check into The Langham instead of staying with my parents. After I settle in, I book my return flight to Italy, since I now know I won't be here long. Five days is enough time to say my farewells, get my affairs in order, and leave all of this behind.

As soon as I'm back in Italy I'll have to figure out how to get my feet under me. I don't have any money of my own, or a job, or any experience to get work.

I was brought up to be a rich man's wife, and that's turned out to bite me in the ass. But for once, I have faith in myself. I'll figure out my life or die trying. Now that I think about it, I probably can try for a job at a restaurant. Maybe. I'll have to look deeper into the requirements.

With a sigh, I flop down on the pillow top mattress and decide it's time to text Blake. Whatever he wants, that's what I'll give him.

CHAPTER 41

Blake

"I don't understand," I slur, leaning heavily against an irritated Roman. We're at *Leonidas* and he's been listening to me rant for the past fifteen minutes, or half hour. I don't know how long we've been here, but my head buzzes and my thoughts blur together.

"I am well aware that you don't understand, Baron, because if you did you wouldn't be here getting trashed." He sips his two decade old Macallan. "I warned you about getting involved with Ginevra. Actually, I specifically recall telling you that I *wouldn't* be there to pick up the pieces when it all went to shit. I'm usually true to my word."

"Usually," I agree. "But I had to call you. Turns out I don't have many friends."

"What a surprise."

I ignore his snarky comment. Deep down, in his recently revitalized heart, I know he cares about me like I do him. We've always been there for each other and that'll never change. Except this time he let me fall flat on my face. Or maybe that's my own doing and not his fault.

"She tore my heart out with a single sentence." I shove my phone in Roman's face and he swats it away. "Who does that?"

"You don't have a heart, remember?" he quips.

"But I do. Roman, I found it. And this... this crushed it." I down another shot of bourbon and read the text reply from my wife.

WIFE

Fine. I'll sign the divorce papers.

That's not the answer I expected when I sent that email. Her reply is cold, aloof. It makes me believe I could drown in this fucking bourbon bottle and she wouldn't give a shit. Is she still angry with me? I'm at a loss as to what to do. This can't be the end, can it?

Roman sighs. "Fine. Show me the email you sent to her. Let's get to the bottom of this."

I hand him my phone and he reads it, his face impassive. I go over the words again in my head, recalling each and every one of them.

Dear Ginevra,

I know you've been angry with me and I hope a month apart has given you the time and space to gain a clearer perspective about us. I know I've gained clarity.

I've come to the realization that blackmailing you into marrying me was wrong. I whole-heartedly apologize. To right this wrong, I think we must dissolve our agreement, including our marriage. I'll have the divorce papers drawn up immediately.

I hope you take this in the manner it is intended. That we should both be free to make our own decisions moving forward.

Sincerely,
Blake Baron

"Christ, Baron, what the fuck were you thinking? This makes it sound like you can't wait to get a divorce."

My head snaps up. "What? No, that's not what it says at all. See this line here? I'm being a better man and releasing her from our contract. I'm absolving her of her crime."

"Who the fuck signs off a personal email with *sincerely?*"

"It's courteous."

"It's impersonal."

"I was trying to be succinct."

"You managed that all right. This reads like a corporate email." Roman curses. "And you're shit at being a *better man.* What the fuck does that even mean?"

I glare at him. "You know. You made yourself better for Sophia. I'm trying to do the same thing for Gin. I'm setting her free, so she can choose me if she wants me, because..." I swallow hard. Why is it suddenly so hot in here? "I think I love her."

For a long moment, Roman simply stares at me. It's unnerving. I haven't been this shit-faced since college. What does he see?

"You're serious." His tone softens, "You really fell in love with Ginevra Pontrelli."

It's not a question, but I nod anyway. "Hopelessly. Irrevocably. Devastatingly—"

"Okay, I get it." He waves the server over. "Put all of this on my tab."

"Are we going somewhere?" I lean further against his shoulder, slipping sideways on my bar stool.

"Yes. Home."

"I don't want to go home."

He ignores my protest. "You're going to sleep this off, then you're going to go see Gin in person and talk to her to clear this up. If there's one thing I've learned about relationships, it's that communication is key. You suck at it right now, but you'll get better. Now stand up."

I slide down from my stool at the bar and my knees give out.

"Christ. You're a fucking mess." Roman takes my arm and peels me off the floor. The room spins, and I stumble as he supports most of my weight. "You owe me."

"Are you fucking kidding me? The way I see it, we're finally even."

As soon as Roman opens his front door, we're greeted by Sophia. "There you are. I was beginning to worry. It's late." She kisses Roman and my heart painfully twists. I want what they have—with Gin. With my beautiful, sweet magpie who's the only person on this planet that I want to be around constantly. All of my being misses her.

"How was your day," Roman asks his wife as he dumps me on the sofa.

"Great. Gin stopped by this afternoon and we chatted for hours."

My head snaps up, and I immediately regret the sudden movement. "Gin was here?"

Sophia studies me, a slight frown creases her brow. "Yes. She came to tell me she's moving to Italy."

I glance at Roman. "See? She hates me." My speech is so slurred I barely understand myself. "That's why she's moving to another country."

"Or maybe she decided to move after reading that ridiculous email you sent." Roman pours himself a scotch and downs it in one go.

"She bought the house before I sent that email."

Roman and Sophia exchange a loaded glance, but I can't figure out what it means. Do they think I'm doomed? Did I fuck up that badly? Shit, I did, didn't I?

CHAPTER 42

"I can't thank you enough for getting Elena out of the house to have some fun for a while," Ravenna says, sitting across from me at my hotel room table. Arianna and Sophia sit on either side. "She's been wasting away for years. I never thought to just show up and whisk her away for a while."

"We both needed it," I confess. Even though I had a great time touring Italy, and those memories will always be some of my favorite, I'm ready to face reality and settle into my life—whatever that looks like.

Arianna scrolls through the listing photos of my house in Positano, from when it was for sale. "This place is stunning. I'm coming to visit as soon as I can. That view, just look at that!"

"That's half the reason I bought it." I consider my next words, unsure how to phrase them. "Do you think... Once we're divorced, will I get to keep the house or will I have to sell it and give back all the money I spent?"

Sophia and Arianna exchange a look, they both shrug.

"It depends," Ravenna says. "How much did you spend?"

"Well, I wasn't exactly keeping track, but my best guess is about twenty..."

Arianna frowns. "Twenty? The house alone had to cost more than twenty grand, even for a down payment, I'd guess a few mil. Oh!" Her eyes grow round. "You spent *twenty million dollars* of Blake Baron's money?"

I swallow hard and nod. "Do you think he'll want it back?"

"I sure hope not."

Sophia unexpectedly laughs. "Sorry. It's not really funny. It's just... only you could find a way to spend that kind of money in less than a month."

"I was mad at him. I thought it would get his attention, but it didn't. He never really cared about me, which is fine." The lie eats at my insides.

It's not fine.

Nothing is fine.

"I don't know about that." Sophia drinks her coffee. "Roman dragged him into my living room last night. I've never seen Blake like that before. He was intoxicated, but more than that, there was this vulnerability about him I didn't think a man like him was capable of having."

"Oh?" I hide my curiosity behind my coffee cup.

"Roman thinks Blake is in love with you."

I snort. "Right. That's why we're meeting tomorrow afternoon to sign divorce papers." I set my cup down with more force than necessary and the contents slosh onto my fingers. "Let's change the subject. I don't want to think about him anymore. I'm leaving in a few days, and I want all of you to come visit me. We'll have a house-warming party."

"I'll plan it," Arianna volunteers.

We spend the rest of the day together, going out for lunch and shopping. We visit all of my favorite places in the city, since between my father and Blake, I have no intention of coming back to New York anytime soon.

Late that night I return to my hotel. The receptionist calls me over, handing me a letter that arrived earlier. It's typed, instead of hand-written, and unsigned. But I'm certain it's from Blake, because who else would make such demands?

Meet me in the hotel conference room.
I'll be waiting, magpie.

I scoff. Now he's back to pet names? The arrogance of that man. Why couldn't he wait until tomorrow? He must have met someone else. What other reason can he have for getting this divorce settled as soon as humanly possible?

The thought of him with another woman fills me with blinding rage. While I was pining for him in Italy was he jumping into bed with her? That motherfucker.

Heart pounding, hands shaking, I make my way to the hotel's small conference room. Barging through the door, I start, "How *dare* you—?"

"Ginny, so nice to see you again."

My entire body turns to ice. Frozen in place, I blink at the last man I expected to see in this room. He can't be here. He's in prison. This is impossible.

When my brain finishes malfunctioning, adrenaline washes through me. I turn on my heel, desperate to get away, but Oliver's too fast. He slams his palm against the door, blocking my escape. Frantically, I look around for another exit. There has to be one, right?

"You're not getting away this time, Ginny. Come here." Oliver grabs me by my hair, my scalp burning, and tugs my back into his chest. His other hand comes up, covering my nose and mouth with a too sweet, stinky rag.

That's the last thing I remember.

CHAPTER 43

Blake

Glancing at my watch, I groan. How is it only nine in the morning? I've been up for hours, yet every time I look at the clock it's only been five minutes since the last time I looked. One o'clock this afternoon, when I'm meeting Gin, seems like forever away.

I lean back in my chair, stare at the ceiling, and go over all the things I want to say to her in person. She thinks we're meeting to settle the divorce, but first I'm going to get on my knees, confess my feelings for her, and beg for a chance to make this work between us. One chance is all I need, now that I realize what an astronomical fool I've been. All of my excuses to not fall in love with her aren't important anymore.

She's too young and sweet for me. That's what I love most about her. How much she cares, how she treats me like she really sees me and not just my money.

She's a gold-digger. She's spent twenty-two point four million dollars of my money and I don't give a fuck.

In fact, she can have it all, if it makes her happy. All I want is her happiness.

I always thought I was better off alone, but a month without her has been agony. I buried myself in putting Yve behind bars, not fully acknowledging the aching emptiness in my chest until I went to get my wife, only to find her not there.

Now I have to make a fucking appointment to talk to her? Abruptly, I push to my feet. That's bullshit. I'm not waiting another goddamn minute. Selfless, nice Blake can die a slow death for all I care because this isn't working. This isn't who I am. I can't be a better man for Gin, she'll have to take me as I am, flaws and all.

I'm going to get my wife back. Right. Now.

My phone rings and I pinch the bridge of my nose in frustration before answering. "Baron."

"Blake," Yve voice purrs on the other end, and I stiffen. She's in prison, what the fuck does she want? "I've reconsidered what I told you at the courthouse, you can have your mother's possessions. However, you'll have to get there in thirty minutes or everything goes up in flames."

She gives me an address in Long Beach on the bay, an hour's drive from Manhattan.

"That's impossible," I tell her.

"Well, you're the all-powerful Blake Baron, if you break a few traffic laws and the speed limit, you might be able to make it. Though I'd personally love to see it incinerated." She hangs up and I have the sudden urge to pay off her cellmate to murder her. Actually, that's not a bad idea.

But first, I have to make it to that warehouse in Long

Beach by nine forty-five. Wasting no time, I sprint to the garage and grab the keys to my cherry red Ducati. I'm out on the street in seconds, racing to my destination.

Running several lights, I weave around vehicles in the 495 tunnel, where traffic is a clusterfuck, before emerging onto the freeway. I'm halfway to the 678 exit when my phone rings, another unknown number, and I answer it through my helmet's speaker system.

"What?" I bark, out of patience with Yve's fucking game playing. I wouldn't be driving like a maniac, risking my life and the lives of others, if I didn't want the few things of my mother's that I saved after my father tossed everything he could, right before her funeral. They're my last connection to her after her death—besides Liam. I've never told him this, but he looks so much like her it's gut-wrenching at times.

"Baron, why the rude greeting?" Oz's smug voice comes through my helmet's headset.

I keep my eyes on the road. "What the fuck do you want? Prison not to your liking?"

"It was fun while it lasted. Kind of a short stay though. You see, you're not the only one with resources and powerful friends. Now I'm breathing the fresh air of freedom." He deeply inhales. "It's so good."

Motherfucker! He broke out of prison. How did I not know about this?

"What do you want, Oz?"

"I assume you're on your way to a warehouse in Long Beach, probably racing to get there in time. But you didn't think we'd make it that easy for you, did you?"

"What the fuck do you want?" I yell at him.

"I've got something precious to you. Ginny's out cold

at the moment, but she'll come round soon enough. Stupid bitch keeps putting up a fight when she should know better by now."

Son of a bitch.

"So, Baron, I'm going to give you a choice. You can either get to that warehouse in time, or you can come save your little slut. We've just pulled up to her parents' house. The decision is all yours."

The call ends and I shout in frustration. My chest clenches at the loss of my mother's last remaining worldly possessions, because it already knows the choice I've made.

No one touches my wife and lives. Not anymore.

Cutting across traffic, I get off at the next exit, turn my motorcycle around, and head back the way I came. The sooner I get to the Pontrelli house the better. Who knows what that psycho has done to my wife. I can't wait to kill the fucker.

Ginevra

"He won't come for me," I explain to Oliver after overhearing his conversation with Blake. "We're getting a divorce. He doesn't love me, so there's no way he's going to come here, which is obviously a trap. He's not that stupid."

Oliver backhands me and I cower in the passenger seat. We're right outside my parents' home, and I'm not sure why.

"He'll come." Oliver gets out of the car, unlocks my side and drags me out by my hair. His other hand holds a gun. "Let's go see Mommy and Daddy."

"Why? Why are we here? You don't need to involve them in any of this."

Oliver glances down at me like I said something stupid. "How else am I going to get your father's approval? I need to show your parents how good I am for you, how much I love you, so that they'll accept me into the family."

I stare at him, speechless. He's fucking insane.

The side of my face throbs, and the cool September air brushes against my clammy skin. Panic keeps pushing at the corners of my mind, but I hold it back, I can have a meltdown once this is all over—assuming that I'll still be alive.

A foreign sense of calm settles over me at that thought.

Our housekeeper answers the door and Oliver barges inside, firing two shots into her head. I scream, unprepared for the violence.

At the sound, the two guards on duty run into the foyer, where Oliver holds me in front of him like a shield and guns them down. Papa rounds the corner, weapon in hand, and for a second I think that he'll take the shot right through me to kill Oliver.

I see my life flash before my eyes in vivid detail. The good, the bad, and the painful, until the last image lingering in my mind is Blake's handsome face. If only I could see him one last time before I die. That's my wish.

Some unreadable emotion flickers in Papa's eyes right before he slowly lowers his gun. "I don't want trouble. Let her go."

"Move into your office. Keep your hands up and don't try anything." Oliver pushes me along in front of him, his attention on my father. We step into his office, the most secure room in the house, right as Mama appears in the hallway. Oliver gestures with his weapon. "Inside. Now."

Once we're all in the office, Oliver closes the door. He ushers my parents to the open space before the cold hearth and has them down on their knees, hands behind their heads.

Dread wraps around my insides and squeezes so hard I struggle to draw a single breath. "What are you going to do to my parents?"

"That all depends, babe. Right now we're just going to wait until our guest of honor arrives." He holds the gun to my temple, and my heart hammers against my ribcage.

"He won't come. Believe me, he doesn't care about me like that." It's true. There's no reality where Blake would give up his mother's possession—that he's spent *years* trying to find—and come rescue me instead. It's simply not possible.

Oliver ignores me. "It's so good to see you again, Mr. and Mrs. Pontrelli. I'm sure you heard that Ginny and I broke up, but that was all just a misunderstanding. You see, we're fated to be together. She's my soulmate, and today you both are going to come to realize that."

Mama stares up at Oliver, her expression neutral. While the man who is not my biological father silently fumes, if the redness of his face is any indication. Papa is not going to forgive Oliver for breaking into his house and murdering his staff. But that's something to think about *if* we all make it out of here alive.

Which right now, I'm doubtful will happen.

"Leave my parents alone, Oliver, you don't need them. I'll go with you, willingly, I swear. I'll do whatever you say, as long as you don't hurt them."

Oliver shakes me by my hair, the sting causes my eyes to water. "You'll do whatever I say no matter what, you stupid slut. You hear me?"

I nod through the pain. A sob escapes my throat.

"Good. You know what, I'm tired of waiting. Let's

get this family drama started." He points the gun at Papa. "You don't treat your daughter very well, Mr. Pontrelli. But since I'm going to be part of this family soon, I can't have you treating her like that anymore. She's mine to degrade, and yell at, and tell her what a useless whore she is—that's not your job any longer. Do we understand—"

The office door bursts open, banging against the wall, and Oliver trains his gun on the man standing on the threshold.

Blake. He came.

My lips part in shock. I blink through the tears in my eyes to make sure I'm not hallucinating his appearance. He's here, in all his sinister glory. Violence rolling off his broad shoulders in waves.

He came for me. Does he love me after all?

He gave up... so much. I can't believe he'd do that for me unless he cares.

"Get your filthy hands off *my wife*."

I hear the smirk in Oliver's voice. "I knew you'd be joining us. Welcome. Come in and shut the door. Do it, or I'll blow her fucking brains out."

Blake steps inside, kicking the door closed behind him. He takes in the scene, my parents on their knees, Oliver's fingers twisted in my hair and the gun in his hand.

"Now that everyone's here, let's resume. Where were we?" He points his revolver at Papa, then trains it on Blake. "Oh right, Mr. Pontrelli, tell me how you will no longer tell your daughter what a worthless little slut she is, now that it's my job to do that instead."

Papa grunts.

"That's not an answer. Say it or I'll make your wife bleed."

"I understand," Father blurts, his body swaying closer to Mama's and I know he wants to throw himself in front of her, to offer his body as a shield.

"Good. That's good. Now we're on the same page. Next order of business... Mr. Pontrelli, tell us you give us your blessing. I'm going to take Ginny as my wife just as soon as she becomes a widow. But first, I need your blessing."

The room seems to tilt as I make sense of Oliver's words. He lured Blake here to kill him. *Oh my god.*

Papa nods, once. "You have my blessing."

"That means so much to me, Daddy. I can call you Dad now, right? We're almost family after all."

My stomach lurches, threatening to spill what little it has in it from dinner last night. How in the hell did we all end up here? I need to do something, anything, to get us out of this. Blake can't die because of me. That's not what's supposed to happen.

"Now, *Daaaad*, I'm a very perceptive kinda guy and I have this hunch that Ginny here's real fucked up. She's my beautifully broken babe. Unless I'm mistaken, I have you to thank for that. Did you fuck her when she was little?"

Papa's crimson face pales to a ghostly white. "Absolutely not!"

"Hm. Not you then. But you know who did, don't you?"

We all lock eyes on my father, waiting for his response. A hush falls over his office, the whirl of the air filtration system the only sound.

Finally, he nods. Mama gasps, then her stoic mask slides firmly back in place.

"Do tell, Daddy. Who is the man responsible for breaking my sweet Ginny?"

"My brother. Her uncle."

"So you knew about it?"

Hesitantly, Papa nods again. He swallows hard and his eyes fill with remorse. "I'm so sorry, Ginevra."

Oliver mocking repeats my father's words. "*I'm so sorry*. So sorry. Like that's going to fix anything." He scoffs. "You knew she was being molested and you didn't do a damn thing about it. Did you?"

"No," his confession's a whisper.

I've held this against him for years, hating him for not believing me, for not taking my side and protecting me against Uncle Lorenzo. For years I acted out, trying to get his attention, to make him see me, but it didn't work.

His single *I'm sorry* is too little, too late, but it's more than he's ever given me. I finally know why he's always hated me—which is a secret I'm keeping with those closest to me—and now everyone knows why I hate him. There's nothing he can do to right that wrong. But maybe that's okay. Since finding out that I'm not biologically his, I've hated him a bit less.

Maybe that's part of the healing process—letting go of the anger and hatred for those who have wronged us.

My back to the wall, Oz's gun pointed at my chest, I watch the scene before me unfold. None of this is new information to me. After I won back my wife, I had every intention of asking her what she wanted to do about her non-bio father. Does she loathe him for what he did—or rather, what he *didn't* do? I'm prepared to do anything from giving him a piece of my mind, to breaking his knee caps, to slitting his throat.

What I don't yet understand is why Oz is bringing this up. What's his angle? Is he beating me to the punch?

Pontrelli sags, suddenly transformed from a mafia don to a frail old man. "I should have protected you, but you have to understand that Lorenzo was my older brother, he was the don before he died, and he'd always been a bully. I was weak—I *am* weak."

I sneer at him, disgusted by his pathetic excuses. Gin deserves so much better.

Our eyes meet, hers wide with terror. I attempt to silently communicate that everything is going to be okay.

I'm not sure if I'll succeed, given I haven't figured out how it's going to be all right yet. I rushed here so quickly that I barely had time to come up with a plan, much less call for help. I just needed to get to Gin as soon as possible.

Though maybe my lack of planning is a blessing in disguise. Roman, or anyone else, barging in here right now could rapidly deteriorate this delicate situation. Before I do anything, I need to understand Oz's motivation. Get inside his head. Then take him down.

Mrs. Pontrelli speaks for the first time. "What do you want with us? You already have our blessing, and my husband's confession of his sins. Why don't you let us go?"

Oz shifts his attention to her, though his aim never leaves my chest. "What do I want? I want you to realize that I'm the best thing to ever happen to Ginny. She's mine, she'll always be mine." He shakes her by the hold he has on her hair, and she whimpers, her eyes screwed shut.

I see red. My fingers ball into fists at my sides. "Why don't you pick on someone your own size, Oz?" I snarl at him.

"Wait your fucking turn," he snaps. "I'm still dealing with Daddy dearest first. We'll get to you later. I'm sure you did bad things to my Ginny, and you'll pay for your sins, too."

Guilt crowds out some of my rage. He's right, I did fail Gin. If I'd killed this motherfucker when I had the chance, none of us would be here right now. This—all of this—is my fucking fault for being an arrogant prick. I truly thought I was untouchable, that Oz would never do anything to draw my attention or earn my wrath after he turned himself in, out of fear of what I'd do to him if he wasn't behind bars. But he's more of a maniac than I anticipated.

For years, no one dared cross me for fear of retribution. Until Oz, and I greatly underestimated him. He's a threat I never saw coming. I've obviously been blinded by pride. I'll have to remedy that flaw.

"Ginny, I know you don't see it now, but you'll come to see me as your savior. I'm going to give you vengeance. Today. Right here and now. While I can't kill your dead uncle, I can do the next best thing and kill Daddy. He never loved you and he's going to pay for that."

"No. Please don't," Gin begs. I'm not sure why she's feeling so forgiving of her piece of shit parent right now, but she is.

"If you love her, you should respect her wishes," I tell Oz.

"No one is fucking talking to you, Baron! Shut the fuck up or I'll shoot you."

"You don't have the balls."

"Want to bet?" His hand steadies and his tendons flex like he's about to squeeze the trigger.

"No!" Gin shouts.

Oz spins her around and smacks her across the face with his gun. She crumples to the floor. He lifts her to her knees, again using her thick blond curls like a leash.

My teeth grind together so hard I wouldn't be surprised if they crack. I need him to get his goddamn hands off of my wife. Even though I have my knife on me, I can't do anything while he has that weapon pressed to her head. I won't risk her getting hurt.

"Now listen to me, you ungrateful bitch, you're going to kneel right here and watch me bring you what your heart really desires. Afterwards, you're going to thank me by wrapping your pretty lips around my cock. I'm going to fuck your face while your soon-to-be dead husband watches. It's the least he deserves." Oz tugs on her hair until she makes eye contact with him. "Now tell me that you love me."

Gin opens her mouth, but no sound comes out.

"I said tell me!" He presses the gun harder against her skull.

"I-I"

"You what? Let me hear you say it."

"I l-love you."

"Convince me, Ginny."

"I love you," she whispers, her gaze drifting to mine. My heart leaps.

"That's more like it. Now look at your daddy." Oz points his weapon at Pontrelli. "Say goodbye, Ginny, it's time for Daddy to die."

Oz moves both of his hands to his gun and pulls the trigger.

Gin screams.

Mrs. Pontrelli's shrieks blend with her daughter's broken sobs. She cradles her husband's body. Gin lurches toward them.

"Ginny, get back here," Oz warns. "Do as I say, bitch, or I'll put a fucking bullet in you." He takes aim at my wife, and time seems to creep forward.

My pulse slowly, deliberately pounds in my ears. Oz

spews threats at Ginevra, and I just know that he's unhinged enough to see them through. My body acts before my brain has time to catch up.

I throw myself toward my wife, to cover her body with mine.

A deafening *bang* sounds just as my side explodes in white-hot agony.

The floor meets my face.

Darkness.

CHAPTER 46

Chaos. Chaos clashes all around me, tearing at my sanity. Mama screams and sobs over my father as his blood pools beneath his body and soaks the rug. Oliver's yelling at me, but I can't make out a single word he says. Then there's another earth-shattering *bang*. My heart wrenches, fearing the worst.

Blake falls beside me, his eyes closed, crimson seeping into his white button-down shirt.

Someone screams, but the sound seems to be coming from inside my head. I hold his pale face between my palms, but he won't look at me, he won't wake up.

"Mama!" I call, and she appears at my side, immediately applying pressure to his wound. She checks his pulse and the hard lines of her face briefly soften.

"He's alive," she whispers quietly, so Oliver won't hear us.

He's alive. Her words ring in my mind. They flip a switch in my conscience and rage replaces my fear.

Suddenly I'm grabbing Blake's knife and hurling

myself at Oliver. His eyes round, he slowly blinks, apparently unable to process that I'm attacking him for a change. The blade sinks into his shoulder, right above his heart. The gun falls from his grip and clanks to the floor. Disarmed, he shields his face with his arms.

But I don't stop. I can't.

I slash and jab. Blood flies in every direction. I'm relentless, never giving him a chance to go on the offensive.

Muttering a string of curses, he turns and runs out of the office. I have half a mind to go after him, until I turn and see Blake lying unconscious on the carpet.

I kneel beside him, agony coursing through me. "What do we do?"

"I'll call 911. Apply pressure, and wait until they get here. He needs a hospital."

I nod, doing as Mama instructs. "What about Papa?" I'm afraid to hear the answer.

Her features twist before that unreadable mask slips back on her face. Mama's so strong, I don't think I've ever really noticed it before. Not like I do at this moment.

"He's gone." Her tone lacks emotion, but I know it's because she's feeling too much right now.

"I'm so sorry." I mean it. I've hated him for so much of my life, but I never wanted him dead, especially since my mother loves him so much. She won't show it, but I know she's devastated by the loss of him. He was the love of her life.

"Who here is either Mr. Baron's blood relative or spouse?" The nurse's gaze slides over the sea of people in the waiting room. I hold one of my mother's hands in my lap, the other is in Sophia's. Arianna sits beside her with Ravenna. Roman, Dimitri, and Cian stand off to one side, while Liam and Lexa sit across from us.

I stand up. "I'm his wife."

"We're his siblings," Liam announces.

The nurse eyes us. "He's in recovery so he shouldn't be overwhelmed with too many people at once. Who'd like to see him first?"

My shoulders slump in deference, and I glance at Liam. "He's your brother, you should go first."

"Are you *serious?*" He looks at me like I've sprouted horns. "If that was Maks in there, I'd go feral if anyone got to see him before I did, and we're not even married. Go see him—if that's what you want."

"But you're his family. Surely he wants to see you first."

Liam scoffs. "Yeah, right. Trust me, the only person he wants to see when he opens his eyes is you."

My heart beats a little faster and hope blossoms in my chest. Can he be right? There's only one way to find out.

"Okay. Thank you." I hurry and follow the nurse to Blake's room.

He rests in a hospital bed, eyelids closed, looking so much more vulnerable than I've ever seen him. Quietly, I enter his room, and he stirs.

His bright blue eyes land on me and my heart stutters. "Magpie, how are you more beautiful every time I see you?"

"Shh. You're heavily medicated."

He slowly shakes his head. "Doesn't matter. Every time I open my eyes and you're there, you're more gorgeous than the last. So much so, that sometimes it hurts. Here." He places his hand over his chest. "It feels like something's growing in the barren soil of my heart. I didn't think that was possible after all these years, but turns out it just needed a bit of sunshine. The kind of sun and warmth you bring into my life."

I'm at a complete loss for words, so I reach out and entwine my fingers with his, giving them a gentle squeeze.

"You saved my life." This same thought has been replaying in my head for hours now. "That's why you were shot. You jumped in front of Oliver's gun, didn't you? You took the bullet meant for me. You saved my life."

He grunts. "Not the first time I've been shot. I doubt it will be the last either."

"Don't say that." I can't bear the idea of him getting wounded again.

"You sound like you care about me, baby girl." The corners of his mouth quirk up.

"Of course I care about you. I care about you very much. I—"

"You love me." His smile transforms his handsome

face into something divine. "I heard you. When you said to Oz *I love you*, you meant it for me, didn't you?"

"Yes," I breathe out the truth.

He grows serious again. "Then why did you try to leave me?"

CHAPTER 47

"I'm not the one who tried to leave you." She almost sounds hurt by the very idea, but my assumption could be distorted by the painkillers running through my veins. "You broke up with me. *Via email*. Who even does that?"

I shake my head, but the movement feels funny so I stop. "I'll admit, sending that email was a mistake. A terrible mistake. I was hurt, and confused, when I went to find you in Italy and Elena told me you planned on moving there. That you only returned to New York to say your farewells."

"Is that what she told you?" She groans, her cheeks growing pink. "Just so you know, I may have vented to Elena about our relationship. She doesn't like you very much—or at all."

"So she lied to me?"

"Not exactly. I did buy a house. But I came back to ask if you wanted to move with me, or we could use it as a vacation home, or... whatever. Honestly, purchasing that place was a spontaneous decision. Once I found out how much it cost, I thought I might finally get your attention."

"You've always had my attention. Every hour of every day. Do you have any idea how each passing day I had to stay here and deal with business ate away at me? How much it pained me to be apart from you? I hated every second of it. As soon as I was free to leave, I went after you, but you were already on a flight home. Then I sent that stupid email and ruined everything."

Her hand covers mine. "Everything was only ruined for a moment." She swallows hard. "I heard your conversation with Oliver in the car. Your mother's things— I'm so, so sorry you lost them. Given the choice you had to make, at that moment I fully accepted that you'd go get your inheritance and leave me to my fate."

Is she *fucking* serious? I study her beautiful, sweet face, and those sad eyes. She's telling the truth. Which means I've failed her far more than I realized.

"Gin, listen to me. If you never hear a single other word that I say, hear this and remember it forever. Okay?" I ask, and she nods. "I love you."

She chokes on a sob, covering her mouth with her free hand.

I continue, because I need to make her understand like my life depends on it. "I love you. I love you more than anyone else in my life, more than anything— including the tangible reminders of my mother's memory. I love you more than nostalgia, certainly more than money, and more than life itself. If I had to do today over again, I'd make all the same choices, right down to stepping in front of a loaded gun and getting shot. I'd do anything to show you how much I love you. Do you understand?"

She nods, tears trickling down her cheeks. I wish I could lick them away.

"I was a fool when I chose Liam's spot at the company over avenging you."

"Don't say that. He's your brother."

"Yes, he is. But you're *my wife*." I lower my voice. "Don't tell him this, but I love you more than my own flesh and blood. I'll never make the mistake of choosing him, or anybody else, over you again. You had every right to leave, to revenge spend your way through Italy, to try to hurt me in return. In truth, you did manage to hurt me, but not by spending my money. Your distance is what tore at me day and night."

"I'm sorry."

"Don't be. I deserved it." I sigh, content at having her so close. "What I meant to say in that email was that I don't want you to be with me because I blackmailed you into this relationship."

"I'm not here because of that anymore. In fact, that threat of jail time hasn't been a motivating factor for me in months."

"All I wanted to do was set you free. To let you choose me of your own free will."

Gin leans forward, finally placing a kiss on my lips. Fuck, I've missed her so damn much.

"I choose you," she says against my mouth. "All I've been waiting for, is for you to choose me, too."

"You have that. You have me, all of me. My body, my heart, my soul." I deepen our kiss, unable to get enough of her sweet honey scent and decadent taste. Pulling back a little, I confess, "Our wedding was the most real experience of my life. That's the day I realized I was in love with you, though I couldn't admit it to myself yet."

"I was terrified to walk down that aisle because I knew I'd fallen for you, but was afraid you'd never feel the same," she says so quietly, I hardly hear her.

I thread my fingers gently through her hair. "How could I not? You're my perfect match, magpie." My attention drifts to her blond locks. "Has anyone seen to your injuries? Nurse!" I shout, pressing the button for assistance.

"Stop. I'm fine. Yes, I got checked out. Just some lost hair and bruises." She pats her cheek. "I think I did an okay job covering them up."

Rage hits me like a sledgehammer and my grip on her tightens. "I swear to you that you'll never have to cover your bruises with concealer again. No one will ever hurt you again. I'll make sure of that, or die trying."

"I love you."

Her beautiful words calm my raging temper. "I love you too. Say it again, Mrs. Baron."

"I love you, husband. Now and forever."

Ginevra

The news called what happened at my parents' home a burglary gone wrong. Their recounting of the situation makes it sound so simple, instead of the convoluted mess that it actually was with Oliver holding us hostage in his twisted game of heroics.

The worst part is that the man is still at large. Oliver is out there, somewhere, watching and waiting. Because of that, I haven't gone anywhere without multiple bodyguards.

After reading that article, and several nights of waking up in a cold sweat, I signed myself up for therapy. Honestly, it's something I've needed for a long time. I found a brilliant therapist who works specifically with women who've been through what I have. It's such a relief to be able to talk to someone, to have them listen, and the hope of healing myself with effort and time.

Blake stayed in the hospital for several days. He was discharged yesterday, just in time to attend my father's funeral this morning.

I stand beside my family in the graveyard on a bright, sunny late summer day. Birds chirp in the trees above us, it's a harsh contrast to the priest's solemn prayers over Papa's coffin. The deep hole in the earth is surrounded by our extended family, as well as the other mafia Italians: Casella, Rizzo, and Valente. My family, the Pontrellis, are the fourth pillar of power in this world. Today, we not only mourn his tragic passing, but also anticipate the upheaval brought on by the loss of a don.

Who will succeed him?

After the burial, we all make our way to Mama's house, which is open for visitors throughout the day so they may pay their respects and offer us condolences.

I drift aimlessly through my childhood home, feeling so detached from what happened here. So many secrets, lies, and bloodshed. Papa wasn't the best of dons, but he was far better than his older brother Lorenzo.

"Honey?" Mama catches my attention. "Can I talk with you?"

"Of course." I let her guide me upstairs to her private sitting room. She seems so frail. Grief has left its mark under her eyes, on her body and skin. My heart aches for her.

We sit on the sofa. This room is home to all of my mother's personal heirlooms and sentimental pieces that she likes to display.

She takes my hand in hers, her gaze finding mine. "I want to clear the air, as well as answer any questions you may have." Mama clears her throat. "You are my daughter and I love you. I'd hoped that my husband would have done the same, but I know he didn't—he couldn't. I'm so sorry that I turned a blind eye to how he treated you. That was wrong of me."

My fingers squeeze hers. "So you knew how he mistreated me?"

Flinching, she nods. "I'm so sorry. Not that this is any excuse but it was our compromise. He let me keep you, and I didn't interfere with how he raised you. I regret that now. I should have put my foot down. I should have protected you in every way possible."

"It's okay, Mama."

"It's not, honey. It's not okay at all. I'm so sorry."

I nod. I'm sorry that I'm a child of rape, but neither one of us can go back and change the past. It's best left buried.

"Your father was a weak man in many ways, but I did love him. His brother, Lorenzo, was the one who kept pressuring him to get rid of you. But in the end, he chose me, and us. Even though is brother bullied him about it endlessly. At least Lorenzo got what he deserved in the end." Mama vibrates with sudden anger. "I'm sorry that I didn't know what he did to you."

She didn't know. Not until Oz made Papa confess to that secret, to put everything out in the open.

Mama's husband kept a lot of things from her. Now she knows how he treated me, and how my uncle abused me, yet I can't blame her for continuing to love him. I don't understand it, but I don't hold it against her either.

"I just want to move forward. Let's let go of the past. Okay?"

"If that's what you want. But if you ever have any questions, you can always come to me. If you ever need to talk, I'm here for you."

"I know."

We kiss each other's cheeks, then stand up. Her energy seems lighter, as if the secret of my parentage, and her guilt, had been weighing her down.

She goes off to meet with some new arrivals, and I meander through my the house, processing the conversation we just had. It did feel like clearing the air. No more secrets between us.

As I enter one of the rooms, I spot the aunties gathered around a table playing cards. Not once in my life have I ever grown tired of listening to them gossip. Most people avoid the meddling women, but I've always found comfort in their company—as long as I'm not the subject of the hour.

"With Davide gone, who is going to be the new don? He doesn't have any more brothers."

Thankfully. I lean closer to better eavesdrop. I'm curious about that too. I should have asked Mama.

"Don't you know? I do."

"Then tell us, you old tease."

"I'll give you a hint. His last name is Pontrelli. He's young and handsome and... broody. I've already come up with a list of seven eligible young ladies for him to court."

"You're still being a tease. The Pontrelli men are all dead."

"Not the ones in Italy."

"But—"

I feel a presence behind me right before an accented voice speaks, "My condolences, Mrs. Baron."

I turn, finding a distant relative that I never thought to see in New York. "Maximo Pontrelli."

"That is me. I am at your, and your family's, service."

"They're talking about *you*, aren't they? You're going to be our new don?"

"Yes. My father does not want to leave Italy, so the honor passes to me. Why... why do you frown?"

"Aren't you kind of young? You're not married either, are you?" I don't know why I'm grilling him. I'm just surprised, I guess.

"Yes, well, I'm sure I will have to prove myself before the family in New York sees me as worthy of my new role. But I never back down from a challenge." He stands straighter, squaring his shoulders.

"Easy there, tiger. No one's putting you on the spot, yet."

"You just said I am too young."

"Good point. If I said it out loud, then you can bet everyone else is thinking it."

He scowls, surveying those in the room.

"There you are, magpie." Blake loops his arm around my waist, pulling me into a possessive hold. "Want to introduce me to your friend?"

"This is Maximo Pontrelli. We briefly met when I was in Italy. Maximo, this is my husband, Blake Baron."

They both grunt in greeting and shake each other's hands. Maximo politely excuses himself, leaving me and Blake to ourselves.

"How are you feeling?" I ask him, concerned since he's still healing.

"I'm fine. Don't fret about me. However, I wouldn't mind getting out of here soon, if you're ready to go. I have a surprise waiting for you."

"Oh?"

He's been out of the hospital for only one day, what has he been up to in that short amount of time?

"I think you'll really like it," he murmurs close to my ear.

A shiver runs through me, peaking my nipples. We haven't had sex in what feels like forever and I'm in desperate need of him.

"What is this surprise?"

"Let me give you a hint." From his pocket, he retrieves a small enamel pin, in the shape of a magpie.

Four for death.

"For my father's death?" I ask.

"It's kind of a two for one deal."

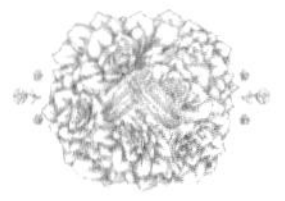

"Blake, what is this place?" The hairs on the back of my neck stand on end as we move further underground, deep into the bowels of a shady looking warehouse.

"I call it storage." He grips my hand more firmly. "Don't worry, nothing can hurt you down here. Promise."

"What do you usually store down here?"

"Contraband. Secrets... People."

Oh my god. "And we're here because..?" *Death.* But what does that mean? Whose death?

"Because today is the day that you put all of your demons to rest. This morning you buried the man you knew as your father. This evening you'll bury another man who hurt you." He shoves open a squeaky metal door and a dim light flickers on.

My gaze immediately latches onto Oliver's nude form. He's strapped to a chair in the center of the room.

Relief. That's my initial feeling. If Oliver's here, tied down, then he can't hurt anyone.

I lick my suddenly dry lips. "H-how long have you had him here?"

"Three days. It took my people longer than expected to find him, but they did, they always do. I was going to take care of him myself, but then I thought that you might want to do this together. Was I right?"

I give his question some serious consideration. Do I want to be down here? Do I want to have a hand in Oliver's fate?

He raped me.

He murdered my father.

He shot Blake.

"Yes, you were right." My voice comes out surprisingly steady. I fidget with the magpie pin in my pocket, its meaning has become crystal clear. My ex dies today.

"Good." Blake revives Oliver with smelling salts.

He jerks awake, an animalistic cry tears from his throat, but no words.

"What's wrong with him?" I ask, my gaze traveling to all the stab wounds I inflicted on him at my parents' house.

"I cut out his tongue. He didn't have anything nice to say, and honestly, I was tired of hearing his voice."

Oh.

"So, how would you like to end this?" Blake gestures toward a rolling cart fully stocked with what I'm assuming are torture instruments. "We can do it slowly, over the course of a week if he has a strong constitution. Or it can be quick: a bullet in the head or a knife to his throat. You call the shots, magpie."

I've fantasized about vengeance, about what I would do if I was in a position of power to do something, for so long that this feels like a dream. If I can really have anything right now, then it's the fantasy that I've spent the most time imagining.

"Can you... can you cut off his dick and have him choke on it?" *Ew.* That sounds terrible to say aloud. But when I think about everything Oliver did to me, of how frightening and painful... How I felt all alone and had no one to turn to afterwards. He deserves to burn in hell for all of eternity. I guess my job is to send him there.

"If that's what you want, then it will be done." Blake slides on a pair of plastic gloves.

Oliver screams, his eyes wide and pleading. I'm not sure why he thinks I'd be merciful, not after everything he's done. Maybe to him it was all a game, but to me... to me it was my life, my body, my psyche. Things that clearly mean nothing to him.

"That's what I want," I clearly state. "I want to watch the spark leave his eyes. Send him to hell."

Blake picks up a knife and a pair of tongs, then takes a blow torch and heats up the metal blade. He approaches a shaking, incoherently blathering Oliver, whose expression shifts from terrified to outraged. The rank scent of urine permeates the air and I realize he's pissed himself.

Not such a big tough guy now, are you?

Luckily, Oliver's a shower, not a grower. Blake

pinches the end with his tongs and pulls Oliver's dick up and out, leaving enough clearance for his slashing, glowing hot knife. He quickly severs the thing. Surprisingly, Oliver manages to only pass out for a moment, then he's screaming again. The deafening sound echoes through the space.

The sound cuts off abruptly when Blake shoves the dick into Oliver's open mouth. Using the tongs, he shoves it down his throat, cutting off his airway.

Oliver's eyes bulge, his skin reddens, then purples, and his body convulses. For the first time in his life, I think he's experiencing true terror. Too bad it will be relatively short-lived. I could have Blake take it out before he dies, and then subject him to this all over again.

But I've wasted enough time and energy on this monster. I'm done.

Standing there, I watch as the light leaves Oliver's eyes, feeling no remorse. No guilt or even pity.

All I feel is avenged.

CHAPTER 49

Blake

"Are you sure you're okay to fly?" Gin's been an angel, taking care of me for far too long. It's time for us to have a break, a vacation, and get away from the routine we've fallen into.

"I'm fine, baby girl. Here let me strap you in. We're about to take off." I secure her seat belt around her waist, swoop in for a taste of her sweet lips, then settle into my seat across from her on my jet.

This stupid wound took an entire month to heal, which is a fucking waste of time if you ask me. Luckily, Oz used a low caliber revolver or the thing would have gone right through me and still hit Gin, instead of lodging in my rib. The reality of how close I was to losing her still wakes me up in a cold sweat at night. But she's always there, her limbs tangled with mine, easing my frantic heart and worried mind.

Even with the down time, I've been anything but idle.

While Dante Barbaro complained about it, as usual

when I insist on his unique services, I've put him to work these past four weeks. Thanks to my little birdies, I've managed to track down almost every man who's laid a hand on my wife in the last four years—all except for one. Carl Jones III is currently out of the country, whereabouts unknown. But the rest of them... Dante has taken care of each and every one.

I've been in a good mood since we offed Oz. The rest of those fuckers should be grateful that I'm feeling merciful enough to offer them a quick death. Dante is a master at his work, just as any good assassin should be, and made quick work of it.

My wife has been avenged.

Yve is another story. She tragically died in prison two weeks ago after being repeatedly tortured. Apparently, her cellmate, and everyone else in her block, hated her as much as... well, most people once they got to know her better.

Good riddance.

I've also been busy planning this vacation for us. We'll be landing in Italy this evening. Our life together has been on hold for over two months now and enough is enough. It's time to start living our dream together.

"I see why you bought this place." I gaze out at the turquoise waters, a soft breeze blows in from the sea. It's...tranquil. "Besides the price tag, I mean."

Gin tucks herself under my arm and giggles. "I mean,

I think it really is worth thirteen million dollars. You can't put a price on this view. I think it's a good investment of your money."

"Our money," I correct her. "Everything I have is yours, too."

"Do you really mean that?"

"Absolutely." I drop a kiss on the top of her head. "Let's live here."

"Are you serious?"

I chuckle. "That's what you want, isn't it? To live in Italy?"

"I thought so, but now I'm not so sure. I love Italy, but I also love New York." She sighs, as if she's really struggling to choose between these two locales.

"Why don't we do both? We can live in the brownstone part of the year, then here for the other part. Or at least keep this place as our vacation home."

Her gorgeous brown eyes light up. There's the sunshine I've been missing.

"Y-You're serious. We can do that?"

"We can do anything we want, sweetheart. The world is our oyster. There's nowhere else I'd rather be than at your side, it doesn't matter where in the world we are, so long as we're together." I mean that with every fiber of my being.

"But your work is in the city. How—?"

"I can work remotely. Liam is doing fine with Titan Enterprises. I'm not as needed in the family business as I once was. I'm all yours."

"Yeah?"

"Yeah."

"Well, in that case..." She steps back, taking my hand

in hers and leading me into the house. "I think we should properly bless our new home. I want you in every single room. We can start with the kitchen."

I quirk a brow. "There are fourteen bedrooms."

"I know." She beams at me, causing my heart to skip a beat.

"Then I'll make you come in every single one of them." I strip off my tie, quickly followed by my shirt and trousers. It's been far too long since I've been inside my wife and I'm aching for the feel of her, for her whimpers and moans.

Lifting her, I set her ass on the marble island and dive between her legs, inhaling her earthy, honey scent. Her fingers tangle in my hair. No panties, just the way I like her. Placing her knees over my shoulders, I devour her like a starving man.

I lap at her pussy, tease her clit, and tongue-fuck her entrance until she's writhing, begging me to let her come on my face. She painfully tugs on my hair and I relish the sensation.

She's so wet her thighs glisten. Her arousal slides down to her ass, and I finger her hole with one hand while I tease her nipples with the other. I bite down on her clit and she so very beautifully falls apart for me. Her screams echo through the sparsely furnished house.

Before she has the chance to come all the way down, I thrust my cock into her dripping, spasming cunt, once, twice, three times.

Then I climb onto the island, cage her body between my thighs, but keep my full weight off of her. Gathering her gorgeous tits in my hands, I press them together, gliding my thick cock between them.

I groan. "Fuck. You have no idea how long I've wanted to fuck your tits. You're so damn perfect."

With a mischievous glint in her eyes, she opens her mouth wide, an invitation. *Fuck me.* I love this woman. I fuck her pretty breasts and plunge the head of my dick into her mouth. She sucks on me like I'm her favorite flavored hard candy, driving me wild with lust, with my need for her. I hit the back of her throat, and groan.

Fucking ecstasy.

"That's my good girl. You're taking my cock so well in your greedy little mouth. *Yes.*"

My first spurt of cum lands in her mouth. I pull out, finishing all over her perfect tits, painting them white. The sight of her covered in my cum has me so turned on that I spread her thighs and bury my still hard cock in her hot pussy.

With my index finger, I write a single word across her tits with my cum. *Mine.*

I fuck her like a man possessed. No matter how much time we have together, it won't be enough to get my fill. Ever.

She screams my name as she shatters around my dick, her pussy trying to milk me dry. I grit my teeth to hold back my own release. My palms roam her body, toying with her peaked nipples and her swollen clit. She's so fucking beautiful. My wife.

Adjusting my angle, the crown of my cock rubs over her g-spot and she comes for me a third time. I follow her over the edge and into oblivion.

When I'm finished, I slide from her pulsing cunt and watch my release leak down her ass and thighs. She's covered in drying cum, her cheeks and chest flushed. The most gorgeous sight I've ever seen is right before me.

"Are you ready for the next room, magpie?"

"Oh dear god," she groans. "I may have been overly enthusiastic, or optimistic, I'm not sure which."

"We can do this, baby girl, we have all weekend." I scoop her into my arms, carrying her into our fully furnished bedroom, then into the en suite. "Let's get you cleaned up."

I wash her in the shower, making sure to clean every inch of her delicate skin. By the time we're finished, I'm hard again, my cock straining toward her. She fists me, but I don't let her get far before carrying her to the bed.

Gin lies back, dropping her knees to show me her pink pussy. Desire courses through me, but this time it's tempered with something else—emotion.

I climb on top of her, easing my length into her until we both moan. Sweeping her hair from her face, I cup her cheeks and softly kiss her lips. My hips rock, slowly, deliberately. Our tongues glide against each other. My heart swells and I realize that I'm no longer fucking my wife, I'm making love to her.

Our gazes lock, her hips meet mine for each thrust. We rock together, every nerve-ending alive with desire and love, until we come at the same time.

"I love you." I nip at the soft skin of her shoulder.

"I love you more."

I scoff. "Not in a million years. And I'll prove that to you each and every day."

CHAPTER 50

Ginevra

That's the last box, all packed up. I glance around the guest room that housed my childhood things. Finally, the time feels right to pack them away and put them in storage. I haven't visited them in months.

The painting crew will be in here next week, then I'm turning this room into my own personal space. Meditation has been part of my therapy, so I'm dedicating this space to rest, relaxation, and mindfulness. I can't wait to decorate and furnish it eventually.

Switching off the light, I head downstairs to the living room and flip through the open tabs on my laptop. A sound up the hall catches my attention.

Lexa huffs as she comes out of Blake's home office. We're back in New York for a while, through the holiday months, then January second we'll be flying to Italy and spending the rest of the winter months at our new home. By spring we'll be back here.

"That man is impossible," she complains with a sigh. "I don't know how you live with him."

I close my laptop and gesture for her to sit down on the sofa. "What happened?"

"Okay, so the whole reason I came here was to ask him for a place at Titan Enterprises." She flops down across from me. "I really want a job there. But Mr. Gatekeeper won't give me one because he says it could be a conflict of interests."

"How so?" When she showed up this evening, I had no idea she was seeking a job from my husband.

"Because of Eion Bane." Lexa folds her arms. She greatly resembles an angry pixie. "Yes, I had Eion rescue me from that disaster of a wedding, but that doesn't mean I'm now the enemy. I don't even like Eion—he's a pompous ass. I swear if I get the chance to work at Titan Enterprises I will be completely loyal. I'd never tell a *Bane* any of our trade secrets. I'm a Baron, after all, my loyalty is to this family. I swear it."

"You should be in there begging Blake, not me, there's nothing I can do about it."

She leans forward. "But there is. You have him wrapped around your little finger. If you tell him to give me the job, he will. I just know it. I probably should have come to you first," she mutters. "Could have spared myself the humiliation."

"I don't think he'll give you the job just because I ask him to." I let out an awkward chuckle.

"But he will. I know it. Will you *please* ask him?"

I sigh. It's not my place to interfere with his business, but he should give Lexa a chance. She deserves a position at Titan Enterprises as much as Liam. "Okay, I'll talk to him."

She claps her hands. "Thank you! It means a lot. Really. You're the best sister-in-law I could ever wish for."

I laugh. "You win. That's the best flattery I've heard in a while."

"I mean it." She leaps up, hugging me. "You're the best. Good night."

"Good night," I call after her, as she's already halfway to the door. Lexa even moves like a fairy, or a sprite, flitting here and there.

"I see how it is," a deep voice speaks right behind me and I squeak in surprise. "You two are teaming up on me. That's hardly fair. I might be able to deny my sister something she wants, but not my sister *and* my wife."

"It's good to know your limits," I tease.

He pours a scotch and sits beside me. "You understand my concerns though, don't you?"

"I can see your point of view. But keep in mind your brother's boyfriend is a bratva underboss, and you're not worried about him selling family secrets to the Russian mob."

"*Touché*. Though they don't own a rival real estate development business like Eion Bane."

"I don't think Lexa has it in her to betray you. She's far too sweet." I think back to when she helped me poison and steal from her mother. "Mostly sweet. You should give her a chance."

He groans. "I will." Blake tips his head at my laptop. "What are you looking at on there?"

I pick it up and set it on my lap. "I was just scrolling

through cooking school websites. It's nothing really, just an idea for the future. Maybe."

"Gin."

"What?" I glance over at him.

"Cooking is your passion—and your talent." He takes the laptop from me, clicking through the tabs. "Barilla Academy in Parma, Italy. Le Cordon Bleu—Paris, London, Australia, even Thailand. Where do you want to study, magpie?"

"Um... Is that a serious question?" I swear Blake continues to surprise me every single day. Beneath his grumpy, rude exterior, he has a heart of gold and the soul of a poet. If I didn't know any better, I'd think he was a romantic.

"I'm always serious, you know that. Just say the word and we'll be off to whichever destination you choose."

Wow. Okay.

"Paris?" I lick my lips, and this time say it with resolve. "Paris."

Blake closes my laptop. "Good choice. I know a realtor in Paris who can help us find a place. We can start looking online tomorrow."

My pulse stammers. A warm, glowing sensation fills me from head to toe. This is happening, like really happening. I've had all the information about each school's programs sitting in my email for a couple of weeks, including links to their applications.

I just... I thought the idea was more of a dream than a reality. Until now.

"This is really happening. We're moving to Paris so I can go to school?"

Blake draws me in for a sensual, unhurried kiss. "Of course we are."

"That's a dream come true."

"I want to make all your dreams a reality. You deserve every single one of them."

I melt against him, happier than I've ever been in my entire life. Our relationship may have started as fake, but what we have together now is the most real thing I've ever experienced. I want it forever. I want *us* forever.

Epilogue

GINEVRA

"Happy birthday!" We shout, and I can tell from the murderous expression on Blake's face that we managed to surprise him. I told Arianna a surprise party might not be the best idea, but she assured me it would be fine. I made sure Blake came here unarmed, just in case.

"Magpie," he growls.

I shake my head. "This is not my fault. Blame Arianna, it was her idea."

Dimitri must have overheard me. "If you lay a finger on my wife, Baron, I'll have your head decorating my Christmas tree next month."

Blake stares at him, unfazed.

"Okay…" I drag him away from my sister's husband so he can mingle with the rest of our guests. "Happy thirty-fifth birthday, old man." Lifting to my tip-toes, I kiss him.

"Old man?"

"Yep. It's official now."

He swats my ass. "Once all of these fucking people are out of our house, I'm going to show you what it's like to be punished by an old man."

I giggle. Honestly, I can't wait, and we both know it. By the time we have our house to ourselves, I'll be begging for his flavor of wrath.

"Look, there's Sophia and Roman. Let's go say hello." We weave our way through the crowd. Arianna must have invited half of Manhattan to this party.

Sophia hugs me as soon as we approach. "I heard you were accepted into Le Cordon Bleu. In Paris!"

"Arianna must have told you."

She nods. "When are you leaving us to go live in Paris, lucky girl?"

"Not until late spring. We're going to find a house, then school starts in August."

"That's wonderful. I can't wait to be done with college. Three and half more years." She groans. "Then I can live and work anywhere I want, too."

"You could always transfer," Roman points out.

"No. I want to finish here. But maybe after graduation, I'll get a museum curator job in Paris. What do you think?" Sophia gazes hopefully up at her husband.

"Anything for you, *principessa*."

I've always been envious of my oldest sister's blissful marriage. Now I'm glad to finally know what it's like to be loved, cherished, and adored. I entwine my fingers with Blake's. He gazes down at me, his eyes softening. I love the way he looks at me.

Arianna and Dimitri join our circle. Even though I

know they are also happily married, seeing them together is still jarring at times. She's so perfectly put together, a good girl with a strand of pearls around her neck. While he's a tatted up *pakhan* who oozes bad boy vibes. They couldn't be more opposite if they tried.

"I hope the party's to your liking," Arianna says, glancing from me to Blake.

He grunts.

I barely manage to hold in my giggle. "It's absolutely per—"

The front door bangs open, drawing everyone's attention in the foyer.

Blake, Roman, and Dimitri shove us behind them, creating a shield with their bodies as Roman and Dimitri draw their guns. Blake curses.

But the person who walks through the door is hardly a threat.

"Ravenna?" I move around Blake to approach my cousin. She's wearing a wrap dress with nothing over it, soaked through and shivering from the November rain. I open the coat closet and drape one across her shoulders.

My sisters join us, and together we usher a stricken Ravenna through the house to a rarely used sitting room. As soon as I close the door, the party sounds quiet.

Sophia sits Ravenna on a couch. "What happened? Ravenna, what's going on?"

"I was worried when you RSVP'd but didn't show up tonight." Arianna settled on her other side, leaving the armchair for me.

Ravenna's shaking, and I don't think it's only from the cold given the tears in her eyes.

"Ravenna?" I call her name, and she seems to snap out of her daze.

"I'm sorry. You're the closest to me and I knew everyone would be here tonight. I didn't know where else to go."

"Why don't you start by telling us what happened," Sophia suggests in a soft tone.

Ravenna slowly nods. "H-he hates me." Her voice cracks. "He p-put a g-gun to my head and t-told me he never wanted to s-see me again." She breaks down into sobs, the rest of her words incoherent.

"Who?" Arianna presses, concern etches her features.

I lean forward to catch Ravenna's response.

"Cian."

Cian put a gun to his wife's head and told her he never wants to see her again? What the actual fuck? I thought they were happy together. The Cian I know would never, ever treat his wife like that. What happened between them?

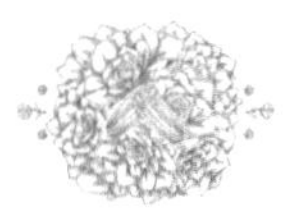

Thank you for reading *Forever Fake!* Please consider leaving a review, they are like tips for authors. If you enjoyed Blake and Ginevra's story, I'd really appreciate it!

Want more of Blake and Gin? Read their bonus scenes here: subscribepage.io/sFB4hI

He's a dangerous criminal who's been betrayed too many times. She secretly swaps places with her identical twin at the altar.

Read Cian and Ravenna's story in *Corrupt Promises*.

XX,
Cassia

Newsletter Signup

For works in progress updates and new release announcements, as well as giveaways, author life snippets, and more, sign up for Cassia Quinn's newsletter: www.CassiaQuinn.com

Acknowledgments

First, I'd like to thank you, dear reader, for your patience and enthusiasm for Blake and Gin's story. I hope the wait was worth it!

Thank you to my wonderful Alpha readers. Jay and Andra, you're the best.

I'd also like to thank everyone on my growing ARC team, you make each new book release better than the last. I appreciate you so much!

Last but not least, thanks to my lovely cover designer, and to GP Author Services, for fitting me in last minute. You ladies rock!

xx,
Cassia

About the Author

Cassia Quinn writes billionaire romance with steam, angst, and dark themes. She currently resides in the Pacific Northwest with her husband and kitty fur babies. Her favorite activity is reading on rainy days with a glass of wine.

Also by Cassia Quinn

Twisted Arrangements

A series of interconnected standalones

Stolen Vows

Forced Union

Forever Fake

Corrupt Promises